And Nothing's Been the Same Since

by
Bill Wood

Introduction

C hristmas is perhaps the simplest and yet most contro-versial holiday celebrated. It is supposed to be a time to celebrate the birth of Christ, the main figure in Christianity. For some, it is a time of peace and joy and giving. For others, it is a time of despair and loneliness. I've heard that more suicides take place around Christmas than any other time of the year.

Some Christians celebrate in late December while others celebrate in January. And still others, who claim the name of Christ, don't celebrate at all. For most, Christmas is a time to show their love for friends and family, carefully selecting or making gifts and edible goodies that will bring joy to the receiver as well as to the giver. For others, both those who believe in Christ as well as those who don't, Christmas is a time to show appreciation for the folks in their lives by giving expensive presents. Retail businesses focus much of their attention on the Christmas season in order to increase sales. A few folks declare that Christmas has become too commer-cialized and refuse to have any fun during this season of bright colors, happy songs, and genuine friendliness shown towards family, friends, acquaintances, and total strangers.

And then, of course, there are the atheists who try to put a damper on the festivities of the season, because in their minds they are far too intelligent to believe in God. While they cringe at the uninformed pushing their beliefs onto them, atheists swell with pride while attempting to push their enlightened views on the rest of humanity. They probably are angry because they only got a lump of coal in their stockings... if they hung stockings up at Christmas.

The ACLU (referred to as the American Communist Lawyers Union by some folks) demand that cities, towns, and villages in the United States adhere to a strict interpretation of the Constitutional concept of "separation of church and state", threatening lawsuits against any religious public displays of the "ornaments" of Christmas. Problem is, there is no concept of "separation of church and state" in the US Constitution, nor have the words been added by amendment since they were "discovered" in the early 1950s in a private letter from Thomas Jefferson to a Virginia state legislator written in the late 1780s. These same "guardians of American liberties" do not seem to have a problem with Jewish, Muslim, or Kwanza decorations on public property, however.

And then there are the religionists who argue that the modern celebration of Christmas was chosen to coincide with a pagan holiday in which the sun god was worshiped. They proceed to explain all the "reasons" why late December should not be celebrated as the birth of Christ, beginning with the weather, and conclude by demanding that true believers not worship Christmas at all... on any date.

So why write a novel about Christmas? Perhaps just to add to all the controversy. I do not claim that my ideas or characterizations are absolutely fool-proof. And I realize that "scholars" will find fault with most everything. But the bottom line is, I wish to produce the story of the first Christmas in a believable, human way.

The idea for this story came to me while driving back to my home in California after visiting my children and grandkids in Texas and Louisiana during one Christmas season. As I listened to my collection of Christmas songs, and pondered the Scriptural backing of those that had the actual birth of Christ as its theme, I began to think about the reactions of the people involved in that first Christmas season. The people involved were not stained-glass saints; they were just ordinary people who had the opportunity to respond to unusual things that were happening around them... and even to them. And I began to see a true love story... between Joseph and Mary... between Zachariah and Elizabeth... between God and His people. I also began to wonder how the participants might have felt as these extra-ordinary events happened, and I began to ask myself questions. Why didn't anyone else see the light from the star and hear the Angels proclaiming the birth of Christ like the shepherds did? And was it Joseph or Mary who was the subject of the "jokes" in Nazareth before Jesus was born? Has the innkeeper gotten a bum wrap all these years because his place of business was full? Was the innkeeper being greedy or simply recognizing the need for privacy when he offered Joseph and Mary the stable for the birth of the child? And just who were those wise guys from the East anyway, and why did they really come to Jerusalem? Why did it take them about two years to make a journey that should only have taken a couple of months? And why did they bring the particular gifts that they did bring?

Most of this work is based strictly on scripture and/or Jewish customs; other parts come from an active imagination. To the reader I say, take what you wish to, throw out what you can't accept, but enjoy reading. And... Merry Christmas... God bless us one and all.

Contents

Chapter One

The Unusual

There was nothing particularly unusual about that sabbath morning of the tenth week during the 33rd year of the reign of Herod the Great over Jerusalem. Roman soldiers strolled the streets of the City of God like they normally did, mostly to remind the somewhat rebellious citizens of Israel that Rome controlled their lives. The market place was closed because the Jews did no servile work from sundown to sun up during the weekly Day of Rest. Several inhabitants of the once great city made their way to the Temple to offer sacrifices for their sins, hoping to appease Jehovah's judgment while seeking His mercy.

Zachariah, an elderly priest, arose early, as was his custom, to pray for his family and his ministry. This tall, dignified man-of-God still walked and stood straight despite the fact that his age was past the retirement of most priests. He had been serving in the Temple for the past three weeks and had not seen his beloved wife, Elizabeth, or his home in the hills of Judea since he had walked through the gates of Zion just days before the Passover feast.

King David had recognized the fact that the Jewish priesthood was growing and so established a schedule, dividing the priests into twenty-four groups according to their ancestral connection to Aaron, the first High Priest. Zachariah was of the course of Abijah and was scheduled to perform his priestly duties during the eighth week of each year. Of course all able-bodied priests were required to serve during Passover and Pentecost due to the sheer numbers of Jewish pilgrims entering the Holy City.

Zachariah, known for his piety and integrity, longed to see his wife who was also known for her devout spirit. Elizabeth, also a descendant of Aaron, had grown old with her husband. She had been his helpmate for more years than either could remember. Their only remorse was the fact that Elizabeth, though some ten years younger than Zachariah, had never borne any children for her beloved, and now the years were no longer her friend. She had seen her childbearing time disappear many years before. Still, Zachariah prayed faithfully that the Lord would open her womb and end her rebuke from the women of their small village in the Judean hills. The old, grey-bearded, country preacher no longer believed that their "special prayer" would be answered. But he continued to mention the old couples' dreams of a son to Jehovah during his prayers each day because he had promised Elizabeth that he would.

Not long after the old priest began his duties at noon on that particular sabbath, he was chosen to enter the Holy Place and offer incense on the altar while praying for the people. Some prayers were specific while most were of the more common and general in nature. Those for whom he prayed awaited his exit from the Place of Prayer with the proclamation that their offerings and requests had been accepted.

It was during this time of normal activity that the unusual occurred. Suddenly a great light filled the small room that was ordinarily lit only by the glow from the seven-pronged golden candlestick. Zachariah had turned his back away from the altar of incense for only a short moment when it happened.

"Don't be afraid, Zachariah," said a calm voice behind the aged priest. Zachariah turned ever so slowly, for despite the voice's admonition, fear gripped the ancient servant-of-the-Lord from the top of his head to the soles of his feet. No one else was supposed to be in the Holy Place at that moment, except Zachariah.

As the antiquated preacher turned, he saw what appeared to be an ordinary-looking, young man wearing a long, white robe standing in front of him just to the right of the altar. The face of the man gave the appearance that he had come from the Lord God Jehovah Himself.

"My name is Gabriel," said the man, "and I normally stand in the presence of Jehovah. I've got some good news for you. Your prayers have been answered."

"Which... prayers?" asked the visibly shaken old priest. "The ones for the people... or my own?"

"Actually... both," replied the angelic-being. "God has heard your request for a child. Your wife, Elizabeth, will conceive and bare a son. You are to call his name John, because 'God is gracious'. Lots of people, including you and all your kinsmen will rejoice over the birth of this child."

"Are you sure you're talking to the right man?" inquired Zachariah with just a hint of irony in his voice and a grin on his lips. "My wife is far too old to bare children."

The angel sighed slightly. This wasn't the first time that he had brought a special message from God to a skeptical human. He just thought that Zachariah would be different. "Believe me, Zachariah," said Gabriel with just a bit more sternness in his voice. "You will father a son by Elizabeth, and you will name him John. He will be used by the Lord to convert many souls to God's way, and he will prepare them to receive the Good News of the Messiah." The angel paused to let his announcement register in the old priest's brain. "Your son will go before the Messiah with courage and zeal and holiness. He is to be a Nazarite from his birth, and he won't concern himself with earthly interests and pleasures. But your son will bring the disobedient and rebellious back to the wisdom of their forefathers and guide them to the knowledge of that Just One who shall walk among them." The heavenly-messenger smiled broadly. He knew of Zachariah's devotion to reading and preaching the Scriptures to anyone who would listen. The constant theme of the old preacher's messages was the coming of the Promised One. Gabriel supposed the shocked look on the aged priest's face was his realization that the announcement of the birth of Messiah's forerunner meant Messiah Himself would soon appear.

******

Another old man by the name of Simeon walked slowly to the Temple that day, stopping to lean on his staff every hundred steps or so, as he searched the faces of those entering the massive place of worship. Like so many days before this one, the elderly gentleman sat down under Solomon's porch to watch and wait.

"Any signs today, Simeon?" asked a silver-haired woman carrying a tray of grain to be cooked into bread for the priests who served in the Temple.

"None yet, Anna," answered the retired businessman. "But one day, He will come!" The old man pulled his hands from under his long, flowing beard and gestured as usual by lifting his hands and face towards the heavens. A resolute, spiritual glow accentuated his heavily-wrinkled countenance. Simeon had been praying for most of his life to see the Lord's Messiah. He had received a vision many years before, in which he insisted to anyone who would listen to him, that he would not die until he beheld the Messiah with his own eyes. The old man was convinced that the Promised One would make Himself known in the Temple.

"Keep looking, Old Man," said Anna while placing her hand atop his. Anna, the daughter of Phanuel and herself a widow of 83 years of age, had dedicated herself to waiting on the priests in the Temple. Though she had lived with a husband for seven years before his death, she was childless and therefore had no one to take care of her. She loved Jehovah and enjoyed doing "little things" for the priests each day. She spent most of her day running errands for God's servants, sometimes cooking for them, sometimes repairing their clothing, and sometimes cleaning their quarters. Often she would get so focused on her work that she would miss a meal. Sometimes she would fast on purpose, especially when seeking an answer to a specific need that she had heard about. Whenever she could, the old woman would pray with those who seemed to need a personal touch. This aged lady was quite content with her ministry, and she often looked in on Simeon. She usually had a smile and a warm greeting for everyone. Because of her words of encouragement, many of the more devout worshipers believed her to be a prophetess.

The advent of the Messiah was a promised reality to these two servants of the Most High. Many in Israel had forgotten God's words to Moses, but these two were among the few who longed for the coming of the Lord's Christ.

******

There seemed to be nothing out of the ordinary going on in Nazareth, a small town nestled in the hills of Gallilee some seventy miles north of Jerusalem, that sabbath, either. Nazareth, "the branch" in Hebrew, was home to perhaps a hundred or so individuals that called the tiny village their own. As he had for several weeks now, a young man named Joseph took the lead in the small synagogue that day. He, his brother Eleazar, and his father Jacob, had recently returned from their annual pilgrimage to Jerusalem for Passover, and the young carpenter-by-trade was describing the beauty of the Temple to the men sitting at his feet. The little synagogue had no regular leader since the death of their long-time rabbi, Levi, so Joseph had been appointed by the other men to help expound on the Scriptures and read from the Torah. Everyone in Nazareth was well aware of the carpentry skills of Joseph and his family, and they all recognized Joseph's gift of teaching God's word. He had a way of making everything so easily understandable through his use of little stories that made the Ancient Writings come alive.

One of his many admirers was a young teenage girl named Mary. Mary and her married sister, Rebekah, like all the other women and children, stood in the balcony at the back of the small synagogue, eagerly taking in every word that the young carpenter spoke, especially about the work of the Promised One.

"How can any one man be so talented with his hands," Mary had once asked rhetorically to her sister, "and still possess such deep understanding of the Scriptures?"

"It is amazing, little Sister," replied Rebekah as the two spun thread to make a new blanket for their father, Eli. "Do you have your eye on him, Mary? I think you waste your time on this artist-with-wood. He appears to have a wooden heart when it comes to women."

"That may be so, Rebekah," commented the young, dark-haired lass, "but I'm one of only three marriageable females in the village, and he is able to support a wife and family now. Or perhaps I will settle for being the mother of the Messiah," she teased while batting her long, black eyelashes at her sister.

"You and every other young woman in Israel. We all pray for that honor, Mary," answered Rebekah with only a hint of scolding in her voice.

"True. But Joseph says that the prophet wrote that a young virgin would give birth to Messiah," added Mary with a smile. "You and Ishmael have been married for a year now, big Sister, so, I'm sure you no longer qualify." Both girls grinned and blushed and then giggled.

"Well, Joseph is wise and handsome and talented," suggested Rebekah after a couple of stitches, "but he doesn't have the final say in these matters. Everyone knows that it is impossible for a virgin to conceive and give birth to a child. I am sure the prophet must have meant that Messiah's mother would simply be a young woman." Rebekah spoke with such authority for a fifteen-year-old.

Mary looked up and grinned slightly, and then continued her sewing. With God, she thought to herself, nothing is impossible. If He created the world from nothing, surely He could figure out a way for a virgin to give birth to His Chosen One.

******

There was nothing of noteworthiness happening in the great city of Susa, the former capital city of the Persian Empire, some 700 miles to the east of the former capital of the Kingdom of Israel that day, either. A part Jewish scholar and teacher by the name of Meshech searched ancient documents to develop new lessons for his class. Meshech had always admired the writings of Moses and the Hebrew prophets. He especially liked the writings of another Hebrew scholar from long ago named Daniel. Meshech was a direct descendant of one of Daniel's friends who had been taken captive to Babylon by Nebuchadnezzar some 600 years earlier. In fact, his ancestor was his namesake and a hero to the Hebrew side of his family. Many of Meshech's ancestors had chosen to stay behind in Persia when Nehemiah had taken the remnant back to Jerusalem. Through intermarriage with the native Babylonians and Persians, almost everyone in the former Persian capital had some Jewish blood flowing through their veins. Meshech seemed to be more proud of his heritage than most, including his younger cousin, Abimael.

Abimael focused his education on science, instead of philosophy like Meshech. The young Easterner believed that the stars guided the destiny of men and so looked to the heavens to provide the answers to the great questions of life. He just had not found many of those answers yet.

"Have you observed any new stars, Abimael?" asked Meshech as the two strolled through the streets of Susa.

"No, Meshech," replied the young astrologer with a sigh. "No new king born to the Jews."

The young scholar hounded his star-gazing cousin every now and again. Meshech had been studying the ancient writings of his Hebrew ancestors and making calculations as best he could to determine the entrance of the one Daniel prophesied would come to Israel. Abimael did not believe in the Hebrew myths any more and neither did most of the other educated men of the palace, including Aramazar, an uncle of the two boys who kept his real ancestry a secret.

Aramazar was a priest of AlQaum, the warrior god who protected the caravans. AlQaum was one of the key gods of the Nabataeans or, as the Romans called the area, the Province of Arabia. No matter what it was called, it was the foremost trading nation of the Middle East at that time. As a night god, AlQaum protected the souls of the sleepers in the form of stars, accompanying them on their nightly journey through the heavenly realms. Aramazar was also an advisor to Aretas IV, King of the Nabataeans. At least he was an advisor when the King was in Susa instead of Petra.

"Well, keep looking, Abimael," cautioned Meshech. "The Writings of Old suggest that a great ruler will soon be born in Israel. Perhaps he will be the one to free the world from the wicked oppression of the Romans."

"You should watch what you say, Meshech," advised the young star-watcher. "There are many who do not share your views of the Romans, Cousin. Do not bring dishonor and disgrace to your family by having to hide from the governmental authorities. Besides, the Romans do not rule over the Nabataeans. We are not part of their Empire, but so much of our economy depends on the Romans and their lust for our spices."

"Someday, my learned cousin," replied Meshech, "the Romans will grow tired of buying so much incense from us so that they can worship their multiple gods... and they will try to become our masters to control the frankincense and myrrh trade as we do now. But a man will come who will free us from tyranny. The prophets have foretold his coming. The time is near. I know it is."

"I fear that you will become an old man still hoping for your Deliverer to show up, Meshech," stated Abimael matter-of-factly. "Or a young corpse who followed the wrong political ideology."

******

Zachariah stared at his heavenly visitor. "I understand what you are saying, Messenger," said the old priest emphatically. "A man will come in the spirit and power of Elijah to prepare the way for Messiah. And to be the father of that man would be a great honor, indeed. But apparently you do not understand that it cannot be expected that Elizabeth could bare a child in her old age. This I find too hard to accept."

"That's too bad," stated Gabriel. "You have been given a great gift, but because of your unbelief, you will not be able to share this revelation with the people outside. From this time forward until these things come to pass, you will not be able to speak of what is to come, nor will you be able to answer the questions of the people, for you shall not hear them. But mark my words, Zachariah, for they are the words of God. Elizabeth will bare you a son, and you will call his name John."

And just as suddenly as God's messenger had appeared in the light, he vanished. Zachariah's eyes took several seconds to re-adjust to the dimmer light of the Golden Candlestick. As he regained his bearing, the old priest exited the Holy Place slowly.

"We were wondering what took you so long, Zachariah," stated Jonathan, one of the younger priests of the course of Abijah. The crowd began to murmur amongst themselves as Zachariah opened his mouth to speak, but no noise came forth.

"He's seen a vision!" said someone in the crowd.

"Yes! He must have seen a vision!" cried another. "Look at his face! It seems to be glowing!"

"And his hair has turned snow white!" exclaimed another. More and more of the people began conjecturing about what had just happened in the Holy Place. Each offered their own interpretation adamantly to the persons standing close by.

Zachariah could see the lips of those around him move, but he heard no sounds. He tried to speak again, but could not utter a word. He tried to gesture with his hands but became aggravated when no one could understand him. The old man turned to his younger protégé with great anxiety in his eyes.

"Here, Zachariah," said the younger priest, "let me help you to your quarters. Perhaps if you lie down for awhile, you'll be alright later." Jonathan took his old friend by the arm and slowly led him through the Temple past the Great Altar to the quarters of the servants of God. The frustration on the face of the old priest grew deeper with each step he and Jonathan took. Zachariah kept trying to speak, but Jonathan heard only grunts from his mentor, while Zachariah heard nothing.

Simeon stood to his feet as the two priests passed, followed by the puzzled on-lookers, who continued their own investigative conjectures of what had just happened to the elderly priest. The old businessman caught the eye of the widow, Anna, and winked while shaking his head. Then he settled down, grinning from ear to ear, to continue his waiting and watching.

******

The truth of that usual day that set so many events into motion is simply that the time God had previously set aside had come. Man is the only creature who seems to be amazed at God's plans for the ages. The plan had been conceived by God Himself to redeem mankind by the future sacrifice of His only Son. Each day had brought the world closer to the time when the plan would be revealed.

The Romans controlled the world with their Pax Romana. These conquerors built good roads to connect their ever-expanding empire, and while Latin had become the universal language of business, Greek had become the universal language of the common man allowing for better communication.

While many of the Jews simply went through the motions of worship, the true believers longed for the coming of the Messiah. God always has a people, no matter what the political or economic situations of the time. God always has power to do the extraordinary within the realm of man's faith or despite their lack of the same.

God's timetable set unusual events into motion using ordinary people. And nothing has been the same since.

****

Chapter Two

The Announcement

C ounting travel time and the time Zachariah had spent in Jerusalem being examined by three different doctors who came to no consensus as to what malady had befallen the old priest, Zachariah had been away from his home in the Judean hills for almost two months. He longed to see his beloved wife, Elizabeth, and tell her about his experiences in the Temple. He was not sure just how he would communicate what the angel Gabriel had announced since he had been unable to speak because he questioned the Heavenly Messenger's words. The old country preacher was concerned, too, about the health of his elderly bride. He had seen many younger women die in childbirth during his lifetime, so his fears were reasonable. He had a deep faith in God; he believed in miracles because he had seen the unexplainable happen, but he also had no desire to live his waning years raising a son without his wife's help. Most of his travel time back home had been filled with prayer about the coming months. And he wondered if Elizabeth would conceive immediately.

"Elizabeth," said Jonathan with a hint of foreboding in his voice, "something has happened to Zachariah. Many of the people believe that he saw some kind of vision while offering prayers in the Temple. Only he can't tell us what he saw." Jonathan could see the deep look of concern on the furrowed brow of his older friend, so he spoke quickly. "Zachariah can't speak… and from the look on his face… he can't hear, either."

Elizabeth's heart sank to her stomach. For many years she had feared that the trek to Jerusalem was too much for her ancient husband. Perhaps now he would listen to her and turn all his duties over to his younger charge, Jonathan. The old woman walked as quickly as she could to Zachariah as he entered the doorway of their humble, country home. The two old servants of Jehovah held each other tightly. Both were genuinely glad to be reunited after such a long separation. Zachariah had so much to tell the love of his life. Perhaps, in private, later in the night, he could find a way to explain the prophecy he had been given. Elizabeth knew her companion of so many years well enough to see from the look in his eyes that he had something amazing to announce to her. Then she noticed a little twinkle in his eye that she had not seen for many years. She blushed slightly as she reckoned that tonight would be a night to remember for awhile.

****

"Mary! Mary!" exclaimed Eli. "Set the table with the engagement cups! A young man is coming to call!" Eli, a short, overweight man with a slightly nervous disposition, hurried about the room. Eli was excited about the prospect of marrying off his last daughter to the most eligible bachelor in the hills around the small village of Nazareth.

Jacob, the father of the local synagogue's leader, had contacted Eli two days earlier about the prospect of his son, Joseph, marrying the young maiden. A time had been set for the formal meeting of the fathers on the traditional appointed time, the romantic day of Tub'Av, or the 15th of Av, a day of matchmaking, in the home of the intended bride to set the payment price for the girl, which would be paid by the future bridegroom. This tradition brought joy to the entire village after the announcement was shared with the locals, for in Nazareth, everyone would be invited to the wedding supper.

****

Abimael had just finished recording his previous night's study of the stars from high atop the old Palace of Susa. As the official astrologer to the king, the young wise man was responsible for making a daily, general prediction for the use of the Court. Aretas IV was highly superstitious and planned his activities according to the placement of the stars. Most of the time, the young, part-Jewish star-gazer saw nothing significant in the movement of the stars, but he had mastered the art of reporting the "news" in a way that allowed for an ambiguous interpretation.

"Good day, Cousin," said Meshach the scholar as he entered Abimael's apartment. "Anything to announce today?" Meshach grinned his usual expectant grin for his skeptical cousin.

"No, Meshach," answered the young magi, "nothing that interests you."

"I've been studying the great prophet Daniel," began the young teacher, "and I'm convinced that the Promised One will come this year."

"Is there anyone else who studies those old manuscripts like you do, Cousin?" asked the astrologer.

"I don't think so, Abimael," responded Meshach, "there's dust on most of them. But that doesn't mean that they aren't accurate... just forgotten by the average scholar."

"Perhaps there is a reason that they are forgotten," suggested an adamant Abimael while raising one eyebrow.

"Perhaps... still, they are a part of our heritage," replied the young Palace instructor. "All the Hebrew prophets write of a man of peace who will deliver Israel from her enemies. I've calculated the years from the time that Nehemiah took the remnant back to Jerusalem and rebuilt the Temple with the prophecy of Daniel. The time is this year, Abimael... this year. You wait and see. A new king will be born to the Jews who will set them free... and perhaps us, too."

****

Jacob sat directly across from Eli as the two future in-laws discussed the bridal price for Mary. Joseph stood in the shadows behind his father, while Mary and her sister, Rebekah, listened from an adjoining room, but out of sight of the negotiators.

"So how did you get Joseph to notice you, little Sister?" inquired Rebekah.

"I did as you did with Ishmael, Rebekah," answered the young maiden. "I dropped a little reminder where he would find it at the market place last week." Mary grinned shyly.

"What reminder did you choose?" asked the older of the two girls.

"A little wooden cup with the family symbol on it," replied Mary. "Joseph always goes to the market with his mother each morning during the third watch. He likes fresh fruit," added the young lass with a slight grin.

While it was traditional for marriages in the East to be arranged by the parents, and the fathers negotiated the deal allowing for the betrothal of a man and a young woman, most couples found a way to "choose" their intended before the parents met over the engagement table. Mary had done nothing particularly out of the ordinary, for she had seen the way Joseph had looked at her on the occasions when their paths crossed after the synagogue meetings. Neither had actually spoken with their mouths, yet their eyes had communicated volumes.

"And when did you decide that the young scholarly carpenter was the one for you?" coaxed Rebekah.

"Since the day I watched him and his brother repairing the engagement table for you two years ago, sweet Sister," answered the dark-haired beauty. "I brought him a cup of water... in the little cup Papa gave me when I was a little girl. You know the one... with the mark of David on the side to remind us of our kinship to the great King."

"There are many of those cups around, Mary, especially in Nazareth. I'd be willing to wager that Joseph has one like it himself. He's also of the lineage of David, you know," suggested Rebekah.

"Yes, I know," replied Mary, "but this one has tiny teeth marks all around the bottom of the cup. I put them there to help me identify my cup. I chipped a tooth... remember," mentioned the young virgin. "He asked about the teeth marks that day, and when I told him why I bit the cup's bottom, he laughed... and then he thanked me ever so graciously and handed the cup back to me. And when my hand touched his..."

"Shhhh...," whispered Rebekah. "I think Papa is about to pour the wine into the betrothal cup."

Eli and Jacob had indeed settled on a price for Mary. Since Eli had two sons and an already married daughter, he felt the price entirely reasonable. The money would be used to supplement his retirement.

"Are you sure you can't come down a bit on the price, Eli," inquired Jacob. "That's a hefty price for a poor carpenter, and the lass is so small and a bit scrawny."

"Scrawny?!!" said Mary, a little too loudly.

"Shhhh... little Sister," cautioned Rebekah. "All of the fathers of the grooms say things like that. They're negotiating, you know. Besides, it's what Joseph thinks you're worth that counts. He has to pay the price to purchase his bride."

Mary knew her older sister was right. Each Jewish couple started their lives the same way. That's one reason most Jewish men were several years older than their young brides. The groom not only had to pay the bride's price set by her father, but he had to be established enough to support them both and a future family. Children were important to the social and religious customs of Israel and were seen as a sign of God's blessings on the family. Parents with sons had someone to take care of them in their old age. Parents with daughters relied on the bridal price to carry them through their final years.

"Mary is a hard worker," said Eli. "And very devout. She will make a good wife for your son and will bare many grand-children for you to tell stories to in your old age."

"So much for being the mother of the Anointed One, huh little Sister," whispered Rebekah. Mary grinned and blushed.

"I still think the price is too high," said Jacob as he leaned back in his chair. "But it is up to Joseph to accept or reject this bargain." The older carpenter motioned for his son to come forward.

Joseph stepped out of the shadows and looked momen-tarily into the eager eyes of his future father-in-law. Then he grinned at his own father and reached for the betrothal cup and poured a generous portion. The muscular shaper-of-wood lifted the cup and declared, "Blessed art Thou, o Lord our God, Creator of Heaven and Earth, who has given us the fruit of the vine." And with another grin like he was planning their future, Joseph drank to seal the bargain.

As the young carpenter set the cup on the table, Eli called to his youngest daughter to enter the room, for she could still reject the deal if she had had her eye on another suitor. She didn't.

Mary entered the room where her father and Jacob the car-penter had been negotiating the marriage contract between her and Jacob's son, Joseph. She approached her future groom and circled him. Eli took Mary's hand and placed it on top of Joseph's. "I entrust her to you, Joseph. The law and the ruling recorded in the Book of Moses assign her to you as your wife. Take her; take her home to your father's house with a good conscience. The God of Heaven grant you a good journey in peace." There seemed to be a long-time of silence with each of the older men staring at the two young lovers so mesmerized by each other.

"Joseph has agreed to the bridal price, Child," stated Eli matter-of-factly but with a gleam in his eye. "Do you accept his proposal?"

Before her father could finish speaking, the young maiden had the cup to her lips and drank all the remaining wine, indicating that she accepted the young carpenter as her husband, pledging allegiance only to him. As she lowered the cup, the two locked eyes again, and a joy flooded their beings as each began to mentally plan their future. Joseph grinned broadly as he placed the betrothal ring on the index finger of Mary's right hand.

"So, when can we expect the wedding feast to begin," asked Eli.

"I don't know," responded Joseph while staring straight into the eyes of his betrothed. "No man knows the day or the hour. Only my father knows. But watch. In my father's house, there are many rooms. I go to prepare a room for you, Mary. A room that will contain treasures beyond your imagination. That is my *mattan*, my special gift to you. And if I go, I will come again to receive you unto myself that where I live, there you may live also. And so shall we ever be together."

And so with the drinking of the cup and the traditional announcement, Joseph and Mary were betrothed. To the villagers of Nazareth, they were as husband and wife, but could not live together until Joseph built a special room onto Jacob's house where he could bring his young bride. Jacob would inspect the room from time to time to make sure this addition to his house met his approval. Then, whenever he was satisfied with Joseph's work, he would tell his son to go snatch his bride back to her new home. Mary would just have to be ready to leave her father's house on a moment's notice. Traditionally, this betrothal time would be about a year... long enough for the groom to build the room onto his father's house and long enough for the local women to inspect the bride to make sure that she was not pregnant. But with Joseph being such a good carpenter, Mary had every reason to believe that her kidnapping by her beloved carpenter would come sooner than later.

God's timetable was right on schedule. However, Jacob became ill, and there were a couple of houses to rebuild after a summer fire. So almost four months elapsed before Joseph could even start on their room. Mary, ever diligent, kept herself ready for the bride groom's shout. She knew that from that time on things would never be the same again.

******

Chapter Three

The Visit

Just as the angel had predicted to Zachariah, Elizabeth did conceive. At first, she thought her discomfort was caused by some bad food she had eaten. Zachariah had tried to tell his wife about the Messenger's visit, and the message that their son would be the forerunner of the Lord's Christ. The elderly couple had to resort to writing notes to each other using pieces of chalk in order to communicate. Unfortunately, Zachariah's handwriting was barely legible, and his spelling was even worse. Therefore, Elizabeth had to "interpret" many of his messages. The fact that the two had been together for so long actually helped. More often than not, the elderly lady got the message right.

As soon as Elizabeth discovered that the Lord had removed her disgrace, she wanted to brag to the other women in their small village. Zachariah convinced her that most would taunt her and make jokes about her until there was visible proof that the elderly woman had indeed conceived a child. So, she hid herself in their small farm house for five months, as was the tradition. The servants and Zachariah made excuses for her centered around her mysterious illness. The fact was, her body had a difficult time adjusting to the pregnancy, as Zachariah had feared. The changes in her body were not beyond normal, the problem was her age. For awhile, her body rebelled against the physical changes. Satan used her morning sickness to try and discourage her from carrying the baby to term. None of his schemes worked. God's plan was in motion, and old Slewfoot couldn't stop it.

******

Mary had spent the last few months preparing for the day that she would hear Eleazar shout, "The bridegroom's coming!" as others in the wedding party would blow horns to alert everyone of her eminent kidnapping, which would begin the seven-day wedding feast. She wanted to visit her and Joseph's new home, but was advised against that by her sister.

"Let it be a total surprise," suggested Rebekah. "That way, it'll be more than you expected. Besides, your man has been asking around about your favorite things. This room he is designing will be made especially for you."

Mary was trying to be patient, but her young heart grew increasingly impatient as she longed for the day when her young carpenter would steal her from her father's house. The young farmer's-daughter proudly wore the veil that signified to all that she was promised to someone who had paid a special price for her, that she was no longer available for any other man to consider her as a potential bride. She was set apart and consecrated to her hammer-swinging, synagogue-teacher. She was his and his alone, and Mary longed to be with Joseph for ever.

In the meantime, Mary busied herself with her duties as hostess in her father's house for the upcoming Festival of Lights. She had planned the meals for the eight days of celebration commemorating the time when the oil did not run out in the Temple. She had also found or made little toys for her young cousins who would visit their home to play games and have a good time.

Mary sat combing her long, curly black hair, when suddenly a light filled her room much like it had done several months before in Jerusalem's Temple. There before her stood a man dressed in a long, white robe.

"Don't be afraid, Woman," said the Messenger. "For the Lord is with you. Among all women, you are most fortunate and are chosen."

Mary had been taught, as had all the other Jewish girls, that this greeting meant that the Promised One would come through her. Still, she was startled by the sudden appearance of the angel, plus she was curious about why she had been chosen out of all the young women in Israel.

"I am Gabriel," continued the man in the robe, "who stands before the very face of Jehovah. God has examined your heart and found it favorable. You will conceive and bring forth a son, and you shall call his name, Jesus, for God Himself will be among you."

Gabriel paused momentarily to study the expression on the young girl's face. The angel sent by God did not see fear or disbelief in the eyes of the young girl. Nor did this ordinary-looking man see an "it's-about-time attitude of pride", either. Then he continued, "He will be greatly admired; he will be called the Son of the Highest. And He will sit on David's throne where He will reign over the house of Jacob for ever. And His kingdom will never come to an end."

The messenger could see that the young maiden was puzzled by his visit and his announcement. "You look like you want to ask a question, Mary. Ask through your faith," said Gabriel.

"Well… right now, I am still a virgin," she stated, "but I am engaged to a fine man named Joseph… the carpenter. Maybe you know him? Anyway… is that when… it will happen?" asked the young girl.

The Messenger understood that Mary posed her question not as a lack of faith or disbelief, but because she genuinely sought understanding and clarity. "Joseph will not be the physical father of your baby. The Holy Ghost shall come upon you, and the power of the Highest shall overshadow you. Therefore, the Holy One which shall be born to you shall be called the Son of God." The angel paused for a moment to let his message take hold. Then he smiled and continued.

"With God, there is nothing that is impossible. For example, your cousin Elizabeth has conceived in her old age and will bare a son. This is the sixth month for her. Though she had been barren, she is barren no more. Go visit her and see for yourself that what I say is true."

Mary pondered the words of Jehovah's messenger. She only partly understood the implications and ramifications of what the angel had told her. But she possessed a servant's heart, and she remembered Joseph's words from several weeks before in the synagogue.

"God chooses special people for special tasks," her young carpenter had said. "But the specialness comes from being chosen by God. He knows what He is doing, even when we don't. It is the attitude of availability and acceptance of His plan for us that makes us most useable in His eyes."

Mary bowed herself reverently and said, "Here I am, Lord. If You want to use me for Your purposes, then I submit myself to You. Do with me according to Your word."

And just as suddenly as the angel appeared, he left the tiny room of the young maiden of Nazareth. Mary sat down on her bed and stared out the window of her room at the stars twinkling above the hills of Galilee. And she wondered just how she would tell Joseph of the angel's visit.

******

The village in which Zachariah and Elizabeth lived was only a three or four day journey from Nazareth, and Mary had decided to join a small caravan going towards her cousin's house and use the time to think about the events of the last few days. She had visited Joseph while he worked on a neighbor's house the day after the angel had appeared to her. Joseph was happy to see her, and the two took a few moments to talk. Joseph was so excited about the plans he had for their room, and the young girl found it difficult to interrupt him. She liked to hear him talk. Perhaps it was the smoothness of his voice, or the authority in his tone, or the way he used his hands to accentuate his words, or perhaps it was the way he drew the blueprint for their room in the dirt, or maybe it was the way he smiled at her as he explained his plans and apologized for not having the room completed yet. Mary decided that her news could wait. She did manage to tell him that she was going to visit Elizabeth.

"Yes," said the young carpenter with a smile, "I've heard that she has conceived. One of our other cousins from the same village dropped by yesterday and told us the good news. I've always admired Zachariah's devotion to the priesthood. And his devotion to Elizabeth. He is a good role model for us younger men."

Joseph's smile was absolutely enchanting to Mary. She noticed that he smiled at most everyone, which sometimes caught strangers off guard. But his smile always relaxed those around him. And his ability to remember the names of everyone in their village and the circumstances of their last meeting caused all to admire the carpenter-sometimes-scholar. It was his smile that had first captured the young girl's heart. He had a special smile for her. She dreamed of what that smile might look like when she told her man about the angel and his message. The young farm-girl would miss seeing that smile of his while she visited Elizabeth, but there were so many questions she had, and she hoped her older cousin could supply the answers that her mother might have supplied had her mother still been alive.

****

As Mary approached the house of Zachariah and Elizabeth, she saw her cousin carrying a small bowl of fruit. The older woman was obviously with child.

"Hello, Cousin," said the young girl. "May God's blessings be on all who enter your house."

As Elizabeth turned towards the voice of the one who delivered the salutation, she felt the baby in her womb move as if he had leapt for joy. And then she felt a sudden rush from the Holy Ghost fill her very being.

The older woman spoke loudly, much to the amazement of those in the courtyard, "Mary... you are truly blessed among all women. And the babe in your womb is blessed also. I stand amazed in your presence. Awed by the fact that the mother of my Lord should come to visit me here. Let me tell you, young Lady... as soon as I heard your voice, my son leaped inside of me." Elizabeth hugged Mary as if she had not seen her young cousin for many years. At the end of the embrace, the older woman held Mary at arm's length and continued her greeting.

"I see the joy in your eyes because you have believed," said an overjoyed Elizabeth. "Zachariah told me about the angel's visit to him. Our son will be the forerunner of the Messiah. I just had no idea that you, my dear young Cousin, would be the mother of the Anointed One. Continue to believe what you were told, for everything will happen just as it was told you by the Lord." Mary's countenance was beaming.

Mary and Elizabeth walked arm in arm into the house of the country preacher. Inside, Zachariah joined the two women who were glowing with the presence of the Holy Spirit. Instinctively, the old priest knew of Mary's wonderful news. Though he heard nothing, he watched the facial expressions of the two women as they conversed at the table.

"Are you OK, my Dear?" asked her older cousin.

"Yes, Elizabeth," answered Mary. "My heart is so full of so many emotions. My soul praises God for what He has done. I'm not sure why he picked me to be the mother of the Messiah. I've done nothing notable. My father is a simple shepherd from a small village, and yet, people will think of me as someone special because of the honor the Lord has bestowed upon me. But He is the special one, Elizabeth, not me."

The old woman held Mary's hands tightly and grinned her understanding. Mary continued pouring out her heart to her cousin. She just couldn't keep the good news bottled up inside her any longer.

"Jehovah has shown His mercy to those who honor and respect Him for as long as time has existed," continued the young girl. "He shows his strength in ways and at times that we least expect. Those who claim that they have no need of the Lord, He pulls down in their own pride. Those men think that they are something special, until He makes them wallow in the mud of their own feeble intelligence and strength. God provides for those who hunger for his righteousness, and He destroys those who are self-righteous. He has constantly protected Israel and given us numerous chances to praise His name and return to Him. And despite the hardness of our people, He shows us mercy. Now He has sent His Promised One to free us from the evil that surrounds us. And He has chosen me to carry His Son into the world."

The eyes of the young maiden displayed her extreme joy as well as her fears about the future. Zachariah wanted to comfort the young woman, but could only pat her arm gently. Mary turned to him and looked deep into his eyes.

"People won't believe me if I tell them, will they," she said, knowing the answer before she spoke the question. She had pondered that very same revelation in her mind for days now, and she still found no comfort in her answer.

"No, Mary," answered Elizabeth. "Most people won't believe you." The old woman looked directly at Zachariah as she continued speaking. "It seems that we pray for God's mercy and His guidance, but when He sends it, we have trouble believing what He says." Then she grinned at her husband. Zachariah knew without hearing that she was speaking of him. And he knew that she wasn't nagging or scolding... just stating a truth. He exchanged her grin and placed his left hand atop those of his beloved's. "Time will always prove Him right, Mary," continued Elizabeth. "He has touched me...

and He has touched you… and nothing will ever be the same for us again."

******

Chapter Four

The Delivery

It had been three months since Mary had arrived in the little village lying in the Judean hills where her cousin Elizabeth and Zachariah lived. The older woman had offered her younger kinsman the comfort and understanding that Mary's mother might have offered had she still been alive. Mary had spent most of the days before the Passover Feast cleaning house for her aged cousins, because Elizabeth was not quite up to moving all the furniture outside the simple rural dwelling in the Judean hills northwest of Jerusalem. The entire house had to be cleaned to remove all leavened products, which was quite an undertaking for all the walls, floors, windows, and furniture had to be scrubbed with boiling water so that the house could be declared clean. Mary was used to the process of this annual spring cleaning since she had performed the same tasks for her father's house since her mother had died. This year, her father Eli would have to eat Passover at Rebekah's house.

This would be the first Passover that Elizabeth and Zachariah had spent together in more years than she could count. The old priest was usually in Jerusalem during this special holiday, but had remained in their small village partly because of Elizabeth's condition as well as his own. All preparations had been made to declare the house ready for the

Passover meal which would be shared that evening. Mary had made all the correct foods with Elizabeth overseeing the preparation.

Elizabeth walked slowly into the main room of the little country home, holding her hands beneath her swollen belly. The old woman leaned against the wall and spoke with urgency.

"Mary," said Elizabeth, softly at first, because she was still trying to catch her breath. "Mary!" she exclaimed. "Mary, go get Shiphrah... quickly! Tell her to bring the delivery-stool!"

Mary dropped the sponge in the bucket at her feet when she looked into the eyes of her aged cousin. She could see that Elizabeth was in a great deal of discomfort, so the young girl hurried through the door of the little cottage as quickly as her two feet could carry her. As she ran, she clutched her own stomach, only slightly swollen from the child she carried.

Since the time of Moses, Jewish women had given birth while sitting on a small, short stool, aided by a midwife only in rare cases. As the stories were told and re-told of the difficulty of Rachel in Genesis, everyone in the small village where Elizabeth and Zachariah lived knew that the old woman's delivery would be a difficult one. Shiphrah, one of the two women in the village who performed the duties of a midwife, had been put on alert by Jonathan, Zachariah's young assistant, for several weeks now. Her sister, Puah, would also be summoned to whisper in the ear of Elizabeth during the delivery... to calm her and soothe her... and hopefully make the delivery less complicated. Both women had been well trained to perform their duties flawlessly.

Although in tremendous pain, the elderly wife of Zachariah glanced at her husband who had risen from his studies to come to her side. The old priest helped his beloved back into her room. Tears filled his ancient eyes as he thought about the many possibilities that could take place in a manner of minutes.

****

"The room is taking shape nicely, Joseph," said his brother Eleazar. "Father will be pleased. Do you expect Mary home, soon?"

"Yes, big Brother," answered the young carpenter while wiping his brow with a damp cloth. "She decided to stay with Elizabeth… to help her out during her time of… well, you know what can happen to a young woman when she's with child," stated Joseph rather modestly, "and Elizabeth is rather old to be going through all those birth pains."

Eleazar knew all too well what his younger brother meant as his own wife had lost two babies of their own before their first son was born healthy. While many doctors of the time and even some priests were acquainted with the science of delivering babies, complications were a norm in many parts of the Jewish kingdom, especially in small villages.

"I understand what you are saying, Joseph," noted Eleazar with just a hint of sadness in his tone. "I'm sure Mary will be a great help to our cousin in her time of labor. She might even assist one of the midwives. That could come in handy when the two of you are ready to start your family," grinned the older of the two men.

The young carpenter smiled one of his you-can't-get-me-rattled smiles at his older brother. "Everything will happen in due time, Eleazar," offered Joseph. "Mary will be home in a week or so. And the room will be finished soon, also, if father will ever stop finding me little jobs to do that take up my time. He comes in here every day or two… walks around… inspecting everything… and just makes little noises with his throat. He never comments or makes a suggestion… just grunts."

Eleazar laughed at his younger brother's description of their father's routine. "He did the same thing to me when I built the room where Miriam and I spent our first year," added the more experienced of the two. "He's just like that. Remember this room will be a part of his house even after you and Mary leave to establish your family. He sees these rooms as a part of his legacy. And he uses them to persuade folks in the village that his work and the work of his sons will last throughout the ages. Believe me, if there was something of which he did not approve, he would tell you to rip it all out and start over," said the older nail-driver with a grin. "He did it to me several times."

Both men laughed as they recalled how their father had wanted everything to be so perfect in Eleazar's room. But Jacob was that way in everything he did. It did not matter that he and his sons were the only carpenters in the tiny Galilean village of Nazareth. Pride in workmanship was a way of life for most Jewish men, and Jacob was no exception. His sons might be impatient when it came to bringing their brides home to their father's house, but he wanted everything to be absolutely perfect for his daughters-in-law. The bridal chamber had to be beautiful and perfect. One doesn't honeymoon just anywhere, and it had to be stocked with provisions since the bride and groom were to remain in that room for seven days. And it was also true that the old carpenter wanted no idle gossip concerning the craftsmanship of his work.

****

For the first time in over ten months, Zachariah actually heard the sound of the door of his country home open and the sound of a woman's voice. He turned his head towards the noise of two women hurriedly entering his residence. The old priest's countenance took on a look of puzzlement mixed with fear of what might happen.

"Where's Elizabeth?" shouted Shiphrah, as if talking more loudly would make the old priest understand. Zachariah moved his head so very slowly towards the room where Elizabeth sat on the side of their cot. Shiphrah paid no attention to Zachariah's apparent understanding and rushed in to aide the old woman. Mary followed close behind. The old, country preacher's reaction didn't register with Mary, either. She had other things on her mind at that moment. Still, Zachariah heard the conversations of the women. The sounds seemed almost foreign to him. He moved to the doorway and leaned against the opening.

"Puah can't come, Elizabeth," said the elderly mid-wife. "She's sick with the disease that vandalizes all women. Mary will have to take her place."

"But I've never done this before," protested the young farmer's-daughter. "I wouldn't know what to do... or say... I can't do this." Mary took two steps away from the older women in front of her.

"It'll be alright, Mary," said her ancient cousin in between gasps for air. "Just talk to me... whatever comes to mind will do fine." Elizabeth reached out her hand towards the young maiden.

"She's right, Girl," said Shiphrah, "doesn't much matter what is said at a time like this. Just try to take her mind off the pain." The experienced midwife spoke as she helped Elizabeth squat on the delivery stool. "Pray with her... recite scriptures... tell her a story... or just sing softly. Nature will take care of the rest if we're lucky. You'll understand better when it's your time to sit on the stool."

Mary looked into the mature eyes of her kin who smiled reassuringly at the novice-to-the-birth-process. Both women knew a secret about what was happening that could only be shared for the moment between the two of them. Elizabeth reached out, took Mary's small, young hand, and pulled her close. "Sing to me of the Messiah, Little One," whispered the elderly priest's wife. And the mother-to-be of God's Anointed tenderly repeated scriptures into the ear of the old woman along with the stories she remembered her beloved telling in the synagogue.

****

Abimael rechecked the calculations which he had made the night before very carefully. The moon wasn't coming up where it should. His first instinct was to double-check his calibrations. The young scientist did not like "making up" his daily predictions to the King, but this time he would have to do so. He would have to search a little to recycle some old prophecy, one that he hoped Aretas would not remember.

"Good evening, Cousin," said the happy-go-lucky educator, Meshach, as he entered the apartment of the young astrologer in his normal fashion. "Seen anything good in your star-gazing?"

"I'm not sure, Meshach," answered the befuddled soothsayer, "probably just wrote something down wrong."

"Was there activity like I said?" inquired the jubilant teacher. "Has the new star arisen?"

"No, Cousin," stated Abimael, "nothing so dramatic. No new star... but something seems to have happened to the alignment of the stars which has caused the moon to not come up where it should. But the error must be mine because the difference is not even noticeable... unless you look at this every night... and every morning."

"But something is happening!" exclaimed an excited Meshach.

"As much as I hate to deliver good news to you, Cousin, which might encourage your research... something is happening. Maybe," retorted the young forecaster for the King. "But it is too early to determine just what."

"We need to start making plans to get to Jerusalem," mentioned Meshach as he began pacing back and forth in front of the little table where Abimael was working. He seemed to be talking more to himself than to anyone in particular. "Perhaps we can persuade Aramazar to go with us. King Aretas leaves for Petra next month in time for the festivals." The young instructor of the King's court stopped momentarily in front of his cousin. "You know Aretas enjoys the directing of the caravans that will leave Petra with the goods that make us Nabataeans so wealthy that even the Romans envy us. Of course, everyone knows the routes are the same ones which have been traveled for centuries."

"What do you mean by 'we'?" asked Abimael in a rather incredulous tone.

"Cousin... don't you want to be near Jerusalem when the new King of the Jews is born? You can even tell everyone that you knew in advance that it would occur," declared the young researcher of the prophets. "And I know that Uncle Aramazar would want to be there... to give the new born babe the blessings of AlQuam."

"I don't think I want anything to do with your scheme, Meshach," suggested the young astrologer with a hint of disbelief in his voice.

"At least consider the possibilities, Abimael," proposed the young reader. "We could visit King Herod, unannounced, ask about his new son, and make an everlasting impression on him. And that would put us in good with Aretas, which might get us both transferred to Petra." Meshach's eyes sparkled with excitement as he spoke, trying to convince his cousin of the opportunity that lay before them, which apparently no one else in the Susa palace was even aware of.

The two men discussed the possibilities on into the night, with the young star-searcher trying his best to distance himself from his older cousin's plans. Meshach just seemed to ignore each and every objection that Abimael proposed.

****

"Anna," said the old Jewish businessman who frequented the Temple every day, "do you feel the tension in the air? Have you seen any new people here at the Temple? Have I missed anybody?" Simeon seemed to be more anxious than usual and there even seemed to be a little spring in his step.

"No, Old Man," answered the elderly prophetess, "nothing has really changed. Everyone is getting ready for the festivals coming up, that's all."

"Has the old priest, Zachariah, arrived yet? I'm sure he knows something," said Simeon. "Last night I had another dream about the coming of the Messiah. Elijah stood right outside the gates of the city, and said, 'Behold, the voice of one crying in the Wilderness. Make straight the way of the

Lord'. It was so real, Anna, so very real." Tears filled the eyes of the old man as he relived his dream and remembered his promise from God about seeing the Messiah with his own eyes.

Anna smiled at the ancient businessman and just shook her head. She wanted so much to believe the old man. But nothing unusual had happened in or near Jerusalem in quite awhile, with the exception of the news about Herod's sons and favorite wife being executed for treason. But the old prophetess failed to see how that bit of information, gory as it was, could possibly fit into Simeon's quest to visibly see the Messiah.

Herod was always doing something strange because he feared the people of Israel trying to take his throne from him. That's why he had Mariamne and her sons, Alexander and Aristobulus murdered. He feared that these family members were more popular with his subjects than was he. The executions made Antipater the exclusive successor to the old king's throne.

****

Shiphrah had not watched or paid attention to the activity and exchange of words between Elizabeth and Mary, but Zachariah had. Friends and neighbors and a few kinsmen had gathered outside the little dwelling that housed the two aged workers of the Lord, praying that the delivery would be as uneventful as possible. And when the noise of a new born's cry filled the air, they all rejoiced because the Lord had shown great mercy upon Elizabeth.

Zachariah also heard the baby's cry and watched in awe as Shiphrah cut the cord, cleaned the baby quickly, and then wrapped him in swaddling clothes to keep him from throwing his bones out of socket. The old priest looked into the eyes of his beloved. He noticed the glow flooding the features of his long-time wife as she listened with a rapturous spirit to the words of the young maiden from Nazareth.

"It's a boy, Elizabeth," said the young virgin with a huge smile and sparkling eyes. This was the first time that Mary had actually witnessed the birth of another human being. The thrill and excitement of the moment filled her soul, and she wondered what it would be like for her when her time came.

Zachariah slowly stood erect as he recalled the traditional teachings that Elijah, who was thought by many to be the one to introduce the Messiah, would arrive in Israel on Passover. Therefore, the people of Israel placed an empty chair at the table during the Passover meal, and the reason that the youngest child would look out the door to see if Elijah had indeed come that night. And a tear trickled down Zachariah's face as the importance of that moment consumed his being. It would be some time before anyone else would make a connection between the miraculous birth of Zachariah's son with the coming of the Messiah, but the old priest knew the connection would be made. And he also knew nothing would ever be the same again.

****

Chapter Five

The Naming

As the small caravan in which Mary traveled neared the little village of Nazareth, the young shepherd's daughter recalled her visit to her elderly cousin Elizabeth in the hills of Judea. She recalled the discussions she and the aged lady had had concerning the miracles they both carried.

A slight grin crossed her lips as she remembered how Elizabeth's husband, Zachariah, had tried so hard to communicate with the two women. The old priest had been unable to speak or hear since he had returned from performing his duties almost a year earlier. Still he tried. He would laugh a bit whenever Mary or Elizabeth did, and the old gentleman continued his life-long habit of praying during certain times of the day. Often Mary and Elizabeth would join him.

During these times of silence, Mary pondered how she was going to inform her betrothed, Joseph, about her blessing. The young maiden believed her carpenter would be understanding, still her mind created several scenarios that could take place. Mary had always worn clothes that had been her sister's and so the garments were just a little bigger than necessary. No one in the caravan had noticed that she was with child despite her small frame. And the three months she had spent in the Judean hill country kept local gossip down. The young girl was grateful to have her older cousin to reassure her that the morning illness she experienced was normal. The older woman also reassured the younger Mary that her body's changes were also within the normal range for a girl her age who was pregnant, but that she would start showing soon and not be able to hide her situation. And then the young farm-girl smiled broadly as she relived in her mind the day Elizabeth gave birth to a perfect little boy. For a moment, just outside of Nazareth, time stood still as Mary recalled the baby's circumcision ceremony, the first she had ever attended.

Eight days after Elizabeth gave birth, close to two dozen of her and Zachariah's friends gathered during the third hour to celebrate the infant boy's *brit milah*, or circumcision. Jews all over the world still practiced the ancient command of God as an outward sign of a man's participation in Israel's covenant with God, as well as a sign that the Jewish people would perpetuate through Him.

How sad, or so Mary had thought that morning, that Zachariah could not be the *mohel* for his own son. The elderly priest had been highly trained in relevant Jewish law and surgical techniques to perform this sacred ritual and had, in fact, done so on numerous occasions. But the old country preacher was still unable to utter a word. Zachariah had been training his younger protégé in the proper blessings, and had turned the ceremony over to him.

Mary recalled how very proud she felt when Zachariah indicated to Elizabeth that their younger cousin should be the *sandek* and hold the new-born babe. Usually that job was reserved for the child's grandparent, but the parents of the elderly couple had long passed away. Elizabeth was very careful to explain the symbols to the young farm-girl.

"We'll place Elijah's chair in the middle of the big room," mentioned Elizabeth the day before the ceremony.

"Elijah's chair?" questioned Mary.

Elizabeth smiled and shook her head slightly. "I keep forgetting that you are the youngest of your Eli's children. You've never been to a *brit milah* have you, Dear?"

Mary dropped her eyes, looking a little ashamed at her apparent lack of knowledge of what was about to happen. "No," she answered shyly.

Elizabeth placed her arm around her young cousin and explained. "Many years ago, the prophet Elijah rebuked the Israelites because they had forsaken the ritual of *brit milah*. Now, an empty chair is placed close to the center of the room to symbolize his presence. The *mohel* must be very careful, as Elijah presides over the circumcision ceremonies to ensure its continuation. The chair itself is nothing special, so the seat of honor is covered with a special cloth embroidered with 'Elijah the Prophet'." Elizabeth walked over to a small cabinet, opened the doors, and retrieved a beautifully made cloth, folded perfectly. As she turned to face Mary, she continued her explanation. "This was used when Zachariah was circumcised so many years ago. We've kept it all these many years... hoping and praying that it would be used again... for our son."

Elizabeth crossed the room slowly, holding the cloth like it was a sacred family heirloom. "The child will be placed in the chair of Elijah at the beginning of the ceremony," she continued. She stopped close to Mary and lifted her gaze to meet her young cousin's eyes. The older woman's pale blue eyes began to fill with tears. "Then the baby will be placed on the knees of the *sandek,* which is you, Sweet Kinsman, and Jonathan will say, 'this is the throne of Elijah the prophet, who is remembered for good'."

On the day of the babe's circumcision, Elizabeth and Zachariah gathered with their friends on the porch of their comfortable house. Mary carried the baby in from an anti-room, and everyone exclaimed, "Barukh Haba!" Everyone that is except Zachariah, who just stood to the side with his hands raised, gently rocking back and forth.

Jonathan then said, "And the Lord spake unto Moses, saying, Phinehas, the son of Eleazar, the son of Aaron the priest, hath turned my wrath away from the children of Israel, while he was zealous for my sake among them, that I con-

49

sumed not the children of Israel in my jealousy. Wherefore say, Behold, I give unto him my covenant of peace."

As the ceremony proceeded as Elizabeth had described the day before, Mary tried to memorize every word and action. She was sure that Joseph already knew every aspect of the ceremony, but she wanted to ponder on the events of the ritual as she looked forward to her own son's *brit milah*.

After Mary sat in the prophet's chair, the baby was placed on her knees. Jonathan, the *mohel,* said, "I wait for Your salvation, O Lord. I hope for Your salvation, O Lord, and I do Your commandments. O Elijah, messenger of the covenant, behold yours is now before you; stand at my right and assist me. I hope for Your salvation, O Lord. I rejoice at Your word like one who finds great spoil. Great peace have they that love Your law; nothing can make them stumble. Happy is the man You choose and bring near to dwell in Your courts."

The friends of the elderly couple responded by saying, "May we be sated with the blessings of Your house, Your holy temple."

Jonathan made his special preparation to perform the circumcision and looked straight at Zachariah, momentarily forgetting the old priest's inability to speak. The ancient preacher's eyes filled with tears as he realized his handicap during this most sacred and exciting time of his and Elizabeth's life. He looked at his bride of many years for help. And if cued by a higher power, the mother of the baby said, "Behold, I am prepared and ready to perform the positive commandment that the Creator has commanded me; may He be blessed, to circumcise my son."

The small crowd of witnesses turned their heads towards the young priest serving as the mohel to see if he would continue the ceremony. Jonathan smiled broadly and answered Elizabeth, "Said the Holy One, blessed be He to our father Abraham," then looking at the baby on Mary's knees he continued, "Walk before me and be perfect. Behold, I am prepared and ready to perform the positive *mitzvah* that the Creator has commanded me, may He be blessed, to circumcise."

At that point, the baby was lifted into the air by the young priest, as if presented to the Lord for His inspection. As the baby was placed on Mary's knees again, Jonathan said, "Blessed art Thou, O Lord our God, King of the universe, who has sanctified us with His commandments and commanded us regarding circumcision."

Elizabeth, who had herself witnessed so many circumcisions over the years as performed by her husband, responded without hesitation, "Blessed art Thou, O Lord our God, King of the universe, who has sanctified us with His commandments and commanded us to bring him into the covenant of Abraham our father."

Mary turned her head to the small group of her cousins' friends as they responded by saying together, "Amen! Just as he has entered into the covenant, so may he enter into the study of Torah, the marriage canopy, and the performance of good deeds." At the mention of the word marriage, Mary's thoughts momentarily turned to her carpenter and their future unification. But her focus was quickly returned to the ritual at hand as Jonathan delicately and precisely clipped the fore-skin of the baby lying on her lap. The baby squirmed and cried, but one of the guests named Martha, one of Elizabeth's closest friends, picked up the baby and held him close, gently shushing him. Another guest, with whom Mary was not familiar, filled a cup with wine and said, "Blessed art Thou, O Lord our God, King of the Universe, Creator of the fruit of the vine." And the small group responded with a hearty, "Amen!"

******

Aramazar looked especially tired and much older than his 65 years as he folded his priestly garments carefully and put them away for the day. As the priest of Shamash, protector of the poor and those who travel, the old man served King Aretas daily while the superstitious monarch lived in the palace at Susa. Of course, the elderly priest also offered sacrifices and gave blessings from AlQuam. But that work was reserved mostly for the people, especially the dignitaries of the old palace. Aramazar had been serving in the temples of the city for some 50 years now, and his naturally curly red hair had grown silver over the years. His face was wrinkled more than most his age and his brow and hands were marked with dark brown age spots. He had become weary of the priesthood and the duties associated with gods he no longer believed in. In fact, the old man believed in very little anymore and considered retiring during this annual visit of the Nabataean king. But the king was a talker, and the old priest knew the superstitious ruler would probably talk him out of leaving his lofty position. Aramazar had even considered running away from Susa, perhaps disguise himself and join a caravan that would take him far away from the kingdom and his responsibilities.

"Good evening, Uncle," said Meshach, startling the aged priest.

"Oh, Meshach," said the tired holy man, "you frightened me some. What are you doing here? Looking for more answers to your studies?"

"Not exactly," answered the young teacher, "but I would like to talk to you about something that I believe in very strongly." Meshach stood across the room from the old minister. The young scholar respected his uncle and his work, but feared him almost as much. He had always kept his distance, never getting close enough for the two to touch.

"Sit down, Meshach," said Aramazar as he gestured towards a bench to his left. "Tell me what's on your mind." The old priest sat down on a small stool facing the bench where the young man had cautiously positioned himself.

"I've been studying the ancient writings of the Hebrew prophets of old," stated the young scholar.

"Yes, I know," commented Aramazar. "Your research has been the butt of many jokes among most of the wise men of the palace. Have you found something interesting, my Boy?"

"Yes, Sir," answered Meshach reluctantly. Meshach had watched his uncle performing his duties many times, but recently had noticed that the old man's enthusiasm had subsided some over the years. He was not sure how Aramazar would take his revelation. "I've been studying the writings of the prophet Daniel," continued the young intellectual, "particularly his prophecy about the coming of Jehovah's Anointed One who will set Israel free." Meshach studied the face of his uncle to see if the old man was actually interested or just making conversation.

"Why would that be interesting to you... or me?" asked Aramazar rather matter-of-factly. The old priest leaned his left arm on his left leg and placed his closed fist on his right.

"Because of our heritage, Uncle," replied Meshach. "Our ancestors were Jews, captured by the great King Nebuchadnezzar and brought here from Jerusalem. But our ancestors chose to stay here when Nehemiah and Ezra were given the opportunity to take the Jews back to Jerusalem and rebuild the city, because they didn't want to lose their social standing. Then they intermarried with the Chaldeans and Persians and each other. Most have forgotten their lineage. My research has helped me discover my roots. Did you know that you have the blood of Levi running through your veins, Aramazar? You would be serving as a priest of Jehovah in the Great Temple of Jerusalem had your ancient fathers returned with Nehemiah so many years ago."

The old man lowered his eyes to the feet of his young nephew without moving his head. He indeed knew of his ancestry, but had spent most of his adult life trying to hide the facts. After several moments of silence between the two men, the aged priest returned his gaze into the face of the young teacher. And although he said nothing, Meshach knew the old man understood what he was talking about.

"Anyway," continued the young philosopher, "I've calculated the timing mentioned by the prophet Daniel... and I believe that the Deliverer he spoke of will be born in Jerusalem this year."

"Don't you think King Herod is a bit old to father a child? And from what we've heard from travelers... a bit too sick?" asked Aramazar.

"He may be," answered Meshach, "but the old king has nine wives. And one of them just might have laid with him on a night when he wasn't feeling so poorly."

The old Nabataean priest sat stoically for awhile, contemplating his nephew's words. "Assuming all this is true," commented Aramazar after taking a deep breath, "what are you planning on doing about it?"

"Perhaps," stated Meshach, "we could put together a special caravan with Jerusalem as our destination... maybe use the occasion to visit Herod... offer him congratulations on his new son... give the lad a special gift from Aretas. Establish a new trade line with Jerusalem... and maybe Aretas would move us to Petra... and we could be closer to the land of our fathers." Meshach looked directly into the eyes of his uncle, looking for a sign of acceptance of his plan. What he saw was a man deep in thought, pursing his lips and staring at the far corner of the small apartment as if watching an imaginary spider spinning a web to catch his next prey.

"Perhaps you're right, Meshach," noted the old priest after a lengthy silence. "It's worth considering. You do realize that it would take many months to plan all the details, arrange for the merchants and the goods and the transportation. And Aretas would have to give his permission. Let me ponder on this awhile. Have you shared your idea with anyone else?" The young scholar could see from the old minister's facial expression that he was serious.

"Only Abimael," replied Meshach, "but he didn't seem too interested. He doesn't believe in the ancient writings. Still, if he thinks you are interested, I'm sure he'll change his mind."

"I'll talk with him, Nephew," stated Aramazar. "Perhaps together we can change his mind. It would be nice for the three of us to visit this boy king together. And perhaps we can impress Herod by offering gifts to the newborn King of the Jews ourselves."

******

The cart that carried Mary and some merchandise back to Nazareth hit a small rock in the road and forced the young farm-girl to grab the sides of the two-wheeled vehicle. The incident jolted her back to reality, and the fact that she would soon have to confront her intended with the news of the miracle she carried. The angel had said that they should call him Jesus. Her mind returned her again to the events she witnessed in the Judean hills just a few days before.

After Jonathan had performed the circumcision on Elizabeth's baby, he continued with the naming of the child. "Our God and the God of our fathers," he had said, "preserve this child for his father and his mother, and may his name be called in Israel Zachariah, son of Zachariah, the priest."

"No!" interrupted Elizabeth as all the spectators gasped at her boldness. "He shall be called John!"

"Elizabeth," said her friend Martha, "don't be so silly. No one in your family has that name. This child may be the only one you ever have. He should carry his father's name."

But the elderly woman insisted, "His name is John." Elizabeth glared at the young *mohel* in front of her while arching her eyebrows in a rather menacing manner.

The small crowd of onlookers began to murmur amongst themselves. Mary giggled like she had that day Joseph had asked her to be his bride when she noticed the frustration in the eyes of Jonathan, the young mohel. It was obvious that he didn't know what to do. He kept turning towards Zachariah, then to Elizabeth, then to the witnesses. Finally, one of the men went over to the old preacher and using a type of sign language, asked Zachariah what the baby's name should be. The old gentleman motioned for a writing tablet, and to the astonishment of all but Elizabeth, he wrote, "His name is John." The mohel read the writing, and again the small group gasped in amazement.

The younger priest turned to Zachariah, forgetting his handicap of the last year and asked, "Are you sure you want to name him John?"

Suddenly, the old country preacher's tongue was loosed, and he replied, "His name is John." That made the crowd really gasp, for everyone in their small village was aware of the old priest's inability to speak. Even Mary and Elizabeth were amazed. "Now, continue the blessing, Jonathan," said Zachariah. The old country preacher sat up as straight as he could, and with a roguish grin, gestured to his young apprentice-priest to complete the ceremony.

The young student of the Torah was visibly shaken, but mustered the courage to continue. "Our God and the God of our fathers, preserve this child for his father and his mother, and may his name be called in Israel... John, son of Zachariah, the priest. O give thanks unto the Lord; for He is good; because His mercy endures forever! John, son of Zachariah,... may this little one become great!"

The people responded rather flatly, still in a state of shock over the events of the preceding minutes, "Just as he has entered into the covenant, so may he enter into the study of Torah, the marriage canopy, and the performance of good deeds."

Then Jonathan responded, "May He who blessed our fathers, Abraham, Isaac, and Jacob, bless the tender child just circumcised... John, son of Zachariah... and may He send him a complete recovery because he has entered into the covenant. Just as he has entered into the covenant, so may he enter into the study of Torah, the marriage canopy, and the performance of good deeds. And let us say Amen!"

Zachariah, filled with the Holy Ghost, began to praise God, a normal part of the circumcising and naming ritual. "Blessed be the Lord God of Israel," prayed the old priest, "for He has visited and redeemed His people. He has raised up a horn of salvation for us in the house of his servant David as He spoke through the mouths of his holy prophets from the beginning of time. Through these men He has told us that He will save us from our enemies and from those who hate us. This salvation comes because He wants to demonstrate His mercy that He promised our ancestors and because He always remembers

His holy promises. He made a special promise to Abraham to deliver from the hands of our enemies so that we could serve Him without fear. Instead we shall serve Him all of our days in holiness and righteousness." Then the old priest walked over to the woman holding his son and said, "And you, my son, shall be called the prophet of the Highest," he said as he picked up the baby and held him close to his own face, "for you shall go before the face of the Lord to prepare His ways, to give the knowledge of salvation to his people for the remission of their sins through the tender mercies of our God." Then he turned his eyes towards Mary, although no one really noticed, and he said, "The Dayspring from on High has visited us so that light might be given to those who sit in darkness and in the shadow of death and to guide them in the way of peace."

The friends of the old couple murmured amongst themselves about the future of the child whose *brit milah* they had just witnessed. Most were convinced that the baby would grow up to be someone used greatly by God for they recognized that Jehovah had already performed many amazing events surrounding his birth.

"There's a feast to be eaten," announced Elizabeth as she took John in her arms once again. "Please stay and help us celebrate our son." And as the small crowd moved to the roof of the simple country house, they wished the proud parents a hearty, "Mazal Tov!".

Mary's experience had strengthened her faith in God's directions, and she realized that He would give her the wisdom to say the correct words to Joseph. She believed, too, that her carpenter would accept her explanation of the events revealed to her which would become their life. And she knew... that nothing would ever be the same again.

****

57

Chapter Six

The Discovery

Although Mary had been back at her father's house for most of a week, she had not had a chance to speak to Joseph about the miracle that grew inside her. The young maiden was determined to see her intended before sundown. Joseph had been busy working with his brother and father in the community while putting finishing touches on the room he was building for his bride.

Mary recognized the familiar tap on her door that meant her sister, Rebekah, had come to visit. "Enter, big Sister," said the young farm-girl with just a slight hint of aggravation in her voice. Rebekah had spent most of the last few days asking question after question about Mary's visit to Zachariah and Elizabeth. She wanted to know every detail of her younger sister's stay in the Judean hills with those "country folks". Mary had shared everything that she thought was of importance except her own personal circumstance. The young maiden wanted to tell her betrothed first.

"Mary," said Rebekah excitedly, "tell me more about the miracle of Zachariah's speech returning. I find the entire story so fascinating. Are you sure he really couldn't speak all that time?"

"He really couldn't speak, Rebekah," replied Mary. "Or hear, either. God had shut his mouth because Zachariah had doubted the message from the angel. He wanted so much to tell everybody that Elizabeth carried the forerunner of the Anointed One, but he couldn't. Only Elizabeth understood his scratches on the board and his attempts to explain what was taking place."

"I can't imagine not being able to share something so wonderful with everyone," commented Rebekah. "And Elizabeth told you everything that had happened to Zachariah... and to her... and you kept the secret? How did you do it?"

"It wasn't my secret to tell," sighed the young shepherd's daughter.

"Well, I just wouldn't be able to keep that kind of secret," commented Rebekah. "Because the birth of their baby means that the Anointed One will soon be here. This is so wonderful, Mary. Don't you understand what's about to happen? Somewhere in Israel there's another young woman who will soon be blessed above all others." Mary could see the excitement in the eyes of her sister, and she wondered if any of the people at the *brit milah* of Elizabeth's son understood as much as Rebekah did. She wondered if news of the blessed event would spread rapidly and be the center of conversations around supper tables across Judea, or would people ignore the miracles associated with the birth of John. Mary wished for the former, but in her heart, she believed the latter would take place.

"I was just about to prepare myself to visit Joseph," stated Mary. "Would you care to help me wash, big Sister? I want to look my best." Mary stood in the middle of her small room, the same room where she had encountered God's messenger three months earlier just before the Festival of Lights. She watched her older sister retrieve the large bowl to where Mary stood and then busy herself with the arrangements of the cleansing. Rebekah continued to chatter away about what had taken place in the little village of Nazareth over the past several weeks.

"Did I tell you that Ishmael talked with Eleazar about a week ago?" asked Rebekah as she carried in the water to pour over her sister. "According to him, the room is just fine. He said Eleazar didn't know what was keeping Jacob from declaring that the room was ready for you two. Eleazar said it looked perfect to him. Joseph is such a talented carpenter. And I understand that father has given him some of your favorite things to make the room feel more like home for you."

Mary quietly undressed and stepped into the large bowl without responding to her sister's remarks. She stood silently, watching and listening to her sister. "Joseph is a good man, Mary. You're a lucky girl to land him. He'll make you a good husband. Do you think the mother of the Anointed One is anyone we know?"

Rebekah turned to face her little sister and dropped the pitcher of water. She stood staring at the young farm-girl, with her mouth wide open. "Mary!" exclaimed Rebekah in a hushed tone. "What happened to you? How did you gain so much weight? You look..."

The young maiden stood erect and looked straight at her sister. "Rebekah," Mary said calmly, "I'm going to have a baby."

"I can see that!" said the surprised fifteen-year-old. "How... who... oh, Mary! What's Papa going to say? Is it Joseph's? Have you two..."

"No, Rebekah," replied Mary as she covered herself, "the baby is not Joseph's."

Mary was about to share her secret with her older sister when they heard Eli come into the house. "Mary! Mary! Where are you? I've heard some good news at the market today," cried the overweight shepherd. "Mary!" The portly, gentleman farmer burst into the room occupied by his two daughters.

"Oh... pardon me, daughter," said Eli turning his back on the two. Mary looked at her father with a disapproving manner while Rebekah stood silently, almost frozen by the shock of her discovery of her little sister's secret. Eli continued his proclamation, "I heard one of the women at the market talking about a friend of hers speaking with the sister-in-law of Jacob's wife. She said the room would be ready in just a day or two, and that old Jacob could hardly wait to tell Joseph to come here and take his bride... uh... Mary back to his house. Judith... uh... your future mother-in-law has been busy buying up all the food stuffs needed to throw the wedding feast." The old man turned to face his daughters. "The time is at hand, young woman. You will be leaving your father's house soon... to begin your life with your husband. I wish your mother could be here to see this day," he added with just a slight crack in his voice.

"I'm glad mother isn't here now, Father," said Rebekah slowly and with deep emotion. "Mary's got something she needs to tell you." The older of the two women turned to her sister and continued, "Don't you, Mary?"

******

"Anna," called the old business man, "did you see Zachariah, the old priest? He is usually here in Jerusalem for Passover. I wanted to talk to him."

Anna came closer to Simeon and took his arm to gently lead him to his usual spot on Solomon's porch. "Zachariah did not come this year, Old Man," mentioned the elderly prophetess. "He stayed home this year. Didn't you hear? His wife, Elizabeth, had a baby boy. They named him John. I'm sure the old priest must be awfully proud. Jehovah is so very gracious to bless him and his wife with such a wonderful experience in their old age. I just hope they both live long enough to get the boy to the age where he is ready to leave the nest. I know how important it is for Elizabeth to have her curse lifted." Anna's eyes filled with tears as she thought about her own life's disappointment of not bearing a child. She turned away from the old gentleman sitting before her. "Pardon me, Simeon, the wind blew some sand into my eyes," she said.

Simeon's eyes began to glow with excitement as he responded, "A miraculous birth... like Abraham and Sarah... late in years... but a miraculous birth of a son." The old man stood slowly, leaning heavily on his staff for support. "This is the beginning, Anna. It won't be long now… it won't be long now."

*****

It was two weeks after Passover in the 32nd year of the reign of Herod the Great in Jerusalem. And for the most part, it was still business as usual throughout Judea, except in the little village of Nazareth. Rebekah had discovered her younger sister's secret, and Mary had informed her father, Eli, of her circumstances. Both Eli and Rebekah heard only part of the story before their imagination and their concern over the family name being disgraced impaired their hearing. Eli ran immediately to Jacob, the father of Mary's betrothed husband, Joseph, to tell him of the news before his daughter, Rebekah, blabbed the information all over town.

"Jacob, my dear friend," stated the portly shepherd, "I fear our children have not been completely honest in their relationship. It appears that they have been getting to know each other a little more intimately than they should at this point in time."

"What are you suggesting, Eli," asked the village's elder carpenter.

"I am not suggesting anything, Jacob," replied his agrareian friend, "I am stating a simple fact. Mary is with child… about three months along. Now what shall we do about this… situation?"

Jacob looked at his friend, shocked by his accusation that Joseph and Mary had been playing at being husband and wife. The betrothal had followed the law explicitly, and the two were bound to one another in the eyes of everyone in the village. The *ketubah*, the marriage contract agreed to by both Joseph and Mary, had listed his obligations to her during the marriage as well as the conditions of inheritance upon his death. And, of course, the contract contained Joseph's obligations regarding the support of any children of the marriage plus Mary's support in the event of divorce. There was no provision however for infidelity or fornication prior to the actual ceremony. Jacob and Eli had not felt the need for such a provision because neither Joseph nor Mary were "that kind of individual". Technically, if Eli were correct, the actual marriage ceremony would have to be performed immediately. Or the contract could be nullified by Joseph, if he insisted that he had not known Mary… that the baby was not his.

"I'll speak with Joseph tonight," responded the elderly wood-shaper. "We'll let you know tomorrow of his decision."

******

Aramazar had been mulling over Meshach's suggestion of putting together a special caravan of trade goods for Jerusalem to honor Herod's son. This could be a perfect opportunity to carry out his plan to "retire" from the priesthood, or more accurately, run away from his responsibilities. The old priest had become weary of the daily routine of offering sacrifices and prayers to a deity that he no longer believed in. Jerusalem was a large town, and Aramazar figured that he might be able to blend into the crowd in the market place of such a city, hide for a day or two, and escape his duties by leaving town through a different route, possibly a northern route back through Syria, where he could catch a ship for parts unknown. The priest of AlQuam sat at his desk in his apartment and re-read the plans he had made years ago to leave his old way of life for a fresh start. He had been trained as a tent-maker before going into the priesthood, and the old man figured that he could find employment in Togarmar or some other Roman colony making tents for travelers. He had heard of a good tent-maker living in the city of Tarsus, and Aramazar thought that he would start there.

As he reviewed his former plans, making updates, changing a detail or two here and there, the worn-out priest's thoughts turned once again to his nephews. What if Meshach was wrong about his calculations of a new born king of the Jews? What if Herod wasn't able to have relations with any of his wives? The three of them bursting into the court of Herod would not make them seem like very wise men to the crazy puppet-king of Judea or to Aretas IV of Petra. Still it would be a good cover with which to carry out his plans. He would share his idea with no one, not even his youthful nephews. If his plan succeeded, it would be best if they did not know anything, for he would never be able to return to the kingdom of the Nabataeans. The old priest weighed his chances and decided it was worth the risk to free himself from the boredom and hypocrisy of serving AlQuam and Shamesh.

******

Joseph sat on the small chest he had made for his beloved Mary, staring at the bed sitting in the room he had added onto his father's house. This was to be the place to which he would bring his bride… where they would spend at least one year getting to know each other before setting up their own home. The young carpenter recalled his conversation with his father about Eli's discovery of Mary's pregnancy. He had remained silent as Jacob related the news that was already causing the gossips in the tiny Galilean village to wag their tongues. Jacob had laid out the possibilities and Joseph's options. Now the young nail-bender had to make a decision.

Joseph paced from one side of the little honeymoon room to the other, struggling to come up with a solution to the unavoidable truth of Mary's situation. He knew that he was not the father of the child, but he could not picture Mary being unfaithful to him. The way she looked at him the day of the *kiddushin,* the day of sanctification, told him that she was only interested in him; that her heart belonged to him. Still, she was with child. Perhaps someone in the caravan that took her to visit her cousin, Elizabeth, had forced her. Or perhaps, it was a Roman soldier, or someone else who was the father of the baby. But surely, the young maiden would have come to him sooner to report the attack, had that been what had happened. Then again, the two young lovers had not had a

64

chance to see each other for more than five minutes since Mary had returned from the hill country west of Jerusalem. Surely his young, beautiful farmer's daughter had intended to tell him about her condition.

Joseph was well aware that he had the right to nullify the betrothal contract.   He   also understood that the legalists in the small community could have her stoned to death for violating the laws of Moses, whether the father of the child was discovered or not. Even if Joseph stepped in to curb the calls for violence intended to root out the evil among them, the young girl's life would be ruined by the rumors and innuendos that would circulate every time Mary stepped foot outside her house. And the baby would not be accepted by the "good folks" in Nazareth, either. Mary's life would be ruined. But the curly-haired carpenter cared too much for the young girl whose image filled his thoughts to see her reputation destroyed in such a way. He truly loved Mary, but now he was not so sure that she loved him as much as he had believed.

Joseph stopped his pacing by the bed he had shaped with his own hands. While most folks in Nazareth slept on straw mats laid on the floor, Joseph wanted something different for himself and Mary. He had been asked several years prior to repair a bed in Herod's palace while the young carpenter was in the city with his family to celebrate the Passover. He gently touched the top and shook his head. The carpenter of Nazareth deeply loved the young farm-girl and could not bear the thought of all the public shame that would accompany Mary everyday of her life. He sat on the side of the bed slowly and made his decision. The strain of weighing all the options had drained him mentally, emotionally, and physically. As he stretched out on the bed, he announced aloud, more to himself than to anyone else, for he was alone, "I will send her away… to another village… where she is not known… and I'll provide for her there. We'll tell everyone in the new village that her husband died while on a trip abroad. Better that she be pitied than she be killed or shamed to death." With his pronouncement he closed his eyes to try and sleep. Joseph's world had been turned upside down, and nothing would be the same again.

****

Chapter Seven

The Waiting

The sound of the *shofar*, the traditional trumpet made from a ram's horn, split the twilight air the week after Mary had decided to tell her secret to her beloved carpenter. Then came the shout from Eleazar, "The bride-groom's coming! The bride-groom's coming!"

Joseph and his friends walked the streets of Nazareth carrying torches so that they could see in the darkness as they made their way to the house of the portly shepherd, Eli. The young village carpenter's intention was to take Eli's youngest daughter to be his bride. The whole procedure was supposed to be a surprise to the future bride and her family, even though this action had been expected since the betrothal of the two Nazarenes some four months earlier.

Mary heard the shouts and knew her dearly loved-one was on his way to her house to steal her away. Tears filled her eyes as she recalled their meeting the previous week. She had been so afraid that her carpenter had changed his mind before she could explain her situation to him.

Mary had walked resolutely to the home of her beloved less than seven days before, ready to face whatever decision he had made. In the middle-eastern world, though still controlled by a liberal Roman government, the decision-making power in a family was given to the man. Mary was well aware of what could happen, but she placed her trust in Jehovah and in the message of the angel who had been sent to announce to her that she had been chosen above all Jewish women to give birth to the Messiah. And although she had not seen her young carpenter for any length of time in three months, she remembered the way he looked at her when she left for her cousin Elizabeth's house, and her mind replayed over and over again the way that he smiled at her. Surely such a man was full of mercy and God's grace.

The shepherd's young daughter stood as straight as she could as she gently knocked on the door of what she believed would be her future home. Judith, Joseph's mother, opened the door of the humble, village carpenter.

"Mary, my dear child," said the elderly woman as she hugged her future daughter-in-law. "Come in, Dear, come in. Let me get Joseph... he's in your room... putting on the finishing touches." Judith hurried off to the rear of the house, leaving the teen-bride standing near the entry way of the humble dwelling. Mary glanced around the room, taking in every detail. It looked like a normal Jewish home, not unlike her own, in the shape of a box, white-washed exterior and plain interior with hard dirt floors. There were three small anti-rooms where Joseph's folks shared their private times. One of those rooms had been added by her young carpenter for their use. The young girl noticed how cool the room felt.

Joseph entered the big room and stared at his intended. The tall, slender, but muscular worker-in-wood looked directly into the dark eyes of the young girl standing so unashamedly straight, as if she were proud of the situation in which she found herself. Then the young carpenter grinned a bit without moving his eyes away from the face of his betrothed. "Mother," he said calmly, "please fetch father to the house. It's time for him to declare the room ready to receive my bride, so that where I am she may be." Then the grin grew into that special smile that he had only for Mary, while tears filled the eyes of the young girl. Judith looked at the two who were moving ever so slowly closer to one another, and she glanced down, moved backwards a few steps, and then turned to exit the room through the back to retrieve her husband.

"I've got something important to tell you, Joseph," announced Mary as she came within reach of her beloved. "It's going to be hard to believe... I mean... it's still hard for me to believe... but I'm going to tell you the truth. Do you trust me?"

"I know all about it, Mary," said the tall woodworker as he reached out for her hands. "Now, I've got something to tell you... and it's not hard to believe at all."

******

Meshach, the Nabataean scholar, walked side by side with his cousin, Abimael the astrologer, down the hallway behind the main temple of Shamesh in the former Persian capital of Susa on their way to the apartment of their uncle Aramazar the Priest. Neither of the two young men were aware of the reason behind their summons to the abode of their silent mentor. Aramazar had long supported and encouraged the two young men to pursue their association with the palace elite, and had, in fact, intervened on their behalf on several occasions, suggesting to King Aretas that the two youngsters were the future of the kingdom and among his most staunch supporters in the eastern portion of the kingdom. As a result, the two Jewish descendents of the Nebuchadnezzar-era gained favor and promotion in the government.

The two stopped just outside the door leading to the humble apartment of their revered uncle. "Abimael," said the young teacher, "surely the stars have told you what we should expect from this meeting."

"I wish they had," replied the young star-gazer, "but I haven't a clue as to why the old priest has summoned us. I don't know if we should be worried or excited."

"Well, he seemed fine a few weeks ago when I last talked to him," added Meshach.

At that revelation, Abimael moved between his two-month older cousin and the door to block his knock. "Wait a minute," said the truth-seeker in a not-so-amusing tone, "you haven't mentioned that cock-a-maimy idea of yours about the birth of a Jewish king have you?"

"Well," answered the young instructor sheepishly, "I might have mentioned what I've found in the prophecies... accidentally... sort of in passing?"

"Now you've done it, Cousin," answered Abimael in a disgusting manner. "That's probably what this meeting is all about. Who else have you told? Don't you know that Aramazar is probably the most influential priest in the Nabataean kingdom? Entire careers have been destroyed by the word of our uncle in the ears of the king. Meshach, what have you done?"

"I've told no one else, Abimael," answered the young scholar in a defensive tone. "And when I told the old priest, he didn't seem to be nearly as upset as you are. He's probably forgotten about the entire thing."

"I pray you're right, Cousin," stated Abimael. He gave one last angry glare at his "older" relative and turned and knocked on the door.

*****

"Blessed art thou, O Lord our God, King of the universe, who brings forth blessing to His people," said Simeon as he began his morning prayers before heading off to his usual place on Solomon's porch in the grand Temple at Jerusalem. The old, retired businessman continued praying for the Anointed One promised to his people so many years before. He believed with all his being that he would see the face of the Promised Messiah, the Deliverer of Israel, the Anointed of God just as he had been promised some fifteen years before, the same year his beloved Martha had died.

The two of them had been devout followers of Jehovah's teachings, never missing a Sabbath worship, never forgetting the instructions regarding the keeping of each of His festivals.

The former shopkeeper and his wife were more than generous with alms for the poor and other outcasts of society, but never revealed to anyone how much they gave to help those who were not as successful as they had been. The old man knew that he had been blessed, though the couple only had had one son. Unfortunately, the boy died at an early age, and the couple was left with their three daughters to stand by them in their end years. But each of the young women had been bought with a great price by their future spouses, and with the selling of his business, the old gentleman had been left with a large sum of money to tide him over in his waning years.

The grey-bearded believer slowly got up off his ancient knees with a bit of difficulty. Each day brought just a bit more pain to endure; he walked a bit stooped now, but the old man's thoughts were continually on the unfolding promise of the Lord God Almighty. He busied himself with his usual daily routine before leaving his home to walk across town to the Temple where he eagerly looked at each individual who entered the outer courts. He believed that the Anointed One would be an ordinary person, perhaps a young boy, who would become extraordinary because of the Lord's touch on the Chosen One's life. Perhaps the Promised One would not even be aware of God's power and anointing, like the stories he had heard of the young shepherd boy who became Israel's greatest King and the ancestor of the King of Kings. The old man pondered on all these things as he approached the Temple gates. Everything still looked normal... he saw Anna talking to a small group of folks who were awaiting their turn to have their offering blessed by the priests. She smiled at him, acknowledging his presence with a simple nod of her head as she glanced his way while continuing her conversation with the folks who sought her wisdom.

The ancient seeker-of-God's-promise seated himself in his usual spot... and awaited the coming of the Messiah.

******

71

The young maiden of Nazareth stood mesmerized by the stare of her betrothed as he related the news he had for her. Joseph took a deep breath and began explaining the decision he had made just a few hours before his young bride-to-be had arrived to tell him of her own news.

"I know all about your… situation," he said without his special smile. "Your father talked with my father," added Joseph as he noticed the puzzled look on Mary's face. Then, he smiled to reassure her that everything was under control. And he continued his story. "Last night… I spent hours praying… talking to myself out loud… pondering… trying to come up with a solution that would not endanger you… or the child you carry. Nazareth is a small town… and no matter what… folks are going to talk. And some, would demand the purging suggested in Moses' Writings intended to remove sin from the camp. I couldn't let that happen to you, Mary… because I love you deeply… ever since you brought me the cup of water… remember?"

Mary nodded as she studied the eyes of her beloved, and then she blushed slightly as she reviewed in her own mind how she, too, had fallen in love with the village carpenter.

"I had decided to send you back to Zachariah and Elizabeth in the Judean hill country. We'd make some excuses to cover your absence here, and after a year or so, I'd move there to be with you. And we'd just live there," continued the young woodworker. "I fell asleep, working out all the details in my mind." The broad-shouldered carpenter smiled, searching the eyes of his soon-to-be bride and saw the vague look of disappointment mixed with hope.

Mary returned the gaze of her intended, looking for some sign of acceptance and approval. She found it in a new, sly, fox-like grin that appeared on Joseph's lips as he continued his revelation. "While I was dreaming," he said with a twinkle in his eyes, "the messenger of the Lord appeared to me." The young craftsman paused to let that thought sink into Mary's head.

"Gabriel", whispered the young maiden as she gasped at the thought.

"Gabriel", repeated the shaper of wood. "He said to me, 'Joseph, you are one of David's descendents. You should not be afraid to complete the marriage agreement you have with Mary, for that which is conceived in her is of the Holy Ghost.'"

Again the masterful woodworker paused for effect... to see if his words shocked or surprised the young girl. He noticed neither in her eyes, so he continued. "Then the angel said, 'Mary will bring forth a son, and you will call his name Jesus, for he shall save his people from their sins.'" Joseph grinned his broadest at those words while his own eyes began filling with tears. "Don't you see, Mary," he asked more to make a point than to explore her knowledge, "this entire thing fulfills the prophecy I've mentioned several times... through Isaiah it is written, 'Behold, a virgin shall be with child, and shall bring forth a son, and they shall call his name Immanuel... God is with us.'" Joseph pulled his young bride close to him and whispered ever so gently. "You are the mother of the Anointed One. You have been chosen above all others in Israel."

"But you, too, have been chosen," whispered Mary as she looked deeply into the windows of Joseph's soul and saw a just and honest man. "For you will have to teach the child all about the Scriptures and the ways of Jehovah. That, my love, is an awesome responsibility that no one could handle better than you."

The young carpenter glanced away momentarily and a look of understanding came across his face. He had realized the same thing earlier that very morning as he awoke from his dream, well rested, but excited about what lay in store for the couple. Joseph fully understood the implications of marrying his betrothed now... the gossip... the whispers from the townsfolk of Nazareth as they did the math in their heads after Mary began to show more. He knew he would be the butt of jokes spoken by the men of the village during his absence from their company. He regretted the shame that would surely fall on his family as tongues wagged on and on about the infidelity

73

of the synagogue teacher or his young bride. And he was fully aware that their son might never be completely accepted in that small Galilean village, but he also knew that his friends and neighbors would not understand what God was doing with and through the young newlyweds.

Joseph looked back into the dark brown pools of Mary's eyes and said, "We must be married immediately. Father must approve our room. We must not wait any longer." Joseph held his beloved close to him as he heard his mother and father approaching from the rear of the small house. He would have to try to explain the situation to his family as best he could without supplying details, for none of them had ever shared his intimacy with the Scriptures. So many things were becoming clear now, and the village builder knew in his heart that nothing would ever be the same again.

Chapter Eight

The Joining

Most nearly a week had gone by since Aramazar had called his two nephews to his private apartment to discuss with them the plans he was making that would take the three of them on a journey that none of them could imagine. For Meshach and Abimael, the plan seemed like an opportunity to gain more prestige in the eyes of King Aretas as well as a good excuse to leave Susa and return to the homeland of their ancestors. For Aramazar, the journey would be the perfect cover to escape the duties he had grown to loathe. But the old priest had not shared his real reasons with his two kinsmen for fear they might let a wrong word slip to the wrong person who might relay the plot to Aretas. The elderly priest anticipated delays to the adventure and figured the cost of the expedition. Businessmen would have to be contacted and contracts signed that would enable the three men to lead a caravan to Jerusalem with a stopover at Petra. The Nabataean King would have to give his approval for the journey, but Aramazar knew how much the King wished to impress the aging and sickly Herod since the small war that had broken out between the two just five years before. So only the finest materials and gifts would be assembled to present to the new born King of Israel, assuming that Meshach was correct in his analysis of the ancient Hebrew writings. The old priest did not know how much time the three actually had before they would be able to leave the walls of Susa, but he knew the journey could take as much as two years depending on how many stops were made along the way and the size of the caravan itself.

And then there would be the ceremonies of blessing that he would have to conduct at each stop. The thought of asking for Shamesh's guidance and protection for the travelers and all those in the caravan made him cringe a bit, but it would all be necessary to get the old man to Jerusalem and then to freedom. The time needed to complete all the details of the escapade made him anxious in his heart, but he knew that he could not let on to anyone what his real purpose was. For now, he would allow his nephews to dream about governmental promotions and celebrations and eventual riches as all congratulated them on their foresight and diligence and loyalty to the kingdom. The two young men dreamed of having their names go down in history because of their actions. Aramazar secretly prayed to an unknown god that the star Abimael searched the heavens for would appear soon.

****

Mary had been waiting patiently in her room for the appearance of her furniture-making, future husband. She knew he would appear any minute, and she had just finished trimming the wick in her oil lamp kept by her sleeping mat. It was getting close to mid-night, the traditional time when most young brides were snatched from their father's house by the bridegroom. The heart of the younger daughter of Eli beat with great anticipation while she eagerly awaited being kidnapped from her father's house, not by a stranger, but by one with whom she had chosen to spend the rest of her life. Stolen by one who loved her so much that he was willing to pay a high price for her. As was customary, Joseph and Mary had not seen each other for the week preceding the wedding day.

As the young farm girl, clothed in her embroidered under-garments and sandals of porpoise skins, placed the wedding bracelets on her wrists and necklaces around her neck, she recalled the reception that her sister Rebekah had hastily given the young couple at the latter's house. Mary smiled as she remembered the "throne" Rebekah had prepared for her to sit upon as the soon-to-be bride received her guests. Joseph was there, too, but he was surrounded by his own friends who sang made-up songs and toasted the scholarly builder. The two, who were soon to be one, were kept separate.

Rebekah, representing Mary's household stood beside Judith, Joseph's mother, and the two women broke the plates of the young couple. "It's official now, Sister," Rebekah said smiling broadly, "you can't return home. Your plate has been broken. And like this plate that can never be fully repaired, so too a broken relationship can never be fully repaired." The older of Eli's daughters raised one eye brow as if warning her younger sister of an unseen danger ahead... repercussions from the premature actions that had prompted this celebration.

Mary had tried telling Rebekah about the visit from the angel, but the older woman brushed off the younger's expla-nation. She chose to believe the rumors that Joseph's sister-in-law had spread at the market about the two getting together before Mary went to visit Elizabeth three months earlier. Most of the little village of Nazareth chose to do the same thing. And while the action was not acceptable in the eyes of the local gossips, it was not unusual. Besides, the villagers rea-soned that the carpenter's son and the shepperd's daughter had signed the *ketubah,* the marriage agreement, and Mary was considered legally the wife of the young man anyway. The *ketubah* would later be displayed in the couple's home, regardless of the circumstances or events preceding the actual marriage ceremony.

The young farmer's daughter heard a commotion outside. As if right on cue, Joseph appeared at Mary's window wearing the traditional white robe worn on Yom Kippur. Both of the newlyweds had been fasting in preparation of their wedding day. Mary looked out her window at the happy faces of just about the entire village as Joseph placed the linen veil over her face and wrapped her in the special silk wedding garment made by his mother amid shouts of joy from the witnesses, most of whom carried drums and instruments of music. After placing ear-rings in her ears, a ring on her finger, and a crown on her head, the young carpenter then helped his betrothed through the window, and the company proceeded through town in a celebratory procession to the *chupah,* the wedding canopy, set up next to Joseph's parents' home.

****

Anna brushed her long, silvery hair while regarding her reflection in the brass mirror she held in her left hand. The lines on her face showed the pains of her long and tragic life. She recalled how proud her father, Phanuel, had been when she had announced that a young priest named Abner would come to sign the marriage contract.

At the age of 15, she had been considered by many living in her small Galilean village as being an "old maid". Then she met Abner. He had been so strong, so educated, and had such a great future in the priesthood. And the two had been so very happy despite the fact that they were childless. The elderly woman of God smiled as she dropped both hands to her lap and raised her tear-filled eyes to the farthest corner in the small quarters she had shared with her husband for seven years.

"Oh, Abner," she whispered to herself, "why did you have to go?" A tear ran down her wrinkled cheek as she pictured her beloved marching off with the small group of men to try and stop the Roman general Pompey from running over Judea with his army. They weren't successful, and Anna never saw her husband again. The small force he led was no match for the best-trained and best-equipped army in the world.

Unfortunately for Anna, her father had died shortly after her marriage to the young priest. So, she stayed in Jerusalem, remained in mourning for a year, and then decided to remain in the Holy City to devote her life to serving Jehovah and his workmen. The old woman enjoyed praying with the people who waited to have their offerings accepted by the Lord God Almighty. She felt inadequate every time one of the women confided in her and asked the prophetess for advice about being a good wife or raising a family. Anna read the scrolls Abner had left behind and spent many hours praying, and she often overheard the other priests discuss solutions to problems people had confronted them with, so the advice she gave was usually what was scriptural and God-honoring. Unlike most women of that time period, Anna had a ministry meeting the needs of the priests and the people they served. She had chosen to join herself to God's work in a way that most other women either could not or would not do.

Anna continued her morning routine, preparing to go to the Women's Court of the Temple, where she shared her knowledge of God's Word daily with those in need. She looked forward to her normal activities of praying and praising God and mingling with various people, some who anxiously looked for the redemption of Jerusalem... like her very good friend, Simeon. With each new day, and with each new wave from the old businessman, her faith grew stronger that the Messiah would soon be made known. And she would tell everyone who would listen that God's salvation would soon be among them.

****

The little village of Nazareth was a-buzz with the excitement of the wedding ceremony elevating Joseph, son of Jacob, and Mary, daughter of Eli. The villagers had been looking forward to the day of celebration for several weeks, ever since news of the couple's *kiddushim* had spread through the market place. Now the young carpenter and his bride were approaching the *chupah,* the four-poled canopy that Jacob and Eleazar had set up outside the couple's new home. The chupah was symbolic of the two dwelling together and of Joseph's bringing Mary into his household and therefore under his protection. Most also believed the canopy to symbolize the sign of blessing given by Jehovah to Abraham, that his children would be "as the stars of the heavens". The gossips in town had already discussed, analyzed, and invented events that explained Mary's condition, though none had actually taken the time to ask the young girl any questions. The older women of the village had decided to forego the traditional *mikveh,* the purification bath of the young bride because the results were a foregone conclusion... or so they thought. The dull voice of the witnesses were interrupted by the cantor who called for the groom with the "*Barukh haba"* invocation.

Mary approached her groom in the usual manner, and then she circled her carpenter seven times. The eyes of the young twosome had locked on one another during this part of the ceremony until the adolescent farm-girl settled on her *chatan's* right-hand side. Everyone who stood close enough to see grinned widely as the expressions on the faces of the young couple displayed their mutual admiration.

Mary's older sister, Rebekah, stepped forward and poured some wine into a golden cup. Looking at the two standing before her, she raised the cup and said, "Blessed art Thou, O Lord our God, King of the universe, who created all things for His glory." In her mind, Rebekkah recalled their mother's death and her admonition to the older of her girls to look after Mary. Mary had always been the more adventuresome of the two and was constantly getting herself into somewhat embarrassing situations because of her curiosity. Still, Rebekkah knew that their mother would be so proud of her little sister on this day.

Eleazar, Jospeh's brother, stepped forward, and taking the cup from Rebekah, continued with the seven blessings of the wedding ceremony. "Blessed art Thou, O Lord our God, King of the universe, Fashioner of man," he said. Eleazar glanced first at Joseph and then at Mary. He had wondered if he would ever witness this day because his younger brother had never shown much interest in girls... at least not until Mary had offered him that drink of water some months before.

Eli, Mary's father, took the cup from Eleazar and recited his part of the blessing. "Blessed art Thou, O Lord our God, King of the universe, Who formed the man in His image, in the image of the semblance of His likeness, and prepared for him from Himself a building for eternity. Blessed art Thou, O Lord, who fashioned the man." Neither Mary nor Joseph noticed the single tear that slowly trickled down the face of the portly farmer. Eli's house would be empty now, and he would miss the girlish laughter of his youngest daughter and the songs she made up while doing her chores. Still he knew that Mary would make the village's young carpenter an excellent wife. The elderly gentleman was looking forward to spoiling his grandchildren as did all grandparents.

Judith, Joseph's mother, smiled reassuringly at the old shepherd as she took the cup of blessing from his trembling hands. She stood erect with her head high to counter the jokes she had heard about her son and his bride as she delivered her portion of the blessing. "May the barren one exalt and jubilantly rejoice through the regathering of her children amidst her in gladness. Blessed art Thou, O Lord, who makes Zion rejoice with her children." This was the first time during the ceremony that either of the youthful duo had acknowledged the presence of others under the canopy as they simultaneously turned to look into the expressive eyes of the groom's mother. But it was only a momentary distraction for they continued their soulful gaze into each other's eyes.

Ishmael, Mary's brother-in-law, took the cup from Judith and said, "Gladden the beloved companions as You made glad Your creation in the Garden of Eden from days of old. Blessed art Thou, O Lord, who gladdens groom and bride." Ismael, who believed that the two standing before him had dishonored the family name, glared just a bit at the young carpenter, though neither Joseph nor Mary glanced his way. They were both too engrossed in expressing their love for one another while looking deeply into the other's eyes and speaking words that only their two hearts could hear. Ishmael had at one time considered Joseph to be his rival for Rebekah's hand, even though Joseph had never indicated any romantic interest towards Eli's oldest daughter.

Ishmael handed the cup to Jacob, Joseph's father, who stood silently for just a moment reliving in his mind some of the words of wisdom he and his sons had shared while working their hands in wood in various projects in the tiny village of Nazareth. The elderly carpenter was very proud of his youngest son because of his skills with tools and his knowledge of the Scriptures. Jacob raised the cup, and in a voice that momentarily cracked said, "Blessed art Thou, O Lord our God, King of the universe, who created joy and gladness, groom and bride, rejoicing, glad song, pleasure, delight, love, brotherhood, peace, and companionship. Soon, O Lord our God, let there be heard in the cities of Judah and in the streets of Jerusalem, the sound of joy and the sound of gladness, the voice of the groom and the voice of the bride, the sound of jubilation of grooms from their canopies and of youths from their feasts of song. Blessed art Thou, O Lord, who gladdens the groom with the bride."

The young couple again broke their gaze into each others soul and turned their heads towards Jacob, who enthusiastically returned their smiles of joy. The old wood- worker reached out his left hand and placed it atop the clasped hands of the exuberant couple standing before him. He, too, had heard the rumors and the jokes about Joseph and Mary getting together possibly even before the sanctification ceremony, but he brushed them off as idle talk and jealousy. The elderly gentleman-carpenter was convinced that the man and woman standing in front of him were made for each other and nothing else mattered. The rumors would soon cease as would the jokes, and he would love their children just as much as he loved Eleazar's two sons.

Rebekah, her face beaming with joy, took the cup from Jacob, lifted it as high as she could and recited in her loudest voice, "Blessed art Thou, O Lord our God, King of the universe, Creator of the fruit of the vine."

With that blessing, Joseph took the cup from Rebekah and drank. Then he offered the cup to his *kallah*, Mary, who drank the remainder of the wine. The young carpenter reached for a glass sitting on a small table and threw it to the floor and smashed it with his right foot. Some thought this gesture would scare away evil spirits while others believed the action was symbolic of taking the bride's virginity. Regardless of what anyone believed, they all triumphantly shouted, "Mazal Tov!"

Amidst shouts and clapping of hands and joyous laughter, Joseph took his young bride to the room he had prepared for her. He closed the door, and both tuned-out the noisy celebration on the other side of the wall. It was here, in this private room prepared by his own hands, that Joseph pulled Mary close and kissed her for the first time. This was the moment both had anticipated for so many weeks, and neither was disappointed. The young couple held this embrace for over a minute.

Joseph gently cupped his huge, rough, woodworker's hands around his young bride's face. Looking deeply into her dark brown eyes, he said, "You are so beautiful, my darling... more beautiful than words can tell. Your eyes look like doves through your veil. Your long, curly, black locks tumble freely in waves around your face, shimmering beautifully like a flock of goats winding down the slopes of Mt. Gilead."

Mary smiled broadly as her beloved carpenter voiced his praise for her womanly charms. She recognized the quotation from Song of Solomon, and she completely understood each of the "country-styled" analogies.

"Your smile is generous and full," continued Joseph, "your teeth are evenly matched making your smile expressive and strong and clean. Your lips are like red jewels... so elegant and inviting. Your veiled cheeks display a rosy, healthy glow like pomegranates." The tall woodworker gently moved his hands to the young maiden's neck as she breathed deeply and closed her eyes. "The smooth, lithe lines of your neck," he continued softly, "command notice. All heads turn towards you in awe and admiration. Your breasts are like the twin fawns of a gazelle, so soft and loveable... grazing among the first spring flowers. The sweet, fragrant curves of your body; the soft, spiced contours of your flesh invite me, and I willingly come to you. I stay until dawn breathes its light, and night slips away. You are entirely beautiful, my love, from head to toe; beautiful beyond compare and absolutely flawless."

Then Joseph turned to a small table where he had pre-pared a simple snack of figs and bread for himself and his bride to break their fast before returning to the marriage feast outside their humble dwelling. The two ate slowly, deliber-ately, taking in every muscle movement of the other as they placed a morsel of food into the mouth of the other. Joseph placed the fig he was holding back into the wooden bowl on the table, looked into his beloved's eyes and said, "Mary, we need to talk."

****

Meshach tapped on the doorway of Abimael's apartment as he walked purposefully into the youthful star-gazer's abode. "Greetings, Cousin," he said smiling broadly. "And what do the stars tell you about our fate today?"

Abimael looked up from his desk looking only slightly annoyed by his cousin's disturbance. The two double-cousins usually got along well except for those occasions where Meshach began promoting one of his schemes to earn the two special recognition from King Aretas. The young scholar could become rather obnoxious and overbearing during those times.

"The stars tell me that we are alive," answered Abimael with just a hint of sarcasm, "and that our future is before us." He grinned slyly at his learned kinsman wondering if Meshach caught the irony in his statement.

"I saw Aramazar yesterday," began the young seeker-of-truth, "and he seems to be getting excited about our journey. You should see the list he's preparing... businessmen to talk to... supplies we'll need... the route we'll take... and the stops along the way... small towns... large cities... oasis. He's planning a large caravan... maybe fifty camels... maybe a hundred!" Meshach leaned back on the small couch close to Abimael's desk and tossed a grape into the air before catching it in his mouth.

"What if you're wrong, Meshach?" asked Abimael. "What if there is nothing in the heavens to indicate the birth of Herod's son? What if the old king is as diseased as we've been told and can't father any more children? Or what if he has fathered another son and that madman goes crazy again and kills the baby or its mother long before we get there? What if we embarrass ourselves and Aretas? Have you thought fully of the consequences of failure?"

"Stop worrying so much, Cousin," answered the young scholar. "I've studied the ancient writings thoroughly. A new king will be born who will be anointed by God. And his kingdom will be great."

"Which god?" replied thy young astrologer, more to himself than in conversation.

"The Lord God Jehovah," answered Meshach sternly, "the God of our ancestors."

Abimael, like his uncle Aramazar, had grown skeptical of gods and answers in the stars and in life as a whole. He had faith in humankind making mistakes, and, like all pessimists, looked for the worst to happen. The young soothsayer sighed deeply and continued revealing his doubts. "Meshach, you know that only a few of our ancestors were Jews. Jehovah is the God of the Jews only... not of half-breeds or mixed races... and most certainly not the god of the Nabataeans."

"He is the God of anyone who accepts Him, Cousin," answered Meshach. "I believe the ancient writings, the Scripture as our ancestors call them, are true, and the prophecies are being fulfilled each day. What has been laid out will come to pass. You and I can't stop it, so we'd best not get in His way," added the twenty-something seeker-of-truth. "Besides… all this activity Uncle Aramazar is planning gets us to Jerusalem!" Meshach grinned big and caught another grape in his mouth.

"You've never seen Jerusalem, Meshach," commented the youthful star-gazer, "why do you want to go there? Our ancestors, as you call them, chose to stay in this land when they had the chance to return there hundreds of years ago. Maybe this land we live in here and now is better than the land of the Jews."

"Jerusalem is God's city, my wise cousin," suggested Meshach. "It is the center of the earth… and it is the home of our ancestors. Good things will happen to us while we are there… wait and see," said the young teacher with a special wink of his eye.

Abimael stared at his older cousin without expression. He knew that arguing with him over the practicality of his scheme was a waste of time. Perhaps, thought the young astrologer, Jerusalem might offer a respite for his ever-growing ideological doubts. Still, Jerusalem was a long distance to the west, and besides, there had been no indication in the heavens that anything out of the ordinary had or was about to take place.

****

The joyous occasion that joined Joseph and Mary as one was followed by a festive dinner. The guests participated in the *Mitsvah of L'Sameach Chatan v'Kallah* celebrating with much music and dancing. Mary mused about Joseph's words to her in their room. She didn't fully understand the words of her scholarly carpenter, but she trusted him completely. She had dreamed of their union on their wedding night with much anticipation. But Joseph's words had made her a bit uncomfortable.

"We must not come together, Mary," said the young shaper-of-wood, "until after the baby is born. It is important for your virginity to remain intact until that time... to fulfill the scriptures."

"I know you love me, Joseph," answered Mary shyly. "But won't people think it is strange that we don't show our love... before then?"

"We will live together and have a normal relationship as newlyweds... as far as the village and our family is concerned. I will hold you close and kiss you tenderly, but we must not get to know each other in that special way... until after the baby is born. It will be hard on both of us... but you are carrying the son of God. The people of Nazareth and our family think otherwise... and I believe that it will be a waste of time to try and explain everything to them right now. They won't listen now because they are not ready to listen. But someday they will listen... and they will understand. And we will have other children that will be totally ours... but we must wait. Trust me on this, my Love... for it must be." Joseph held Mary closely again to reassure her that everything was under God's control.

Mary's thoughts were interrupted by Jacob reciting the special grace after the festive meal, and then Rebekah led the couple's guests in repeating the Seven Blessings once again.

For the next seven days following the wedding, friends and relatives provided festive meals in honor of the newlyweds. The tiny village of Nazareth celebrated as much as they ever had. Joseph and Mary were together, and God's plans were moving along on schedule, and nothing would ever be the same again.

Chapter Nine

The Journey

Joseph reached up to touch Mary's hand as she supported herself in the little cart that he had made for her to help make their journey to Bethlehem more comfortable. Though a bit worried, she returned his special smile that reinforced his love for her. Judith, who had been sharing the cart with her obviously pregnant daughter-in-law had tried to pass the time of day in a pleasant manner. Unfortunately, her tales of her own labor pangs and those of other family members were actually unsettling to the former farm-girl. Mary only partially listened to her mother-in-law's stories. Instead, the young bride chose to relive in her mind the events of the past few months.

The youthful bride smiled as she remembered walking up to the small carpenter shop where Joseph and his family worked. She and her woodworker husband had been married for only three months when word came about the census ordered by Augustus Caesar. The Roman Emperor was curious to find out how many people lived within the boundaries of the Empire. And he was eager to find out how much he could exact from them for tax purposes.

"Joseph," said Mary as she waited at the door for his invitation to enter his workshop. Her young husband had been working on a special project with which he had planned on surprising her. He had asked her not to come to the workshop unless she felt that there was an emergency he needed to attend to. "Joseph," repeated his young bride, this time just a slightly bit louder. She could hear him working in the far shadows shaping something with one of his carpentry tools, but she could not see what he was working on because Joseph's body shielded his project. "Joseph," she said a little more loudly.

The young woodworker stopped what he was doing and turned his head toward the sound of his bride's voice. Looking over his shoulder, he responded, "Mary. What are you doing here? Are you alright?"

"Everything's fine, Joseph," responded Mary with a little grin. Ever since Judith had shared a story of one of her cousin's miscarriages several years ago with the newlyweds, Joseph had seemed a bit nervous with every birth pang that Mary experienced. He kept reassuring her that nothing would happen because she was carrying God's son, and that Jehovah would not let anything happen to her. Mary believed her husband completely, partly because she was aware of his great love for her and partly because she knew that he was trying to convince himself that everything that was happening to her was extra-ordinarily normal.

Joseph hastily threw a covering over his project as he faced his beloved. "What's going on, Mary?" He walked towards his bride while wiping his hands on his tunic.

"I've just come from the market," stated Mary. "Went there looking for the ingredients for tonight's supper. While we were there, two young soldiers hung an announcement on the pole holding up Caleb's canopy. The announcement said that Rome has ordered our people to be counted... everyone is to return to their ancestral home as soon as possible to register." Mary did not anticipate Joseph's reaction. He sighed heavily and smiled a gigantic smile.

"I've been wondering just how the Lord was going to do it," he said with his grin that meant he had just made another discovery of Scriptural proportions.

"Do what, Joseph?" asked the former farmer's daughter.

"Get us to Bethlehem, my Love," stated Joseph calmly, but still with that signature grin. "You see, Mary," he continued, "the prophets of old declared that the Anointed One would be born in Bethlehem. And I've been trying to develop a plan to get us there. And trying to figure out how we can explain the journey to our folks." Mary delighted over the way Joseph's eyes twinkled when he was explaining some truth in the Scriptures. His eyes were twinkling just that way now.

"I'm not sure that I understand, Joseph," offered the young mother-to-be, "how this all fits together."

"Well... Rome has ordered a census to be taken," continued the young shaper-of-wood, "and we are to return to our ancestral home. We both are of the house of David. And David's house... was in Bethlehem. So we have a perfect excuse to journey with our families to Bethlehem."

"But the decree said that we should go as soon as possible," stated Mary. "I am not that far along, Joseph. And the journey shouldn't take more than a week."

"Did the soldiers indicate just when this decree from Caesar was made?" asked Joseph.

"No," answered the former shepherdess, "but I overheard one of the men who read the decree say that it must have been made over two years ago. It just took awhile to get the news all across the Empire."

"True," affirmed the young woodcraftsman, "and we are on the outer edge. Still, even Rome must be aware that this is the planting season. They've waited this long... they'll have to wait until after the harvest. We'll leave the first part of Tishri... and be in Bethlehem for the Feast of Tabernacles." Joseph grinned again, but this time it was his special grin reserved only for Mary.

"And that will be just in time," said Mary, nodding as she began to understand his explanations. "Just in time for the birth of God's son." She looked deeply into her beloved's eyes and matched his grin.

****

Ten-year old Simon had followed his father, Achim, and his older brother, Nathaniel, to the hills above Bethlehem like he had done since he had been old enough to accompany them on their daily trek to find adequate pasture for the family's flock of sheep. The lambs that had been born in the Spring were much more active now and a bit likely to stray from the rest of the flock, seeking new adventures on their own. It was Simon's job to make sure these slightly unintelligent creatures did not stray too far away from the safety of the rest of the flock and the guidance of the two shepherds who depended on them to supply funds to meet the family's needs.

Achim had been leading his flock into green pastures for almost fifty years now, and he was proud of the reputation he had built up with the locals and the priests in nearby Jerusalem for having animals almost always acceptable for the many sacrifices offered through out the year in the great Temple. Of course, he and his family were only one of possibly two dozen families who tended the flocks near the City of David.

Sheep were very valuable to the Jews, and shepherds were looked on with deep respect by most in the region. Those who took extra good care of their flocks, as did Achim and his boys, were respected even more highly. Sheep were a source of milk, meat, and wool, from which much of the clothing of the country-folk was made. But more importantly, sheep were sold in the market outside the Temple area to be used by the more wealthy citizens of Jerusalem as well as the more well-to-do pilgrims who entered the city during the feasts of Passover, Pentecost, and Tabernacles. And with the Feast of Tabernacles just days away, Achim took every precaution to assure that his sheep were well fed and not blemished by the terrain of the area. His lambs would be especially well suited for sacrifice and for the celebrations that accompanied Succoth.

"The grass seems to be especially thick this season, Father," stated Nathaniel as he leaned against his shepherd's staff at the top of the small plateau where Achim had settled his flock. "They will graze well tonight."

Nathaniel was the oldest of Achim's sons by some 18 years, but the third of the old man's children by his wife Hannah. The young shepherd was taller than his father by almost half a foot and his naturally curly, black locks swayed in the gentle breeze that freshened the air atop the small hill. Achim planned on splitting his flock with his son within the next two years, so that Nathaniel could start his own family. The two men watched the skinny lad some 100 yards below them as he hurried the young lambs along.

"He'll make a fine shepherd, Father," commented Nathaniel. "You've taught him well."

"Yes, my son," replied the older shepherd, "your younger brother learns quickly. And he has a heart for the sheep. But I sometimes wonder if he will follow us in our trade. His head seems to be filled with the stories the rabbis tell of the coming of the Messiah. And he gets so excited during each of the festivals. Have you noticed the way he looks at the visitors who stream into the village? "

"Simon has never met a stranger, that's for certain," answered the younger of the two men with a grin, "and he is inquisitive."

"Too much, sometimes," replied Achim. "He makes statements to those strangers that perhaps he should not make... especially concerning King Herod."

"That old fox has nothing to fear from a small shepherd boy," stated Nathaniel emphatically. "He is not David... and Herod is not Saul."

"True on both accounts, my son," answered Achim, "but Herod has had so many of his own family killed because he thought they were more popular than he. Everyone knows that none of them were really trying to plan a rebellion against his power. Still, he killed them. A man like that would not even think twice if word got back to him about a young shepherd boy from Bethlehem who questioned his Roman idealism. He would kill the boy."

"Surely not even Herod would take the life of an innocent boy," stated Nathaniel. "Even he could not be so ruthless as to do that."

The two men looked into each other's face for a sign of agreement. Then Achim turned to gaze on his younger son. "I truly hope not, Nathaniel. Still I am glad that Herod is in Jericho right now, and I pray, as does all of Israel, that his sickness will end his cruel reign soon."

****

It seemed to Mary that her mother-in-law had been talking ever since the small caravan had left the security of their home in Nazareth for the journey to Bethlehem. The cart Joseph had made was much more comfortable than trying to ride on the back of a donkey for 70 miles and much more relaxing than walking that distance. But the noise of Judith's stories was about to drive the young maiden crazy. Surely their journey would end soon. And then she saw it… the tomb of Rachel on the outskirts of the tiny village of Bethlehem.

Joseph and Mary had started out with their families about a week before, crossing over the mountains through Cana to the southern shores of the Sea of Galilee. All along the way, they picked up other families heading south for the Roman census as well as the Feast of Tabernacles. In order to avoid thieves along the way, people traveled these routes in groups. Sometimes, travelers would hire a protector or guide to secure the safety of the journey.

Mary recalled how the small band of pilgrims crossed the Jordan River just south of Beth Shean to the east side of the river. This frequently traveled road was easier and safer down to Jericho, where the travelers crossed back onto the west side of the river. The young maiden marveled at the sight of the castle compound built by Herod as his summer head-quarters. The temperature in this fertile green valley would have been milder than the fall temperatures in Nazareth or in the mountains around Bethlehem, and the topography was mostly smooth.

Mary grinned slightly as she remembered Joseph telling of a merchant who had dared to travel the barren wilderness between Jericho and Bethlehem alone. The foolish man was too miserly to hire protection or to join a caravan for safety. And sure enough robbers attacked him, beat him, and left him for dead. Fortunately, a kind man in another caravan doctored him and took care of him until they reached the small village.

"We're here, Mary." The voice of the former shepherdess' young husband broke her imaginative journey and ceased the chattering of Judith.

"There are so many people, Joseph," commented the soon-to-be-mother, "where did they all come from?"

"From all over Israel, My Love," stated the young wood-worker. "Most of them have come for the Feast of Tabernacles that celebrates the harvest. Jerusalem must be full to capacity by now. Folks are already putting up their tents along the four miles or so to the Great City. And in two days, there will be no vacancies anywhere."

"Oh I do hope that your cousin, Malachi, has kept ample room for us and our animals in his caravansary," added Judith. "He won't want to deal with your father if he hasn't."

"I'm sure there will be room for us, Mother," answered Joseph with a slight grin, the one that Mary had recognized which indicated that her carpenter was not the least bit worried about what was about to happen. And then he looked once more at her and grinned that special grin reserved only for her. And Mary, though frightened as any young girl might be who was about to give birth, felt confident that everything would be as Joseph had so carefully explained to her.

****

Zachariah entered the small apartment he had reserved for himself and Elizabeth and their six-month old baby with a strong sense of accomplishment that manifested itself in the grin on his face. He stood for a moment just inside the little room where he had many times spent his evenings praying and studying the scriptures, preparing himself for the next day's activities in the Temple. He and his wife of over 40 years lived just down the road a piece from Jerusalem, but he seldom ventured into the city except during his appointed times to serve the Lord God Jehovah. He had missed his prior time of Temple service during the Passover because he had stayed behind in his little village in the hill country of Judea to attend to Elizabeth's needs during the latter stages of her pregnancy. The old country preacher looked at the scene of his beloved sitting on the bench beside the small table while she nursed their long awaited boy child... the boy child he had insisted be named John despite arguments from friends in the village. The old priest and his wife believed the Angel's declaration that this little boy would grow up to be the forerunner of the Messiah.

"Elizabeth," said the elderly servant of the Lord, "I've just come from Abihu's room. He agreed to offer the job of adding onto the priest's quarters to Jacob and his sons right after Succoth. So we will indeed have a chance to visit once again with Mary. I've heard that Jacob and his sons and their families are all in Bethlehem now to register for the census and to celebrate the Feast of Tabernacles. And if your calculations are correct, my Dear, Mary should be giving birth any day now." The elderly couple both grinned from ear to ear, for they knew and understood who Mary's baby was... the Promised One... the Anointed One... the Messiah. He would make His journey into the world just as Jehovah had planned, and nothing would ever be the same again.

****

Chapter Ten

The Good News

T he hills and mountains around Bethlehem are porous, providing many caves. Joseph led his beloved into one of these small caves owned by his cousin, Malachi, the local keeper of the caravansary. The young carpenter from Nazareth gently helped Mary past the animals in the outer manger and into the smaller inner room filled with fresh hay. Although the young shaper-of-wood was quite concerned about his teen-aged wife giving birth in a place that housed animals, he did not show his fears to her. He kept grinning that special smile of his to comfort his young bride as best he could.

"Joseph," said Mary rather heavily, "are you sure that this is the best place to have a baby?" The young maiden was obviously having birth pangs as she recalled the scene in her cousin Elizabeth's house some six months before.

"It may not be ideal, Mary," answered Joseph in as calm a manner as he could. "But I agree with Naomi... the caravansary is so crowded with people... and there are small booths everywhere. This manger will offer protection from the leering eyes of all those inquisitive strangers... and protection from the nightly chills, too. The animals in the outer room will provide us with warmth. Now try to relax, Mary. Naomi will be here with the birthing stool soon... and Mother will also attend you... talk to you to get your mind off the birth... as you talked to Elizabeth. Remember?"

Mary did indeed remember. She remembered mostly how frightened she was. But that fear was not to be compared to the fear she now experienced, for the young girl was about to become a mother. She also remembered how Judith had talked the entire journey from Nazareth to Bethlehem with stories of all the things that could go wrong during the birth of her baby. She loved her mother-in-law, but could not conceive of Judith offering her any comfort.

"Joseph," she said in between her short gasps for air. "Please... you perform the function of the comforter... please." The young carpenter looked deeply into his beloved's eyes... and grinned... trying his best to hold back the tears welling up in his eyes. Not tears of sorrow or shame... but tears of empathy.

"Certainly, my Love," he whispered. "Everything else is different about this birth. I might as well have a part in it myself."

Mary smiled as best she could. Her beloved had kept reassuring her that Jehovah was in control. Still, she quickly recalled how Joseph had opened the ark in the synagogue of Nazareth before the reading of the Torah during each sabbath celebration for the past month. She closed her eyes as she recalled the words of the Zohar, "When the congregation takes out the Torah Scroll, the Heavenly Gates of Mercy are opened, and God's love is aroused." The Jews believed that the husband opening those Gates of Heaven would elicit God's blessings making childbirth easy and without complications. Mary prayed that that custom would become reality.

Naomi came into the small cave carrying the birthing stool and several strips of cloth with which to bind the baby as soon as possible after birth. Judith followed closely behind her. The caravansary's wife placed the stool on a pile of hay close to Mary and indicated that Joseph should help his young wife to sit down. Judith stood off to the left of Joseph, wringing her hands. She had not acted as the comforter in many years and was not at all sure that she could perform the duty well.

Joseph noticed the concern in his mother's eyes and offered a way for her to calm herself and ease Mary's fears, too.

"Mother," he said politely, "would it be alright with you if I talked to Mary while she gives birth. Perhaps you could make sure that the swaddling cloths are in order." Judith nodded enthusiastically and turned her back to the trio to measure the length and width of each piece of cloth. Naomi gave a stern look towards Joseph as if to say she doubted the young carpenter's ability to not faint when the actual birth took place.

"Now, Mary," instructed the woman kneeling in the hay before her. "You need to relax as much as possible. Concentrate on the words Joseph whispers in your ear… words of good tidings." The older lady lifted one eyebrow and glared at Joseph, who just grinned as if he had done this countless times and knew exactly what to say.

Naomi pulled up Mary's robe and spread her legs to get a glimpse of just how far along the young girl was. "Oh my!" she gasped. With her mouth wide open and a look of complete puzzlement on her face, she added, "She can't be having a baby! Why, she's still a …"

Joseph quickly took control of the conversation. "It's a long story, Naomi," he interrupted before the older woman could finish her phrase. "I will tell you all about it later." And then he grinned as if to say 'We've got a secret'… and continued, "Mary is going to have a baby… tonight… so you concentrate on your part. I'll concentrate on taking Mary's mind off the pain… the Lord will do the rest." At that he searched the eyes of his young bride who, though in pain, managed to grin a special grin she had saved for just such a moment.

****

Achim and his two sons, Nathaniel and Simon, had just bedded down the sheep for the night. They had found a great pasture during the day and were content to simply remain with their flock on the hillside that night rather than take them into town and risk losing the pasture to another shepherd. They had taken the precaution of constructing a small tent in which they would celebrate the Feast of Tabernacles there in the fields with their sheep. In two days, the old shepherd and Nathaniel would be rejoicing at their harvest, for the lambs would be taken into Jerusalem to be sold for sacrifice.

"Simon took really good care of the lambs, Father," commented Nathaniel as he placed two small twigs on the campfire. "He has watched them very closely. They should bring a good price in the Temple."

The elder shepherd nodded his approval of his oldest son's statement. "The boy works really well with animals... but he does have a short temper that might one day get him into trouble."

"He'll grow out of it, Father," added Nathaniel. "Besides, he believes we are truly doing part of Jehovah's work by taking care of the lambs. You know he has a deep understanding of all the sacrifices."

A crooked little smile came across Achim's face as he thought of his youngest son. Simon was very athletic, very studious, and very mature for a ten-year old boy. He admired his son's inquisitiveness and often became frustrated with some of the lad's questions... especially those concerning the Torah. Still, he was a good shepherd and a good son.

****

"Now would be a good time for you to start whispering into Mary's ear, Joseph," said Naomi who still carried a strange expression on her face. She simply could not believe what she was witnessing.

Joseph sat down beside his young bride, placed his arm lovingly around her shoulders, pulled her as close to himself as possible, and began to whisper into his beloved's ear. "There will be no more sorrow for those who are now in anguish. The people that lived in darkness have seen a great light," he stated, "upon those that tabernacle in the land of the shadow of death, light has dawned." Joseph took a breath as he squeezed the hand of the young maiden at his side and continued, "A green Shoot will sprout from Jesse's stump, and a Branch shall grow out of his roots. The life-giving Spirit of God will hover over Him, the Spirit that brings wisdom and understanding, the Spirit that gives direction and builds strength, the Spirit that instills knowledge and a deep respect of Jehovah."

"Push, Mary, push!" said Naomi rather loudly. "I can see the baby's head!" Mary, drenched with perspiration, looked into the eyes of her carpenter as he continued speaking to her in his calm, reassuring voice. And she pushed.

"He won't judge by appearances, won't decide on the basis of hearsay. He'll judge the needy by what is right and render decisions on earth's poor with justice. His words will bring everyone to awed attention. A mere breath from his lips will topple the wicked. Each morning He'll build righteousness and faithfulness in the land and bring a living knowledge of Jehovah." Mary was breathing ever so heavily, but still managed to grin at her beloved woodworker, despite her groans of pain. Joseph held her even more tightly but with a gentleness that reassured the girl of Jehovah's strength.

"Once more, Mary! Push now!" instructed the middle-aged midwife. Mary groaned loudly and pushed with all her strength. Judith had turned around by this time and had placed her hand over her own mouth as she grabbed her own stomach. Mary only glanced momentarily at her pale mother-in-law who looked as if she were in more agony than was necessary. Judith had been muttering something only half aloud that sounded vaguely like Psalm 4 to the young girl.

"It's a boy! Joseph, God has given you a son!" exclaimed Naomi. "Blessed art Thou, o Lord our God, King of the Universe, who is good and causes good."

"I'll go tell the good news to Jacob and Eleazar," said Judith as she dropped the linen strips she had been preparing for the newborn. Mary let out a laugh of relief and looked into Joseph's sparkling eyes.

"It's a boy, Joseph," said Mary, "just like the Angel said."

Joseph placed two fingers from his right hand gently over his young bride's lips. He grinned his special grin for her and this time added a wink as he continued, "A child has been born... for us! The gift of a son... for us! He'll take over the running of the world. His names will be Amazing Counselor, Strong God, Eternal Father, Prince of Peace." And then Joseph placed his lips to Mary's ear once more and whispered, "Just like the angel said."

****

Achim was about to nod off as his two sons kept watch over their flock of sheep grazing on the hillside near Bethlehem. He was old and tired, and the night was perfect for napping. So many stars shinning, he thought, enough to make it difficult for any kind of enemy of his sheep to sneak up on them. Besides, his two boys were there, and they were young and full of energy and awake.

Suddenly, the angel of the Lord made his presence known to the shepherds. And the glory of the Lord shone like a bright light all around them. It was like the full moon had traveled out of its path and stood directly above them. Needless to say, they were quite frightened.

"Don't be afraid," the angel spoke ever so eloquently and calmly. "I've been sent to tell you about some great news that will make you want to jump for joy. And everyone who hears what I am about to share with you will no doubt be just as happy."

The three shepherds gazed first at each other then back to the heavenly being standing before them.

"A short while ago," continued the angel, "in Bethlehem, David's city, a Savior was born. He is the Lord's Messiah. You will recognize the babe by the swaddling clothes in which he is wrapped, and you will find him lying in a manger."

Before the shepherds had time to react to this news, a multitude of angels joined the messenger of Jehovah in the air just above the hillside camp, all of which made the small hill shine brighter than a new coin. The other angels began praising God, and together they exclaimed, "Glory to God in the highest, and on earth, peace, good will toward all."

And just as suddenly as they had appeared, the angels all vanished, leaving the three shepherds in a state of shock and amazement. Several minutes passed before any of the animal-tenders could speak. They just stood with their mouths open, gazing into the heavens.

"Can this thing be true?" questioned Achim, more to himself than to the others. "Can it be that the Promised One has been born tonight?" The old shepherd looked around slowly at the sheep bedded down for the night. Then he looked first at Nathaniel and then at Simon.

"Father," said the youngest of the shepherds, breaking the silence, "were the men we just saw... angels?" Achim stood glued in his tracks, frozen at the thought that angels had come to deliver such good news to them. Nathaniel took control of the conversation.

"Yes, Simon," he said as calmly as he could, "they were angels. Sent to tell us about the birth of the Anointed One."

"But why us, Brother?" asked the boy shepherd. "Surely this news was meant for the ears of the priests in the Temple."

"I don't know the answer to your question, Simon," answered the more experienced of Achim's sons. "Perhaps we should get over to Bethlehem as soon as we can and see for ourselves if what has been revealed has actually happened."

"But what about the sheep, Father," questioned Simon, "we can't just leave them here unattended... can we?"

For the first time since the angels appeared before them, the old shepherd smiled. "What we've been told is more important than our sheep, Young One. We must go to Bethlehem and see this thing for ourselves. I don't think we need to be afraid for our sheep. They will be safe." Achim motioned for his sons to get moving, much in the same manner that he did daily when herding his sheep towards a particular spot. "Let's go, Boys!"

The three shepherds didn't even take any of their belongings with them, but began hurrying down the hillside towards the tiny village of Bethlehem in search for the right manger housing the new born Messiah. The light from all those stars hastened their journey in the night.

****

Abimael stared in amazement for several seconds as he saw what appeared to be a new star shinning much more brightly than the rest... just above the horizon towards the western sky from where he stood... towards the general direction of Jerusalem. He tried to reason within his own mind just what was occurring. Possibly two of the planets were aligning at that moment which gave the illusion of a new star. Perhaps it was just a reflection of some sort. Perhaps his eyes were playing tricks on him. He looked away, turning towards the northern sky and then towards the eastern sky, but there was nothing that even remotely resembled the bright light he witnessed towards the land of his ancestors. And then the light or the star or whatever it was seemed to vanish. There were millions upon millions of stars shinning that night. What made this one appear to be so much brighter than the others? The young Nabataean star-gazer didn't have all the answers. Had he not been aroused from sleep just a few minutes before, he might have missed it altogether. But he had seen it, even though he did not know what it actually was. Meshach would have an answer for him... an answer Abimael probably would not like, but still, an answer. The young astrologer grinned and shook his head as he imagined the reaction from his cousin as he told him the good news of the appearance of the star the young teacher had talked about for most nearly a year.

****

Simeon was aroused from his sleep by the sound of what he believed to be a bunch of folks speaking in unison, possibly reciting something. He could not make out what was being said, but he could have sworn that he heard something... almost like a chorus of voices... coming from the direction of the small village of Bethlehem.

He arose from his warm bed and peered out the entrance of his sukka towards the southeast. But there were too many buildings in Jerusalem and too many small booths like his where worshippers dwelled for Succoth. These shelters represented the clouds of glory with which Jehovah had shielded Israel from harm during their wanderings in the wilderness after their liberation from Egypt so many years ago. He couldn't be sure, but his spirit told him something had happened... and someone was responding in a joyful manner.

Perhaps it was just the celebration in the Temple that marked the first evening of Succoth. Simeon himself had taken part in that celebration of joy so many times, especially when he was a young man. He smiled slightly as he recalled how he and other prominent Jewish men took part in the torch-dance as they celebrated in the brilliantly well-lit Court of the Women. In his mind he could see the multitude crowded into the double gallery that had been built by the priests and Levites. What a festive night of singing songs of praise to Jehovah and reciting the Psalms by the whole congregation until the cock crowed. It had been many years since the old businessman had attended the entire evening's celebration, for though he truly enjoyed the laughter and happiness on each face, he just could not stay awake for that long anymore. And then the old man recalled how the Levites would sing the Psalms while being accompanied by various musical instruments. These men of God always stood on the steps of the inner court lifting up their praise to the King of the Universe. This must have been the noise that had awakened him. What else could it have been he reasoned?

The old man sank slowly to his knees and prayed until he heard the two priests trumpet the sound from the Nicanor gate that signaled the end of the night's festivities. As he slowly stood erect, Simeon remembered how the people would depart the Temple premises. They would turn around to face the priests just before exiting through the Eastern gate. He could just barely make out the voices of the priests reciting in unison, "Our forefathers in this place turned their backs on the altar of God and their faces to the east, worshiping the sun. But we turn to God." Yes, the celebration in the Temple would explain the sounds that had awakened him from slumber. The old man looked forward to discussing the celebration with his friend, Anna, when he returned to the Temple in a couple of days.

****

Joseph held the new born in his arms as Mary slept. She was exhausted, but the young carpenter from Nazareth could see the peace that engulfed her countenance through the soft light from the two candles he had lit earlier that cast long shadows in the small cave. He grinned as he recalled Naomi gently washing the baby and wrapping him in the swaddling cloths. Then the 40-something midwife laid the infant in Mary's arms, and the young woman smiled larger than she ever had before as the babe fed at her breast.

"May it be Your will, O Lord my God and God of my for-bearers," uttered the young carpenter's bride, "that You provide nourishment for Your humble creation... this tiny child... plenty of milk as much as he needs." Mary looked up into the dark eyes of her beloved and smiled as she continued, "Give me the disposition and inclination to find the time to nurse him patiently until he is satisfied. Cause me to sleep lightly so that when he cries I will hear and respond. Spare me the horror of accidentally smothering my child as I sleep. God forbid. May the words of my mouth and the meditations of my heart be acceptable to You, my Rock and my Redeemer."

"Did you learn that prayer from my mother?" asked Joseph softly.

"No, my Love," replied the former farm girl. "I heard Elizabeth pronounce those words the first time she held John to her breast. Later, she explained the meaning and purpose of the prayer." Mary again smiled at her carpenter more broadly than she ever had before this night. She had already forgotten the pain she had experienced just a few moments earlier. Joseph gently wiped her brow with a small cloth and returned her smile as he surveyed the scene before him. Then Mary raised her eyes towards the ceiling of the semi-dark cavern as if looking into the face of God.

"Blessed art Thou, O Lord our God, King of the Universe, for keeping us alive, taking care of us, and bringing us to this time," recited the former shepherd's daughter while gently stroking the baby's temples.

Naomi stood, looked at first the young mother lying on the blanket spread on the hay and then at the proud poppa kneeling beside his bride with his eyes focused solely on the sight before him. "I'll be getting back to the caravansary, Joseph," stated the midwife, her voice cracking slightly. "You both need to rest awhile. I'll stop back by in the morning to see if you need anything and bring you a bite to eat. Good night, Cousins… and congratulations."

Joseph nodded in the general direction of Naomi, but quickly returned his gaze to Mary and the miracle in her arms. He thought to himself how so many young men like himself had been in the same situation, and yet this situation was so different, for his young wife was holding the son of God. The young woodworker had tried to prepare himself for this moment, but his preparations seemed to have been a waste of time for he could not think of anything profound to say to his new family. The impact of the enormous responsibility he suddenly felt made his eyes tear to the brim. Mary and the baby were content to simply experience the natural wonder of it all, and she did not notice the change on his countenance. Joseph leaned closely to his bride and gently kissed her forehead.

After Naomi had left the young family, Joseph prepared a light meal of dates, figs, and bread that Mary had baked fresh two mornings earlier while her carpenter and his father worked on the sukka that would be their temporary home during the Feast.

"Blessed are You, O Lord our God, King of the Universe, who sanctifies us with His commandments and has commanded us to kindle the light of the holiday," recited Joseph. Then he lit the two traditional holiday candles, sat down beside his young bride, and shared their first Succoth meal together. The rugged woodworker smiled in a joyful manner as his beloved bride awkwardly tried to consume the meal with him. She was not used to eating and nursing a newborn infant at the same time, and she was so afraid that she might hurt the baby or do something that would cause her husband embarrassment during the Feast.

"Joseph," she said humbly, "perhaps we should wait for awhile... before we eat. The baby is almost finished, and he will sleep well while we feast."

"It's all right, Mary," answered the wise shaper-of-wood, "this is a feast of rejoicing... a time to remember when our ancestors wandered in the wilderness in their search for the Promised Land... a time to remember how God dwelt among them and protected them. It is a time for laughter and singing. So relax, my Love... and simply enjoy... the season... and the birth of our son. Tomorrow we will move into the sukka next to my folks and continue the week-long celebration." Joseph had a way of reassuring Mary almost every time he opened his mouth, and her fear of doing something wrong vanished with the echo of a cow's lowing in the adjoining compartment. They both looked in the direction of the sounds of the stable, and they laughed.

When Mary and the baby had fallen asleep, Joseph gently took the small one in his arms and cradled him close as he walked in the shadows.

"Blessed art Thou, O Lord our God, King of the Universe, for keeping us alive, taking care of us, and bringing us to this time," whispered the tall woodworker from Nazareth. As he walked around the small room that was for now their sukka, he spoke the words that all Jewish fathers spoke to their newborns. For like his ancestors, Joseph believed that the first moments, hours, and days of a baby's life are likened to that of a newly planted tree, where the initial care sets the tone for its future growth and well-being. The young carpenter believed, too, that the holy environment that the child entered into established a solid spiritual beginning, which would serve as a firm foundation throughout the child's life.

"I look up to the hills, but my help does not come from there," added Joseph. "My help comes from the Lord, who made heaven and earth." Joseph paused in his pacing, breathed deeply, and continued, "He will not let You be defeated, Little One. He who guards You never sleeps. He who guards Israel never rests or sleeps. The Lord guards You. The Lord is the shade that protects You from the sun. The sun cannot hurt You during the day, and the moon cannot hurt You at night. The Lord will protect You from all dangers; He will guard Your life. The Lord will guard You as You come and go, both now and forever." The strong arms that held the little baby lifted the newborn's head to the lips of the learned carpenter, and Joseph kissed the small life in his hands ever so gently and softly and reverently for he knew that he kissed the face of God. Then he walked over to the feeding trough hewn out of the side of the cave, and carefully laid the babe onto the makeshift bed of hay he had prepared while Mary was nursing the infant.

The small-town wood-smith looked at his young wife resting so peacefully and thought of the prophet's words, "A virgin shall conceive and bear a son, and shall call his name Immanuel." Joseph pondered on that scripture for a moment. "Immanuel," thought the tall woodworker, "God with us... God dwelling with us... God has come to dwell with us... to tabernacle with us... on this day... the first day of the Feast of Tabernacles."

Joseph had spent a great deal of his life studying the scriptures, and hundreds of references flooded his mind as he gently touched the body of the little boy wrapped so tightly that he could barely move. And though asleep, the baby smiled.

Joseph knew what lay in store for his adopted son, and he was quite aware that nothing would ever be the same again.

****

Chapter Eleven

The Time of Sharing

The morning rays of the sun mixed with the light of the lamps Joseph had placed along the walls of the manger giving Mary a feeling of comfort, strength, and extreme happiness. She had just finished feeding her new born son and returned him to the small feeding trough where he had spent the night. She smiled as she thought of the beautiful, little crib that her beloved carpenter had taken such pains to build back in his shop in Nazareth. He was indeed quite a craftsman when it came to shaping wood and making furniture or building houses that would stand the test of time. And the little bed he had shaped for their son was his best effort. Joseph had tried so hard to hide his workmanship from her before their departure from the tiny village they called home to make their journey with their family to the City of David. The young maiden knew all about the crib because her mother-in-law had accidentally shared the surprise with her one day while the two of them were at the village market. Still Mary reacted as she thought her husband wished her to do when he pulled back the canvass to unveil his creation.

Mary looked around at their temporary dwelling. It was not lavish by any stretch of the imagination, but it did provide protection, and it was warm inside. The young couple would be back in Nazareth soon, she thought, and their baby would not grow up over night, so the little bed would still get plenty of use.

The animals in the outer portion of the cave began to move about some, and the young bride turned towards the entrance, expecting to see her beloved returning with the food they would share in their sukkah that morning before moving into the little shelter Joseph and his father had prepared just a few days earlier. But Joseph did not enter... no one was entering. The animals were just a bit restless, perhaps anticipating someone's arrival. It was then that Mary again recalled the strange visit the night before of three shepherds.

Mary remembered how she had awakened from a short nap to discover her beloved lying beside her, leaning on his left elbow and smiling as broadly as possible.

"Is it morning yet, Joseph?" she had asked as she sat up beside him.

"No, my Love," he whispered so as not to awaken the baby. "Go back to sleep... and rest. Everything is fine, just as it should be." He reached over and gently brushed her black curls from her eyes and touched her face like he had discovered the rarest of treasures. And he grinned his special grin just for her. Mary returned that grin with her own, and the two embraced as they did on their wedding day.

Suddenly, there was a slight commotion at the entrance of the cave. Joseph jumped to his feet and instinctively placed himself between the would-be intruders and his family.

Mary thought that perhaps it was her husband's cousin, Malachi the caravansary keeper, or his wife, Naomi, returning with some fruit to eat. The young bride was still quite tired from having given birth, but she was still so very hungry, despite the meal she had shared with her husband only a few hours earlier. She looked at the face of her beloved and read in his expression that their visitors were not recognized by him as friends or family. She sighed deeply. Naomi was right. There were just too many people in the small village, and somebody must have shared her plight with these strangers who just wanted to leer.

"Who are you?" asked Joseph with a sternness in his voice that indicated that this was not the time for these men to be exploring.

"Shalom", said the first man politely as he entered the manger. The old man's clothing indicated to the young carpenter that he was a shepherd. The old man stood just inside the entrance to allow his sons to enter. Joseph could see a young man and a skinny boy of perhaps 10 or 11 years of age. "Shalom", they both repeated in unison.

Joseph relaxed his stance just a bit. "Who are you?" he repeated, but this time with just a tad bit less anxiety in his tone. "What do you want here?"

The older of the three visitors spoke in a humble manner. "My name is Achim. I am a shepherd... these are my two sons, Nathaniel and Simon," he said as he pointed to each. The old man swallowed hard and continued, "We don't mean to intrude... but has a baby been born here tonight?"

Mary, who had arisen from her placemat and now stood beside her protector, clung tightly to the strong arm of her woodworker. Joseph glanced down at his young bride at his side and looked the men straight in their eyes. "What has that got to do with you? Is this your cave where you keep your sheep?"

"No... no," stuttered the grey-bearded stranger, "it's just that...". Achim was having a hard time trying to explain their presence. None of the shepherds had thought about what they would say to the parents of the baby they had been told about if they actually found him. The explanation needed to be believable, but angels weren't in the habit of visiting poor shepherds. That was an experience given only to selected persons who had exhibited a certain form of godliness, like perhaps the High Priest. The old man turned to his sons for help.

"The angels told us to come," blurted out the young boy.

"The angels?" asked Joseph in a manner that did not show surprise or disbelief. Mary's mouth simply dropped open as she heard the young boy's statement and watched all three nod their heads in agreement to her beloved's question.

"Tell me about the angels," said Joseph in a relaxed voice.

Simon stepped forward and bravely began to relate the story of how the three of them had been watching their sheep just a few hours before when an angel shared with them the message of the birth of a baby. "He said that the baby was the Savior... the Messiah who has been promised by Jehovah," added the young shepherd. "Is... is it true, Sir?"

Joseph had not prepared himself for such a question, especially not from one so small. He looked into the eyes of the three visitors and answered calmly, "Yes. It is true." Then he grinned at them the way he did when he was about to impart some great truth in the synagogue. "Come and see for yourself," he said as he stepped to one side to allow the shepherds access to the babe.

Simon walked into the room, and Mary accompanied the lad to the trough where the newborn lay. Nathaniel followed his younger brother slowly into the shadowy area. Joseph took one of the lamps in his hand to aide Achim's approach and view of the infant lying on the straw. All five stood and marveled at the sight before them. The youngest of the group took out a small, flute-like instrument that he used to calm the sheep on the hillside, and he played a gentle, soothing tune that broke the silence of the spectacle in the small cave.

"It is true, Father," stated Nathaniel with just a hint of marvel in his voice. "Just as the angel shared with us... the babe... wrapped in swaddling clothes... and lying in a manger... here... in Bethlehem."

"Is he... is he really the Promised One?" asked Achim, searching the eyes of the gentle carpenter standing at his side. "I had never thought about him being a baby."

"He is the Promised One," answered Joseph, "the Messiah... the Anointed One... the One who is God's salvation."

Mary knew Joseph's words were true. She had dreamed about the Angel's visit to her during the Feast of Lights and recalled the words spoken to her. But she thought perhaps her beloved would wait awhile longer before sharing their little one's real purpose, especially to total strangers. Still, she trusted her carpenter explicitly, and she stood silently at the baby's head. She, too, wondered why the angels had appeared to this group of lowly shepherds. Surely the High Priest would be dropping by for a visit before the next evening.

****

Aramazar unrolled the papyrus he had procured from Aretas giving permission for a special merchant caravan to depart from Suza for Jerusalem as soon as the old priest could get everything organized. This passport had opened doors for the aging preacher because it not only contained the seal of the Nabataean king, but also his complete blessing. Aretas himself had announced the caravan's itenary at a great banquet he had several courtiers throw for him the night before he left his summer palace for his return to Petra. The plan was greatly applauded by all in attendance.

Of course, Aramazar had not sold his king on the idea of honoring a new son of King Herod, but more so on the smoothing over of strained relations between the Jews and the Nabataeans. If Herod had been able to father a child in spite of his severe illness, the cruel King of the Jews might have him killed before the caravan arrived. The old priest calculated that it would take close to two years to reach Jerusalem, not because of the distance, but because the merchants would want to stop at every little oasis along the way to sell and buy. And the dealers in frankincense and myrrh would want to make doubly sure that they sold as much as they could to the Roman garrisons and strongholds along the way, too. In another month or so, the caravan would be ready to depart on the westward journey that would bring great wealth to the area merchants and provide the doubting priest an avenue to escape his duties as High Priest once and for all.

It no longer mattered to Aramazar whether his insightful nephew had been correct in interpreting the ancient writings of a bunch of captured Jews. The battle raging inside his heart and mind would soon be settled. He could bear performing his priestly duties for the handful of months it would take to get to Jerusalem. The old priest hoped that the caravan would arrive in the Holy City during one of the great festivals because it would make his escape easier. Jerusalem had a tendency to swell in population to perhaps over a million people, and the streets became so very crowded. It would be easy to blend into the crowd, find a place to change his garments to those of the common man, and simply walk away from his responsibilities.

The old religionaire decided that he would not share his plan with his nephews. The less they knew, the better for them. Aretas would be so angry, and the old king would take out his wrath on the two novices if he suspected that they knew anything.

Aramazar carefully rolled his precious passport into its traveling position and placed it in a small, but official box of the kingdom. And then he smiled slightly as his mind's eye pictured the journey before him.

****

"Did you hear?" asked a grey-haired woman while examining some dates at the market place in Bethlehem, "a young girl gave birth last night in one of those mangers on the edge of town. Somebody ought to do something about it!"

That was the buzz around the small village just a handful of miles from the big celebration in Jerusalem before the sun could climb very high in the autumn skies of Israel. The townsfolk had been made aware of the newborn's entrance into the world by three shepherds. But the rest of their story was just too unbelievable for most.

"I'm tellin' you I saw him with my own two eyes," said Achim to an acquaintance along the path that led from the hills

115

where the old shepherd grazed his flock to the walls of Zion. Nathaniel and Simon continued driving the lambs towards the Temple. Their sheep would be part of the sacrifice offered the next three days by the priests to celebrate the Feast. The two younger shepherds would let their father tell their remarkable story for now... they had a deadline to keep and couldn't afford the luxury of stopping to talk along the way.

"But how do you know that the men you saw were angels?" asked Micah, one of the fruit merchants doing business in the market that first morning of Succoth in the 32nd year of King Herod. "Have you ever seen an angel before?" The other five men in the small group who were discussing the events of the previous evening all added their two cents worth in agreement. Afterall, none of them had ever seen an angel... at least not that they knew of.

Achim was becoming a bit frustrated at his friends' disbelief as well as their picking at every little detail of his story. And besides, the old shepherd had not yet told them the best part. "No, I've never seen an angel before," he answered wearily, "but who else could it have been?" The other men looked at each other for a plausible explanation. None of them seemed to be able to come up with one.

"Tell us again, Old Man," chimed in Micah, who seemed to be the self-appointed leader of the group. "Start from the beginning and tell us what happened."

Achim took a deep breath, shook his head while peering up at the sky, and began again. "I've told you and told you. We were resting on the hillside... the sheep were all bedded down for the night. And all of a sudden this man appeared from out of nowhere... a big man... long robe... kinda glowing like... and the first thing he said was 'Don't be afraid. I've got some news you just won't believe.'"

"Are you sure you and your boys weren't just dreamin'?" interrupted Micah. "Or maybe you'd had a bit too much of the juice of the vine?" The others laughed at that suggestion.

"No... no... no!" said the old shepherd emphatically. "Now just hush up for a spell if you want to hear this story!" The other men mumbled replies that were unintelligible, and the herdsman continued his tale using great hand gestures and facial expressions like most great storytellers do. "This angel told us that a baby had been born in Bethlehem just a few minutes before he appeared to us... and that that baby... was the Messiah!"

Achim paused momentarily for effect... to let his announcement sink in... and then he continued, "This angel told us how we'd find the baby... in a manger... right here in David's City. And then there was a whole bunch of angels on that hillside..." Achim turned towards his friend Micah who had just started to open his mouth, and the old shepherd put his left hand over the lips of the fruit-peddler. "I know what you're gonna say... I know they were all angles 'cause they all looked like the first fella... long robes... and they were all glowin'. And they spoke in unison... almost like the singin' that the priests do during Tabernacles only there weren't no music. And they said, 'Glory to God in the heavenly places. Peace to all men and women on earth who please Him.'"

"Then what happened, Old Man," asked Azariah, another businessman who specialized in making decorative scripture hangings especially for the Festival of Booths.

"Well, Sir," continued Achim, "they all disappeared... in just a moment... almost like they weren't there at all. Then me and the boys decided to come on down into town and see if we could find this baby that those angels talked about."

"And did you?" asked one of the other men in the small group.

"Yes, Sir. We sure did!" replied the old shepherd. "Just like the angel had said. He hadn't been borned long... but there he was... wrapped up in swaddling clothes... and lying in that manger on the edge of town owned by old Malachi, the caravansary-keeper. His momma was a pretty little girl and his poppa was a tall, strong, good-lookin' carpenter from Nazareth."

"Now answer me this, Old Man," interjected Micah. "You say the angels told you that this baby was the Promised One... the Messiah? Do you think he is?"

"Yes, Micah," answered Achim humbly, "I believe that baby is the Lord's Messiah... the One who will save us all."

"Why do you believe?" asked Azariah. "What sign... what proof makes you draw that conclusion?"

"Because everything was just like the angels shared with us," replied the old shepherd without batting an eye.

"But why would Jehovah announce the coming of the Anointed One to you?" asked one of the other men who still could not take in all that he had heard.

"Exactly," added one of the other men. "If this baby was really the Promised One... wouldn't the angels have announced the birth to the High Priest and his assistants?"

"Well, Sir," continued Achim, "my boy Simon put that one together for me, 'cause I had asked the same question. That boy is mighty smart when it comes to stuff pertainin' to the Lord. He said, 'Father, we're taking the lambs to the Temple tomorrow morning to be offered as sacrifices, right?' And I said, 'Of course we are, Son. We do our main business with the Levites in the Temple.' 'Well,' he says, he says, 'if the baby we just saw is the Messiah who will save us... then he's like our lambs. Who better to receive the message of the birth of the Messiah... God's sacrificial lamb... than a bunch of shepherds? And where better to find a newborn lamb... than in a manger?'" The old shepherd looked at each of the faces of the men crowded around him, and he smiled as big as he could, raised his hands high in the air, and said, "Blessed are You, O Lord our God, King of the Universe, for keeping us alive, for taking care of us, for bringing us to this time, and for showing us Your salvation!"

"Do you really expect us to believe this incredible story of yours, Achim?" asked Micah sternly.

The old shepherd turned to his longtime friend and placed a rough hand on Micah's shoulder. "Micah," he said, "I can't make you believe... but I believe because I was there... and I

saw and heard what I just told you. Believe what you want...
but mark my words... the Messiah is here... salvation is just
around the corner... and nothin's gonna be the same again!"

****

Chapter Twelve

The Season of Rejoicing

M ary looked around the small, temporary dwelling that Joseph and his father had constructed for the two of them the day after the whole family had arrived in Bethlehem for the Feast and the census. The little booth was made with the boughs of trees and the branches of palm trees from Colonia, and she marveled at the craftsmanship. Joseph and his family always took such pride in their work, even if it was just a temporary structure that would be torn down in six days. The young bride inspected the scriptures hanging on the walls which she and her mother-in-law had so skillfully painted. Mary enjoyed making each letter of the Hebrew Scriptures and considered her work a piece of art to be treasured for years to come. The young mother held her baby tightly so as not to drop him as she reached up to touch one of the figs hanging from the ceiling of the sukka made especially for her family. There were other hangings of dates, pomegranates, wheat, barley, olives, and grapes, representing the agricultural harvest for which Israel was so famous. The former shepherdess from Nazareth smiled as she examined the openings in the roof of their sukka… small enough so that the palm branches kept out the heat of the Judean sun, and yet large enough so that the couple could gaze at the awesome sight of the stars during the night and marvel at God's greatness.

"It's perfect, Joseph," she stated as she turned to meet his joyful gaze.

"I'm glad you approve, my Love," he answered as he wrapped his arms around her and the baby at the same time. "Rest for awhile, Mary. Father, Eleazar, and I are going to the Temple with the other men to participate in the morning celebration. And then I will travel with them to register with the census taker. Today we will add a member to our family list," added Joseph with his special grin. "But I will return to share this season of rejoicing with you."

"Will you get to see Zachariah?" Mary asked.

"Perhaps," answered the tall wood-smith, "but he will be busy with his duties. I am sure that he and Elizabeth will come to visit soon. In fact, tomorrow night, we are to share the evening meal with my folks in their sukka. If I get the chance, I will invite Zachariah and Elizabeth to eat with us." He grinned his special grin for her once again, gently kissed her and the baby, and walked briskly through the opening to join with the others heading up to Jerusalem just a few miles down the road.

****

Zachariah had made his way to the Temple early that second morning of the Feast of Ingathering. He had been chosen by lot to lead the celebration that morning and give the *dukan,* the blessing to the people at the close of the morning's ceremony. The old priest had been one of several Levites who had offered sacrifices the previous morning and had been too busy to notice the fanfare involved in the waving of the *lulav* by the men as they marched around the altar. But today, he would be a major part of the festivity as he recited the *Musaf.* He had performed these duties several times before during the past 45 years or so that he had been serving in the Temple, but this time, the entire observance took on new meaning for him and his family. In time, he thought, this day would take on new meaning for the rest of Israel.

Zachriah removed his leather foot-wear as an act of respect for Jehovah and for the celebration itself. He climbed the steps of the altar which had been adorned with willow branches as energetically as he could for a man his age, and Jonathan brought over a bowl and a pitcher of water taken from the laver, so that the aged priest could wash his hands. The old country preacher stood to the right of the altar and looked at the sea of men as they gathered to march around the place of sacrifice. With just a slight nod he acknowledged to himself the presence of his cousin, Jacob of Nazareth and his two sons, Eleazar and Joseph. And then he recognized another face in the crowd... that of his old friend Simeon who had quizzed him about the birth of John. Zachariah knew, too, that this would be the last year that the old businessman participated in the Feast, for his destiny would soon be fulfilled when Simeon would be introduced to the Lord's Messiah.

****

"We leave for Jerusalem at the end of the week." The sound of that sentence from the lips of Aramazar had aroused such hope in the heart of Meshach as he and his cousin Abimael sat in the apartment of their uncle that morning. Since that hour, the young scholar had busied himself with making the final preparations necessary for their journey to the land of their ancestors. He smiled as he recalled the conversation the morning before with his star-gazing relation.

"I hate to be the bearer of good news, Meshach," said the young Nabataean astrologer while sharing breakfast with his slightly older, history-buff cousin. "But there has been unusual activity in the heavens in the direction of Jerusalem."

Meshach dropped a small morsel of food onto his plate, nearly knocking the entire platter onto his lap. "The star?... that signifies the birth of the King of the Jews?... you've seen it?" he asked with his own eyes as large as the pool of Siloam that he longed to see.

"I saw something, Cousin," stated Abimael, trying to remain calm and unassuming. He loved his energetic relative, but hated to admit that the studious teacher was right. "It could have been a star... just above the western horizon... in the general direction of Jerusalem. It was extremely bright, but it didn't last too long. In fact, I almost missed it altogether."

"But you did see it?" insisted Meshach with more excitement in his voice.

"Yes," grinned Abimael, "I saw it. But I'm not sure that it really means anything... from an astronomical standpoint anyway. There may be a simple explanation for the occurrence."

"There is a simple explanation alright," exclaimed the Eastern history-instructor. "It is the prophesy of the Anointed One... just as the prophet Daniel said. We must tell Aramazar this morning. He'll want to speed up his preparations for our journey to Jerusalem." Meshach had already arisen and was pacing the small room, wringing his hands in anticipation of finally walking in the steps of his ancestors... in the streets of the Holy City that he had dreamed of since a small boy.

Abimael took a deep breath and shook his head. He knew that it was a waste of time to try and talk sense to his learned cousin in times like this.

"Yes, Meshach," he said, "we must tell our uncle. And I think he will be pleased. He's seemed to have found a new energy in the past few weeks preparing for this trip. I sense that he is most anxious to leave Susa, though I'm not sure why." The young star-gazer took another bite of fruit and spoke while chewing, "Now sit down, Cousin, and finish your breakfast. There is no rush to leave this very moment. We will see Jerusalem and the new-born king, soon. "

Abimael smiled broadly at Meshach towering above him. And Meshach returned his smile and plopped down to finish the meal in front of him.

****

Joseph looked down at the *lulav* in his right hand that his beloved bride had woven for him just a couple of days before. She had platted each of the branches together so meticulously and with such loving care. And he smiled as his thoughts wandered back to that morning.

"Do you understand the significance of the *lulav*, Mary?" he had asked in a warm, teaching-kind of tone.

"My father told us of the meaning each year," she answered, smiling, "but I would enjoy hearing the story again... from you."

"The palm," began the young carpenter, "bears fruit but has no fragrance. The fruit represents our good deeds... what we do with our lives. But there is no spiritual blessing because of wrong attitude. It represents the person who lives by the letter of the law, but has no compassion for others."

"The myrtle," he continued as he touched that branch, "has fragrance but can't bear fruit. This is like the person who recites scripture by the hour, knows the Torah frontwards and backwards, but doesn't put what he knows into practice... never does anything for those in need." Mary grinned slightly as she pictured in her mind a couple of people in Nazareth she knew who fit that mold, though neither of them would admit it.

"And the willow," he added while gently touching that branch, "can produce neither fruit nor fragrance. It represents the person who just never can quite come to grips with which doctrine to follow. Sometimes he seeks... sometimes he follows for awhile... but he never makes a commitment." Mary nodded slightly to indicate that she understood what her woodworker was teaching.

"Now the citron," commented Joseph as he picked up the fruit with his left hand, "creates both fruit and fragrance. This represents the man who does good works... helps others... avoids temptations... because he recognizes God's hand on his life. He doesn't just study God's laws, but he lives by them daily. He's not a cake unturned... raw on one side and cooked on the other. And those around him see him representing the best of God in his everyday life." Mary smiled greatly because she pictured her beloved. Of course, he would never admit that he lived such a balanced life before God and man, but she knew. Joseph's humility was one of his many qualities that had attracted him to her in the first place.

The tall shaper-of-wood was jolted back into the present with the words of Zachariah as the procession around the altar began. "O give thanks unto the Lord; for He is good! Because His mercy endures forever!" recited the old priest in his loudest voice so that all might hear.

Joseph and the other men began their trek around the altar while waving the lulav and the citron, first to their right, then to their left, then in front, in back, upwards towards the sky, and down towards the ground in an effort to cover all directions.

The group recited in unison, "Blessed are You, O Lord our God, King of the universe, who has sanctified us by His commandments, and instructed us in the waving of the palm branch."

"Save now," shouted Zachariah, "I plead with you, O Lord. O Lord, I plead with You, send us prosperity now."

The circular journey around the altar was not one of solemnity, but one of great rejoicing, the men practically dancing. "Blessed are You, O Lord, King of the Universe, for keeping us alive, taking care of us, and bringing us to this time!" repeated the men in the crowd in a festive manner, as if they were singing praises to Jehovah.

"O give thanks unto the Lord; for He is good; for His mercy endures for ever!" added the old priest. The men continued their journey, saying little prayers of thanksgiving and praise, asking for God's blessing in the coming year as He had blessed them during the previous. As each phrase ended, the men would shout, "Hoshana!" which being interpreted means "Save now!" And with each shout, the young carpenter from Nazareth gazed into the faces of those around him with a grin, for he knew that God's salvation had indeed come into the world to save not just these men gathered around the altar, but all men everywhere. Joseph was so tempted to glance at Zachariah, perhaps pass him a "knowing" gaze, but the people were forbidden to look upon the priest during the procession lest they get distracted with the praise being lifted up to the heavens.

As the procession continued, Jonathan stepped forward to read from the Psalms. "The Lord is my light, and the one who saves me." Zachariah's protégé glanced at his mentor out of the corner of his eye to make sure that his volume was such that all could hear. The older of the two men nodded ever so slightly his approval. "So why should I fear anyone?" continued the old priest's assistant. "The Lord protects my life. So why should I be afraid? Evil people try to destroy my body. My enemies and those who hate me attack me, but they are overwhelmed and defeated. If an army surrounds me, I will not be afraid." The young priest caught himself looking at the crowd beneath him for just a split second and continued. "If war breaks out, I will trust in the Lord. I ask only one thing from the Lord. This is what I want: Let me live in the Lord's house all my life. Let me see the Lord's beauty and look with my own eyes at His Temple. During danger He will keep me safe in His shelter. He will hide me in His holy Tent, or He will keep me safe on a high mountain. My head is higher than my enemies around me. I will offer joyful sacrifices in His Holy Tent. I will sing and praise the Lord. Lord, hear me when I call; have mercy and answer me. My heart said of You, 'Go worship Him'. So, I come to worship You, Lord. Do not turn away from me. Do not turn Your servant away in anger; You have helped me in the past. Do not push me away or leave me alone, O God, my Savior. If my father and mother leave me, the Lord will take me in. Lord, teach me Your ways, and guide me to do what is right because I have enemies. Do not hand me over to my enemies, because they tell lies about me and say they will hurt me. I truly believe I will see the Lord's goodness. Wait for the Lord's help. Be strong and brave and wait for the Lord's help."

Again the men parading around the altar shouted, "Hoshana!" Joseph thought, "If only these men knew what had happened two nights ago, surely their shouts would be even more joyous." He smiled slyly as his mind captured the true significance of the proceedings and the fulfillment of so many years of prayers from the common folks and the priests alike.

Zachariah stepped forward once again and reminded the men of the commands Jehovah had given as written in the Torah concerning the sacrifices that would be made that day. He also read the story of Solomon's dedication of the Temple which was made during this Feast so many years before. Then as if choreographed by an unseen conductor, the men turned their backs to the priest. Zachariah raised his hands above his head and spread his fingers to let the Shekinah glory stream through on the assembled worshippers, and he spoke with his loudest voice, "The Lord bless you and keep you: the Lord make His face to shine upon you: the Lord lift up His countenance upon you, and give you peace!"

****

Simeon returned to his sukka and sat on his mat, filled with excitement from the ceremony in the Temple and his later meeting with Anna and the shepherd Achim of Bethlehem. His heart was about to burst with joy as he rehearsed in his mind the events of the previous hour.

Anna had been searching the crowd for her old friend who so diligently visited the Temple each day awaiting the entrance of the Lord's Messiah. She knew all about his vision and was impressed with his perseverance in examining the crowd in search of the Anointed One.

"Simeon... Simeon.... Simeon!" shouted the ancient prophetess when she saw him exiting the main area of the Temple where he had participated with so many other men in the daily procession around the altar. Finally, she had caught his attention.

"What is it, Anna?" asked the old businessman. "You act as though you've seen a ghost."

"Not a ghost, Old Man," she answered enthusiastically, "but I do have news that we both have been waiting to hear."

"News of what?" inquired Simeon.

"The night before last," began Anna, "I was awakened by a brilliant light."

"You mean the light from the giant candlesticks. I know what you mean, Anna," interrupted Simeon, "those candlesticks are so large and give off such light... the whole city is lit up. Can you imagine what pilgrims in the countryside must think as they look towards Jerusalem during this time? Such light... and the city atop this mountain," stated the old man, shaking his head.

"No, Simeon," said Anna, cutting the old gentleman short in a mannerly way. "I'm not speaking of those four candlesticks that are lit especially during the Feast. I'm speaking of another brilliant light that overshadowed the candlesticks for a moment. It came from the direction of the hills of Bethlehem... where the shepherds keep their flocks."

The elderly prophetess had captured Simeon's attention with her pronouncement as he remembered the sounds that had awakened him that same night. But he had passed it off as part of the celebration in the Temple. "What are you trying to tell me, Woman?" asked Simeon.

Anna smiled larger than the retired businessman had ever seen before. "I'm trying to tell you about a miracle that happened. Let me introduce you to a friend of mine... a shepherd of Bethlehem who sells his lambs for the Temple sacrifices. He can tell the story much better than I can because he was there." Anna pulled the old shepherd over to where Simeon stood. "Simeon... this is Achim the shepherd. Listen closely to what he has to say, Old Man. It is the most amazing story that I have ever heard."

Simeon stood in wonder as he listened to the story of the shepherd and the visit of the angels to his humble camp. By the time Achim got to his finding the babe in the manger as the angels had foretold, the old businessman was shaking and his eyes were filled to the brim with tears of rejoicing. Simeon almost ran to his sukka so that he could spend the remainder of the day praying and giving thanks to Jehovah. It would only be a few days before he would see his dreams fulfilled. He even thought of visiting the City of David in search of the baby Achim had described, but the old shepherd had himself returned to the manger-cave and had not found the young couple. He had asked around, but no one seemed to even know what the old shepherd was talking about. And besides, there were just too many sukkas in Bethlehem and along the road that led from the small town to the gates of Zion. He had waited this long; he could wait a few days longer.

"Blessed are you, O Lord our God, King of the universe, for keeping me alive, taking care of me, and bringing me to this time," prayed Simeon.

****

Joseph and the others filed out of the Temple area and headed back to their own sukkas to celebrate the rest of the day with their families. Zachariah and Jonathan would remain close to the altar to assist the other Levites in performing the many sacrifices offered that day. The young carpenter felt like his ancient cousin would be dropping by within the next few days, probably at night to visit the newest addition to their family. For he had hoped that Zachariah would perform the *brit milah* for the baby boy that Mary had brought into the world. For now, Joseph would almost glow as he read scriptures with his family over the next few days, realizing their true meaning. And he would grin more than he ever had. For he knew that nothing would ever be the same again.

****

Chapter Thirteen

Hosha'na Rabba

Eight days had passed since the birth of Mary's baby in the manger belonging to Malachi, the caravansary-keeper of Bethlehem. And eight days had passed since the beginning of the Feast of Booths celebrated by so many. All the preparations had been made for the circumcision and naming of Joseph and Mary's first born son. It was to be a simple ceremony attended only by the immediate family of the newlyweds from Nazareth. But, of course, the immediate family included Zachariah and his wife Elizabeth as well as Malachi and his wife Naomi.

Mary surveyed the small room where the sons of Malachi and Naomi had once played and laughed. "How sad," she thought, "that both boys had been taken from this home by illness so early in life." The young bride from Nazareth sighed deeply, believing that she and Joseph would have more than ten years with their son. She wished the three of them could be on their way back to their little village close to the Sea of Galilee, as all the others who had flooded Bethlehem and Jerusalem would be headed back to their homes after tomorrow's festivities. But Joseph and his father and brother had been given the opportunity to earn some extra money by repairing the living quarters of the Levites in Jerusalem, and that project would take at least a month. The black-haired beauty from northern Israel smiled as she recalled the look that came on Joseph's face when he heard Zachariah tell him the news. It was like her carpenter was expecting something to happen, but just a little surprised at the specifics.

"This gives us a good excuse to stay here until *pidyon ha-ben* as well as your cleansing, " he had told her later that evening. "Isn't it amazing how the Lord works out every little detail of His plan, Mary? And we get front row seats as we watch this plan unfold. I wish I could tell our folks about this baby boy you hold close to your breast... but they would not understand. So, we must keep the secret a little longer, my Beloved."

Mary had been pondering his words and the words of the shepherds eight days earlier and all the Messianic scriptures that had been read during the last few days. She recalled the words of the angel sent to her and to Joseph. Still, she didn't fully comprehend the meaning of the words. The baby she held looked like every baby she had ever seen before. There was nothing unusual about him. He didn't glow... he didn't have a pair of wings protruding out of his back... or a halo of light around his head... he couldn't talk... and miraculous things didn't happen every time he waved his arms when she changed his swaddling clothes. Nor did a chorus of angels appear every time he was hungry to feed him or wash him when he needed that special attention. How could this normal little baby boy grow up to be the Anointed One promised by Jehovah? But it must be true! God's messenger had proclaimed it so, and Joseph, who knew more about the Scriptures than anyone she had ever met, proclaimed it so. And even Zachariah, her elderly priest-cousin, looked at the baby in a special way and held him ever so gracefully, like he held the Torah. Mary would just have to hold these things in her heart and learn from each day's dawning.

The young mother-of-the-Messiah had her thoughts interrupted by a voice she had grown to love six months earlier. "Mary," said Elizabeth gently, "I've brought you a present, my Dear."

Mary raised her head and gazed wide-eyed at the cloth her older cousin displayed. "That's the covering for Elijah's chair you used at John's *brit milah*," whispered the young bride. Elizabeth smiled broadly as she shook her head.

"We want you to use it for the circumcision of your baby today, Cousin," said the older woman. "It will make the occasion even more special. Which chair will be Elijah's chair, Mary?"

"The one I'm sitting in now," replied the young farmgirl. "Naomi said that it was a family heirloom, too, and she insisted that we use this room for the *brit milah*. How long before the ceremony begins?"

"Not long, my Child," said Elizabeth as she picked up her own baby. "Our men folk will return shortly from the Hosha'na Rabbah ceremony. What a great day this is, Mary! What a truly great day this is."

****

Abimael could not believe the size of the caravan that Aramazar had gathered together to journey to Jerusalem. As he stood on the steps of the summer palace in Susa, the young star-gazer knew he would have to apologize to his cousin, Meshach, for doubting his description of the convoy assembling for their departure. This time his scripture-researching relative had not exaggerated at all.

"This is the biggest caravan to ever leave Susa," stated Meshach just days earlier. "It'll take two days for Aramazar to bless every merchant and every piece of merchandize that is being packed for trade along the way. The new born king of Israel will likely be starting school by the time we get there, " he added with a grin. "I'll bet the old priest has 200 stops planned on this pilgrimage!"

"I'm sure you are adding to the actual numbers, Cousin," commented the young astrologer, "maybe stretching the size of this operation just a bit?"

"Not this time, Abimael," answered Meshach. "Aramazar even made up a map of sorts... placed everyone in a particular spot for traveling. It would be easy to get completely lost in the crowd along the way. And no one would even notice if someone wasn't in their proper spot for days. I doubt we'll make as much as ten miles a day."

"Well, if you are in such a hurry, Cousin," added Abimael, "I'm sure Uncle will let you scout on ahead on your own."

"I thought of that," replied the young teacher, "but I doubt the wisdom of such an act. Aramazar has hired scouts to look for proper places to camp and rest at night. I'll stay with you in the middle of the caravan." Meshach grinned a bit. "I'm adventurous, Cousin, but not crazy. The armed guards will have their hands full protecting us all as it is, once word gets out as to the value of the goods we carry. They wouldn't have time to look for one young scholar who got himself lost along the way. Why I'm not sure they'd even search for the High Priest himself if he were to disappear from the company. "

Abimael shook his head in amazement as he surveyed the scene below him. All of this commotion because of a light that appeared in the skies that just happened to correspond with some forgotten, ancient prophecy that his older cousin had dug up. Still it would be an exciting adventure and perhaps a great opportunity to learn from some of Susa's most distinguished businessmen along the way. Perhaps one of them might offer the young star-searcher a job in which he would not have to chart the heavenlies any longer. Or perhaps, Aretas would indeed be so overwhelmed with respect for the wisdom of the three to grant them permanent positions of honor in Petra. And perhaps in Petra, Abimael would no longer have to waste his time looking at the stars and predicting the day's fortune. Perhaps he would be in charge of young astrologers who would perform that function, and he would just report their findings to the King of the Nabataeans. Speculation... a dream... wishful thinking... he would find out soon. This journey just might be his own salvation.

****

Joseph and his kinsmen were again a part of the crowd of men chanting, singing, praising the Lord, offering thanksgiving, and marching around the altar in the Temple on this eighth day of the Feast. On the other days, the men circled the altar only once and waved the *lulav*. Today, they would march around the altar seven times cheerfully crying out, "Hosha'na… save now!" while they carried palm branches. This was the crowning of all the days of celebration for the Jews, and each man rested from all normal work that day.

The week's celebration was an object lesson in not holding too tightly to materialistic possessions. The daily activities recalled that during the Wandering in the Wilderness, all Jews lived in tents… rich and poor alike. Joseph masterfully weaved the story of the Wanderings in with the scriptures and every day activities common to all men everywhere. "We must seek God's kingdom and not earthly comfort. The Lord is our shelter," taught the young carpenter from Nazareth.

Jacob had handed over the daily teachings and lessons to his youngest son years ago after recognizing the young man's knowledge of the scriptures and his special ability to tell stories that made the scriptures come alive to those listening. Jacob was content to recite the words of Isaiah each day, "Blessed are You, O Lord our God, King of the the Universe. For you take care of the poor people in troubled times; You provide a warm, dry place during bad weather and a cool place when it's hot. You offer shelter from the storm and shade from the sun and shut the mouths of those who oppress us."

The eighth day of the Feast was a solemn assembly. During the day's celebration, the priests would offer one bull, one ram, and seven lambs. In all, one hundred eighty-nine animals would have been sacrificed during the week.

The High Priest offered a special prayer for rain. A golden pitcher holding three logs was filled by one of the other priests from the water in the Pool of Siloam and brought through the water-gate into the Temple. "And you will say in that day," began the priest, "'I thank You, Lord. You were angry, but Your anger wasn't forever. You withdrew Your anger and moved in and comforted me. Yes indeed, the Lord is my salvation. I trust, I won't be afraid. God… yes, God…is my strength and song, and best of all my salvation!' Joyfully, you'll pull up buckets of water from the wells of salvation. And as you do it, you'll say, 'Give thanks to God. Call out His name!'"

Joseph and the other men recited together, "You will receive your salvation with joy as you would draw water from a well!"

Trumpets split the air with blasts of joy celebrating the event as the water was poured out together with a bit of wine into a tube in the altar, through which it flowed, mingling with the libation of wine. From there it went through an underground passage to the Kidron brook. The priest then lifted up his hands high above his head, so that all the worshipers might see that the function had been discharged properly. The people were taught that the ceremony was to remind Jehovah to send them rain during the year so that their crops would grow. But it was to also remind them of the coming of the Messiah. Joseph looked around at the men close to him and longed to tell them that Messiah had indeed come.

Then the men again turned their backs to the altar as the priest pronounced the *dukan,* the special blessing, "The Lord bless you and keep you; the Lord make His face to shine upon you and be gracious unto you; the Lord lift up His countenance upon you, and give you peace!"

And with that pronouncement, the men shouted "Hosha'na!" and filed out of the Temple area back to their sukkas and their families.

****

Mary had awakened in the middle of the night because she thought she heard an unfamiliar noise. She looked first at Joseph sleeping so soundly beside her. He wasn't snoring.

"What a peaceful look he has," she thought, "and even in his sleep, he grins ever so slightly."

The young carpenter's bride turned slowly and quietly from her place of rest so as not to disturb her husband's slumber, and she rolled to her left to the small mat laying close by on which her son slept. The baby rested comfortably... as comfortably as he could after the circumscion rites a few hours earlier. "You're such a fine baby," whispered Mary, "You didn't even cry out when Zachariah cut the foreskin... just a slight whimper... and a tear ran down your little cheeks." Mary touched that same cheek ever so gently and looked up at the stars through the roof of their *sukka* as she recalled the *brit milah*.

Jacob had carried the baby into the room prepared for the ceremony every Jewish boy experienced on the eighth day of life. The room was decorated much like the room used in Zachariah and Elizabeth's country-home. The elderly priest expertly performed the duties of the *mohel,* and the words spoken by him followed all the same traditional words she had heard six months earlier. This time, she heard the words with different ears. This time the words were about her son. Tears of joy filled her eyes as she remembered the old priest declaring the name of her son for the first time.

Zachariah lifted the baby as high as he could and pronounced, "Our God and the God of our fathers, preserve this child for his father and his mother, and may his name be called in Israel..." The old priest looked at Joseph as if to get clarification for a fact which he already knew.

"Jesus," said the young carpenter from Nazareth, "just as the angel declared." Joseph looked neither to his right nor his left as he uttered these words, but he could feel the piercing, questioning eyes of the other folks in the room who did not quite grasp the meaning of the statement. Mary just grinned, as did Elizabeth.

"May his name be called in Israel... Jesus, son of Joseph the carpenter," continued the country preacher. "O give thanks unto the Lord; for He is good; because His mercy endures forever! Jesus, son of Joseph...may this little one become great!"

Mary remembered, too, the rest of the ceremony, the witnesses' response, the tears of joy from all the women present... and she recalled the words of her beloved. She understood that it was tradition for the father of the young boy-child to speak a "prophetic" kind of blessing over the baby, but Joseph's words caused her to experience so many different emotions. She searched the eyes of the witnesses as her carpenter voiced his blessing.

"Blessed be the Lord God of Israel," declared Joseph, "for He has visited and redeemed His people. Lord, you have taught me since I was young. To this day I speak of the miracles that You do. Even as You show us Your salvation."

Joseph lifted his eyes from off the face of the babe in his arms and turned his gaze towards the heavens. "Let Your Anointed One judge Your people fairly and decide what is right for the poor. Let there be peace on the mountains and goodness on the hills for the people. Help Him to be fair to the poor,,, and save the needy,,, and punish those who hurt them," continued the learned wood-shaper. "May all respect You as long as the sun shines and as long as the moon glows. Let This One be like rain on the grass, like showers that water the earth. Let His kingdom go from sea to sea, and from the Euphrates River to the ends of the earth. Let the people of the desert bow down to Him, and make His enemies lick the dust. Let the kings of Tarshish and the far away lands bring Him gifts. Let the kings of Sheba and Seba bring their presents to Him. Let all kings bow down to Him and all nations serve Him."

Joseph stopped momentarily to glance at the witnesses assembled in the small room. Mary noticed a new grin on his face... mysterious, mystifying, and perhaps a bit mischievous as he surveyed the faces of those before him. It was like her beloved was trying to tell them something important... a puzzle... that they would have to figure out themselves.

And then he turned his eyes back to the little one he held so tenderly.

"He will help the poor when they cry out," added Joseph, "and will save the needy when no one else will help. He will be kind to the weak and poor, and He will save them. He will save them from cruel people who try to hurt them, because their lives are precious to Him. He will teach us His ways, and we will walk in His paths. For the law shall go forth of Zion, and the Word of the Lord from Jerusalem. And He shall judge among many people, and rebuke strong nations afar off. And they shall beat their swords into plowshares, and their spears into pruning hooks; nation shall not lift up sword against nation, neither shall they learn war anymore. Let the nations be blessed because of Him, and may they all bless Him."

For what seemed like an eternity, the silence of the witnesses encompassed the room. Then Zachariah said, "Mazel Tov!" and the other witnesses repeated the phrase, some with exuberance, others with amazement that Joseph would say such things. Most recognized the words from the scriptures… words and phrases that were meant to describe the Messiah. Mary knew the words were true, and she hoped that one day all in the room would understand their meaning as applied to Jesus.

In any event, this had been a day of great rejoicing. She wanted to shout "Hosha'na!" but kept the words inside her lest she wake her child or her husband… or her in-laws in the next tent. The young bride turned back to her carpenter, snuggled closely, and smiled with a deep satisfaction that nothing would ever be the same again.

****

Chapter Fourteen

The Redemption

Thirty days is not a very long span of time, unless one happens to be a young bride and mother wishing to be in her own hometown, in her own home, using her own things to take care of her husband and her baby. Mary was looking forward to the return trip to Bethlehem with much anticipation. She recalled how she had been just a bit irritated on the ninth and final day of the Feast of Booths as she and Joseph tore down the sukka they had lived in since the birth of Jesus, their firstborn. But when she looked into the smiling face of her beloved and listened to his smooth, unpretentious teaching, she was encouraged and felt that all was right with the world.

"May it be Your will, O Lord, our God and God of our ancestors," voiced Joseph as he removed the branches from the roof of their *sukka*, "that just as I have stood up and dwelled in this *sukka*, so may we merit next year to dwell in the *sukka* of the hide of the Leviathan." Then he looked straight at his young bride, and with that special grin of his, he added, "Next year in Jerusalem."

The young carpenter from Nazareth took the time to explain to his beloved about the traditional belief that the defeat of the sea monster Leviathan would precede the coming of the Messiah. The Jews taught that Leviathan's skin would provide enough material to make a giant *sukka*, and the righteous

139

would dine on the flesh of Leviathan in that *sukka*. Thus, the essence of the farewell prayer is that Messiah would come within the next year. Of course, most of the Jewish teachers believed that the Promised One would come as a full grown adult, not as a baby.

The rest of that ninth day of the Feast was one of great celebration for *Simchat Torah*, rejoicing in the Torah and the starting over of reading the Torah in the synagogues. There was a parade around the small synagogue in Bethlehem, with just about everyone in the tiny village carrying copies of the Torah as the people danced and sang and drank and spoke blessings over the Torah readings. Even the children of the small town got involved by carrying small, toy Torahs or paper scrolls. The children were given gifts of *challah*, a type of sweet bread, and some fruit because the commandments of the Lord are sweeter than honey. Mary had always compared this celebration to the wedding celebrations she had experienced. The re-establishment of the covenant with the Torah was so very much like the rejoicing of a groom with his bride. And a smile crossed her lips as she relived her and Joseph's own celebration just a few months earlier.

Joseph and his family took an active part in the celebration to begin anew the reading of the Torah. They had been commissioned to repair several of the apartments of the priests near the Temple in Jerusalem, and so they would be spending perhaps up to two months in the little town of Bethlehem with kinsmen. Many of the inhabitants were already familiar with the carpenters from Nazareth, for this was not the first time the family had spent time in the small village. On that day, the men of the town were called up to read from the Torah, but there were so many in attendance that the reading had to be done outside on a specially prepared annex to the synagogue. Jacob was one of several who read the blessing of Moses in which he mentioned each tribe by name and blessed them in the new land. Joseph was among the last of the men to read and was called up with all the boys under the age of thirteen. The tall woodworker smiled and nodded his head as young

Simon, the shepherd boy, stood beside him. Joseph held the baby Jesus with his right arm and placed his left arm around the shoulders of the little shepherd boy who had visited them as the result of the angels proclamation. After the last reading, Joseph, though a guest, was given the opportunity to voice a special blessing on behalf of the boys.

"The angel who redeemed me from all evil," began Joseph, "bless the lads. And let my name be named on them, and the name of my fathers Abraham and Isaac. And may they grow into a multitude in the midst of the earth."

Everyone in the crowd recognized this blessing as the one the patriarch, Jacob, had bestowed upon his grandchildren Manasseh and Ephraim. This was a time of great excitement for the boys of the village who were pre-*bar mitzvah* age, for this was the only time of the year when they were called up to be a part of the Torah readings.

Zachariah was then called up, as the Bridegroom of the Torah, to conclude the day's reading. His young protégé, Jonathan, recited a special blessing for the old priest as he made his way to the place of reading. Zachariah then read the portion of scripture that told of the death of Moses at the age of 120 years, after having seen the Promised Land from atop Mt. Nebo. The words related how God had buried Moses in a place unknown to anyone, and how the children of Israel wept for the great prophet for thirty days, and how God had given them another leader named Joshua, God's salvation.

Mary glanced at her beloved nail-driver who exchanged her glance with that new grin of his. Both recognized the significance of the name's meaning, "God's salvation", for it was the name given to their newborn son. Zachariah, too, paused for just a moment and sought the faces of his young cousins as he mentioned the name, for he also understood how the scriptures were being fulfilled before their very eyes.

For the last verse, the folks in attendance rose to their feet, and at the conclusion of the reading shouted, "Be strong, be strong, and let us strengthen each other!" This brought encouragement to each one to continue studying and living by the Torah during the coming year. And then the Torah reading was begun again like a never ending circle indicating that the people can never finish the Torah.

The clamor in the nearby market brought the young former-farm girl back to her task of washing Jesus. "Thirty days... thirty days," she thought aloud returning the grin of her baby. Thirty days had passed since the young maiden from Nazareth had sat on the birthing stool in Malachi's manger. She peered out the small window in the room that had become her home away from home in her new cousin-in-law's house in Bethlehem. So many things had happened in the past thirty days, and tomorrow, Joseph would take Jesus to Jerusalem to be redeemed according to the law of Moses. Mary sighed deeply as she wrapped her baby in a towel and lifted him from the small basin full of water. She gently dried him and wrapped him again in the blanket she had made before she and her new family had left Nazareth. And she hummed an old lullaby that her mother used to sing as she rocked back and forth on the chair that had doubled as Elijah's chair just a few weeks before. The baby in her arms made typical baby noises and smiled as they each searched the other's eyes. In no time at all, the little bundle in her arms had fallen asleep, and she laid him ever so gently on the floor of their small abode. She was grateful for the generosity shown them by Malachi and Naomi, but she still yearned to be back in her own home.

****

Aramazar, the High Priest of AlQuam and Shamesh, had been traveling for three weeks with his nephews, Abimael the astrologer and Meshach the philosopher-teacher, towards their intended goal of representing King Aretas of the Nabataeans in the court of King Herod of the Jews. The three wise men from the almost forgotten former capital of the Chaldeans had actually spent only a few hours together during one or two of the nightly stops along the trade route designed by Aramazar. The caravan carrying spices and other riches from the eastern world had become much larger than the old priest had antici- pated when he first made his plans to defect into the normal life of an ordinary tentmaker after arriving in Jerusalem. He had spent most of his time taking care of administrative details involved in managing the trading done along the way and mapping out the next day's journey. There seemed to be an endless supply of emergencies that demanded his atten- tion during the day, and countless disagreements among the merchants that had to be settled each night. And, of course, there was the daily public blessing he had to seek from either AlQuam or Shamesh. At each stop, goods were sold or exchanged, and some merchants abandoned the trip, content with the deals they had made. But then there were the new sellers who joined the caravan dreaming of making a fortune somewhere down the line. So after some three weeks on their quest, the caravan had only traveled fifty miles from home.

Part of the burned-out priest's administrative duties required him to avoid the places where the merchants would have to pay exorbitant taxes to the Roman officials or Bedouin tribal leaders. He was well aware of the secret watering holes developed by other caravan leaders over the years. But this meant traveling through regions inhabited by thieves or cris- crossing back and forth across the desert. And the merchants did not like carrying so much wealth long distances without a chance to sell their goods. So the journey had to weave in and out of safe places towards fortresses and resting stations placed strategically along the routes to protect the caravan. At these places, the merchants plied their wares, and the trav- elers rested for a day or two. Animals also needed their rest from carrying the heavy burdens of the spice trade.

Abimael kept busy drawing maps. He kept copious notes about the position of the stars each night matching his find- ings with that of ancient star-gazers. Often times he discov- ered slight discrepancies and corrected them in his journal.

Meshach catalogued the different species of animals spotted along the way. And he enjoyed just talking to the common people at each of the stops. The young scholar had never ventured very far from his hometown of Susa, and he found the men and women that he met fascinating. Each one had a story unique to his or her own experience. Most of all he liked talking to the merchants.

"Did you know we are not traveling westward, Cousin?" inquired the eager seeker of truth as he burst into their shared tent one evening.

"We're traveling southeast," answered Abimael without much enthusiasm in his voice while he studied his calculations.

"We're traveling southeast!" exclaimed Meshach, before he realized that Abimael had already answered his question. The young star-gazer looked up from his work, and just grinned as the young instructor stood before him with a scowl on his face while replaying the previous words spoken.

"How did you know we were traveling southeast?" asked Meshach.

Abimael laughed just a little, the first time he had laughed in quite awhile. "It's my job to chart the stars... to more or less navigate the trip for the caravan, Cousin. Our uncle tells me where he wants to go, and I make sure we stay on course. You could tell, too, if you spent more time looking at the heavens each morning instead of drilling all the merchants with your endless questions." The young astrologer still had a big grin on his face.

"I thought we would be half way to Jerusalem by now," stated Meshach with just a hint of pouting in his voice. "But we are further from our final destination than when we started. And do you know why?"

"Because of the merchants who want to make money selling their merchandise along the way," answered Abimael.

"It's because of the merchants who want to make money selling..." repeated Meshach. The young philosopher stopped short in mid-sentence and just stared at his younger, but taller cousin sitting cross-armed with that goofy grin of his. "I wish you wouldn't study me like I'm some kind of specimen... and I wish you'd have the courtesy to tell me you're going to answer me before you answer me", said the young scholar.

Abimael chuckled as he stood and walked to the back of their tent to pour a goblet of wine for his less-than-excited cousin. "Remember the purpose of this expedition, Meshach, is to bring rich gifts to the new born King of the Jews, Herod's son." The young observer of the stars handed the goblet to his older cousin and continued. "Besides, Aramazar is in no rush. So relax, Cousin. Jerusalem isn't going anywhere. The great City of Jehovah will still be there whenever we get there. Don't you have faith in your own studies and the words of your prophets? According to them, this new King of the Jews will usher in a great new era for all. Surely he will have to grow up a bit first in order to accomplish so many wonderful things."

Meshach looked into his cousin's eyes and realized that Abimael was simply teasing him. As the two of them sipped the wine, the young student of Daniel vowed to be more observant of their location and their journey. Perhaps he would start keeping a journal of each day's activities... of the words of wisdom uttered by the people with whom he came in contact... and of Abimael's comments, too. Meshach perceived an ever so slight change in Abimael's attitude. His star-gazing cousin actually seemed happier than he had been in a long time, and come to think of it, so had their Uncle Aramazar. Perhaps both were beginning to anticipate the three of them walking the streets of God's great city set on the hill... perhaps they thought of stepping in the exact same spot where Israel's greatest prophets had once stood. Their journey would be much longer than the young scholar had figured on, but they would arrive at their final destination triumphantly to welcome the birth of the promised King of the Jews. Meshach would be forced to learn patience, but he knew the waiting would be worth it all. He grinned back at his learned cousin, and finished his pre-supper drink in one gulp.

****

The firstborn son of a Jewish family was originally intended to be the priest of that family. Through Moses, Jehovah had told the people that the firstborn of everything, both man and beast, was to be set apart, sanctified, to serve Him. But while the people traveled towards the Promised Land, they committed the grievous sin of creating an idol in the form of a Golden Calf, which many proceeded to worship. Only members of the tribe of Levi did not participate in this sin. Therefore, the Lord decreed that the Levites were to take the place of the firstborn sons of Israel. Thus, the Levites became the priestly tribe of Israel.

In a matter of speaking, all other firstborn sons became disqualified for priestly duties and had to be "redeemed" from service to God through a special ceremony held on the 31st day after the birth of the firstborn. The father of the child would take the baby to a priest and would pay five silver shekels for the redemption. Joseph had carefully explained the reason for the ritual to his beloved bride to help her understand the proceedings of that day which would fulfill the Law.

"Did you go through this ceremony, Joseph?" asked the young maiden from Nazareth.

"No, my Love," answered Joseph. "Remember, I wasn't the firstborn of my mother and father. Nor did Eleazar. Actually the redemption ceremony applies to only a small portion of Jewish children. Only those males who have opened the womb or were not born after the miscarriage of another child are to be redeemed from service to the Lord. Eleazar was born after my mother had lost a daughter. Our other sons will not have this ritual as a part of their lives, either." The tall carpenter grinned for Mary with that special grin meant only for her. Mary's eyes lit up with joy as she caught his meaning. Then she blushed a bit.

"In nine more days, we will go to the Temple and offer the purification offering for you, my Love," continued her wood-worker. "And we will experience all the joys that God intended for a groom and his bride."

"I would love to go with you today, Joseph," stated Mary, "but I suppose that I should stay here and help Naomi and Judith prepare the festive meal for our friends and family to celebrate this day. Besides, I'm not supposed to mingle with others outside my family according to mother Judith. Elizabeth will be here, too, with young John. I am anxious to speak with her again."

"I'm glad to be seeing Zachariah again, too," added Joseph. "I have some questions for him as well. He will accept the redemption shekels, and the rest of us will return here to Malachi's house."

"All of you?" asked Mary with a slight look of worry on her face.

"Yes, my Love," answered Joseph with a grin, "all ten of us. It will be a great occasion to be remembered."

****

Chenaniah, one of King Herod's many servants, entered the chambers of the aging ruler of the Jews with caution and deep regret. Herod was a man to be feared. He had tried to buy the hearts of the people by restoring Jerusalem and the Temple on a grand scale. And while his massive building projects provided jobs for so many, he was a man whose temper was controlled by his feelings of insecurity. The old king spent his days suspecting everyone around him of treachery and deceit. He had already put several people to death for actions that he believed made them usurpers to his throne. And the people of his kingdom had little respect for his Hellenistic ways.

Chenaniah paused for a moment outside the room where Herod lay sick. The usually overlooked servant to the king did not want to deliver the message he had been given. The young servant recalled how he had given Herod the judgment that led to the death of the king's sons, Alexander and Aristobulus just a year before. The two men had been well-liked by the inhabitants of Jerusalem as was their mother, Mariamne. But Herod had suspected them of plotting to kill him, so he accused them of high treason. Their trial took place in Berytos before a Roman court which found them guilty, and the two sons of Herod were executed. Chenaniah had read the message to Herod from one of the king's informers, and the young servant knew this message would cause great pain to many of his kinsmen.

"O great king," said Chenaniah, "grant me favor in your eyes and bid me enter your chambers. I have a message for you from Dibon the Edomite." The young servant kept his eyes toward the floor and awaited the summons from Herod.

"Come on in, Chenaniah," answered the sickly king. "I've been waiting for word from Dibon for quite some time." Chenaniah entered the sleeping quarters of the king humbly and noticed a strange odor, but dared not mention anything to Herod lest his comment enrage the king. Herod reached out a trembling hand to take the silver tray which held a small scroll. Chenaniah stood quietly awaiting his dismissal. Uncharacteristically, the old king read the message allowed.

"Live forever, O Great One," began Herod, "It has come to my attention that a small group of your enemies, known as Pharisees, have started a rumor that the Promised One of Jehovah will make his presence known soon to the people. These traitors teach that the arrival of this so called Messiah will ignite the spark that will doom your own reign. I know the names of these traitors and will gladly give them over to you. I trust my knowledge will be amply rewarded as usual."

Herod's face showed the hatred and contempt he had for these religious leaders who had continuously opposed his rule, citing his own Gentile heritage to denounce his power. To them, Herod was not legally able to sit on the throne of Israel.

"Send Antiochus to escort Dibon to my chambers," stated Herod. "These men who seek to destroy my kingdom will by their own words be destroyed. No one will ever take my throne from me... not even a Messiah... false or real." The old king's eyes turned red with revenge. He had always feared the prophecies he had heard of this Promised One, but had dismissed the writings as babble from disgruntled religious fanatics. He would show the people once again just how much he respected their prophets by torturing to death those who even attempted to arouse the Jews to revolt against his authority. He would teach them a lesson they would not soon forget.

****

Zachariah had met Joseph and his minions on the outskirts of Bethlehem. He had planned on escorting Elizabeth and John to Malachi's caravansary house and then leave with the others to journey back to a room he had reserved near the Temple for Jesus' redemption ceremony. The young carpenter from Nazareth noticed that his elderly cousin seemed to be a bit out of breath from the short journey to David's City and suggested that he simply perform the ritual in the room where he and Mary were staying. The other men agreed with Joseph's idea, and all acknowledged that the ceremony did not have to take place within the confines of the Temple. The old priest had performed the *brit milah* of Jesus in Bethlehem, and they would not be breaking any law by returning to that same room for the *Pidyon HaBen*. Several of the townsfolk smiled and nodded their approval as the small parade of worshipers headed back for the center of the little village.

Mary had already dressed herself in her holiday finery as had Joseph and Joseph's parents. She smiled broadly as the entourage entered the home of her new kinsmen. Judith took the baby Jesus in her arms while Naomi prepared the silver tray used to carry the baby to the old priest. Judith had given Mary permission to use the special shirt that Jacob's mother had passed down to her for the use of her sons. The little room was packed with family who joyously celebrated the redemption of Jesus.

Joseph approached Zachariah with the baby lying atop the silver tray as the last of the witnesses had finished washing for the *mitzvah*. Zachariah picked up two loaves and held them with all ten fingers while extending his hands. He then recited the *Hamotzie*, the blessing over the bread and broke it.

"My Israelite wife has borne me this firstborn son," said Joseph.

"Which would you rather have," asked the old priest, "your firstborn son, or the five coins which you are obligated to give me for the redemption of this your firstborn son?"

"I want this, my first born son," answered the young carpenter, "and here you have five coins which are required of me for the redemption." Joseph handed the shekels to Zachariah and continued with the ritual blessings. "Blessed are You, O Lord our God, King of the Universe, Who sanctified us with His mitzvoth, and instructed us regarding the redemption of a son."

Joseph lowered his eyes to look for a moment at the baby lying before him. Then he raised his eyes and gazed into the loving eyes of his bride. "Blessed are You, O Lord our God, King of the Universe," he recited, "Who has kept us alive, sustained us, and brought us to this season."

Zachariah passed the coins over the child's head and said, "This is in place of that. This is excused on account of that. May it be that this son has entered into life, into Torah, and into fear of God. May it be God's will that just as he has entered into redemption, so may he enter into Torah, into marriage, and into good deeds."

Then Zachariah placed his right hand on the child's head and pronounced the blessing of Ephraim and Manasah as the patriarch, Jacob, had done so many years previous. The old priest continued the blessing by adding, "May the Lord bless you and safeguard you. May the Lord illuminate His Countenance for you and be gracious to you. May the Lord turn His Countenance toward you, and grant you peace."

The old country preacher then took up a cup of wine sitting close by and said, "Blessed are You, O Lord our God, King of the Universe, Who created fruit of the vine." And with that blessing, he drank from the cup. He then concluded the ceremony by saying, "The Lord is your Guardian, the Lord is the shadow on your right hand. For length of days, and years of life and peace shall they add to you. The Lord will guard you from all evil; He will guard your soul."

A festive meal of meat and wine with cloves of garlic and pieces of sugar capped the celebration. Those gathered sang joyously, and inspiring words from the Torah were shared by each of the men present. Joseph couldn't help but ponder the meaning of the ritual of redemption and the irony of the celebration. Mere men offered to redeem the son of God from service to the Father, but in the near future, this baby that they danced around would redeem each of them with His blood. Joseph thought it best to not tell his beloved of what he believed the Scriptures revealed about the ministry of Messiah. She would learn soon enough... and nothing would be the same again.

****

Chapter Fifteen

The Testimony

S imeon had been sitting on Solomon's Porch for what seemed like an eternity, awaiting the coming of the Lord's Messiah as he had been promised. He had talked ferverently with Achim the shepherd who had witnessed the birth of a boy child in a manger in the small village of Bethlehem. And he had spoken with several young Pharisees who had listened diligently to his story about his dreams and the visits from the angels to the shepherds. The old businessman had felt a bit of remorse when he learned that these young teachers had been executed by Herod because they had been spreading the news he had shared with them. Simeon knew that Herod was a cruel and vicious ruler who feared any and all threats to his kingdom. Still the old man waited, expecting to see the Messiah with his own eyes. And he would speak to anyone who would listen, declaring the time of Christ was here. Simeon did not fear Herod or his cronies, especially if what he had waited for for so long came to be.

There seemed to be a new spring in the old man's step as he entered the Temple area since he had heard of the unusual birth of that baby in Bethlehem. Simeon noticed, too, that Anna seemed to be smiling more and humming more than she usually did. Each morning, he would shuffle into the Court of the Gentiles and examine the faces of the people purchasing animals to be sacrificed. He looked for a couple with a baby, probably he expected, about a month old. Anna had reminded the old gentleman that the baby's mother would most likely come to the Temple for the purification ceremony according to the Law of Moses. He had calculated the 41st day of the baby Achim had spoken of to be this very day. Still he had showed up at his usual spot every day as was his custom, just in case. The old businessman had not been this excited since his wedding day. Every nerve in his body was poised for the joyous occasion when he would gaze upon the Consolation of Israel.

As he surveyed the crowd gathering in the Temple area and preparing to have their sacrifices made an offering to the Lord, he spotted three couples milling towards the tables of the merchants selling their animals. He approached each one individually, and with shaking hands, identified himself and asked to see the baby cradled in the arms of the mothers. Unfortunately, the Holy Spirit did not indicate that any of these infants was the One he had been searching for. Besides, two of them were girls.

So, with a polite smile, he told each mother how beautiful their baby was, and then walked back to his spot to wait. It would only be a few more moments, so the old man reasoned, that have him looking into the eyes of the Lord's Messiah… the Promised One of Israel. Simeon lifted his eyes towards the heavens and whispered praises to Jehovah.

****

Mary was more excited than she had anticipated the night before as she and her beloved carpenter trudged along the road from Bethlehem to Jerusalem. Joseph carried Jesus in his arms like he was carrying a loaf of fresh baked bread to a special party honoring the King. She smiled every time she glanced his way, and he returned that smile with a wink. They were on their way to the Temple to make the required offering that would end her temporary exile from the rest of the world.

The young maiden from Nazareth had not been allowed to mingle with the other folks in Bethlehem at the synagogue or the market since the birth of her little boy. New mothers were considered ceremonially unclean for 40 days after the birth of a male child, 66 days after the birth of a female child. The only exceptions were sharing meals with her close family and the celebrations of *brit milah* and *pidyon haben*. She truly missed the reading of the Torah and the lessons taught in the synagogue, even if the Scriptures were not being explained by her beloved husband. She smiled again as she recalled how carefully he had explained each passage that had been read on those previous sabbath days leading up to their entrance into the Temple.

The young woodworker's bride was amazed and awed by the size of the walled city of Jerusalem. She gasped a bit when she saw the gold and white Temple gleaming in the Israeli sun. Mary had heard Joseph describe the Temple area several times before, but seeing it all in person for the first time since she was a small girl, made her think on the majesty of the Lord. Then, she suddenly remembered who Joseph cradled in his arms, and the impact of that thought in the Holy City made her stop dead in her tracks. Joseph immediately noticed that his beloved bride was not at his side as she had been. He turned to see his young wife standing erect, staring wide-eyed with open mouth at the spectacle before them.

"Breath-taking isn't it?" commented the tall wood-shaper with a new grin Mary had not noticed before. This grin was more akin to a worshipful, peaceful, gentle smile that came across Joseph's face whenever he shared something new about the Scriptures with her... and yet it was different.

"Yes," was all the former farm-girl could muster.

Joseph took a step towards Mary and held out his hand to her. "Come, my Love," he said. "Take my hand. Walk beside me and don't be afraid." His words always had a way of reassuring the young maiden and strengthening her. She smiled at her beloved and took his hand. Together they walked through the Dung Gate and made their way through the narrow streets where the many merchants had set up shop to the Temple itself.

Moses had instructed the people to offer a lamb for a burnt offering and a turtle dove for a sin offering to end the days of confinement for a woman who had given birth. But Joseph had not been paid yet for his work on the priests' apartments, so he bought two turtle doves for Mary's offering from the sellers in the large but crowded Court of the Gentiles.

"You'll have to stay here, Mary," suggested the tall wood-worker, "in the Court of the Women. I'll go yonder, up those stairs to the Court of Israel and give the two turtle doves to the priest." Mary looked a bit frightened at the thought of being separated from her strong, beloved carpenter, but she managed a slight grin for his benefit.

She took the baby in her arms and said, "It's all right, Joseph. I'll wait here for you. Besides, it's about time to feed little Jesus. We'll be fine." The young mother tried her best to disguise her concern of being left alone if even for a short time in such a big and unfamiliar place.

Joseph smiled and touched her hand to reassure her that everything was under control. He turned and walked up the stairs to finish the requirements of the purification offering.

The muscular carpenter handed the turtledoves to the attending priest, who inspected the birds, placed them on the slaughtering stone, and with great dignity, wrung their necks. The blood of these fowl was wrung out, and the priest was careful to collect all the blood of the offerings into a brass container. Then he picked up the birds in his hands and walked up the steps to the brazen altar. There, the priest cut the birds down the middle, and their insides were removed. The crop and feathers were placed on the ash heap at the side of the altar. As the priest placed one of the doves on the altar as a burnt offering, special chants of praise to God were offered by a small group of priests. Then the attending priest sprinkled the blood of the remaining dove around the altar and laid the bird atop the altar while uttering a special blessing for Mary. At that point, she was considered clean again and could mingle with the people.

****

Judith, the mother of the young carpenter from Nazareth sat quietly as her husband of 37 years munched on the fruit and bread she had brought him and Eleazar for their mid-morning meal. She had become accustomed to providing a light lunch for her men for many years now and had plans of not retiring until her husband gave the business over to their sons. But on this day, toward the month of Kislev, she toyed with the pebbles on the ground beneath her sandals. She seemed to be preoccupied with something for she did not make conversation as she usually had done.

"Jacob," said the elder carpenter's wife, "have you noticed anything unusual about Jesus?"

"I'm not sure what you mean, Woman," answered Jacob shrewdly.

"I'm not sure, either," offered Judith, "but he doesn't act like other babies. His eyes..." she added trailing off the sentence.

"What about his eyes?" asked the older woodworker.

"They seem to look right through you," she said, "like he already knows us. And he's only a month old. Don't you think that's strange?"

"Well, I will admit that he does seem to recognize every-body," added Jacob, "and it seems that he's never met a stranger. He does have a terrific little smile, though... and strong little hands. And I do believe that he understands every word we speak to him. Maybe that just means that he's destined for greatness."

"Do you remember Joseph telling us how that little shep-herd boy stared at Jesus the night he was born in that cave?" asked Judith. "And the baby smiled when the boy started playing his flute. I think he really understood. I'm sure Jesus would have reached out to him if he hadn't been wrapped so tightly in those swaddling clothes."

"My nephew is simply perceptive," countered the younger of the two builders. "He's just progressed more than most children his age. I wouldn't be surprised if he starts walking and talking before we get back to Nazareth." The two men chuckled a bit, obviously proud kinsmen. But Judith maintained her puzzled look.

"Have either one of you heard him cry?" Judith asked as the two finished their meal. "I haven't. I don't think he even cried when he was circumcised. At least, I don't remember him crying."

"Perhaps the knife Zachariah used was extra sharp, and the little one didn't feel a thing," suggested Eleazar. "Zachariah has been performing the *brit milah* ritual for many, many years now, Mother. And I am sure he doesn't want to inflict any more pain than he has to. Perhaps he has developed a technique that makes the operation painless."

"You're just being an overly curious grandmother," added Jacob. "If you'll think back a few years you might recall that Joseph didn't cry all that much, either. He was a good baby. Both our boys were good babies. You weren't concerned then. Why now?"

"I don't know," answered the gray-haired lady as she placed the small cloths which had held the lunches back into her leather bag. "I'm not saying that Jesus is a bad baby. I'm just saying that he is… different." Then she smiled just a bit. "I'm just as proud of him as you two are," she added. "I'm just wondering out loud because he seems to be so aware of his surroundings at such an early age. Perhaps you are right, Jacob. Perhaps this child is destined for greatness. Perhaps he will leave his mark in wood and create a masterpiece that folks will admire for generations to come." The old woman sighed heavily as old women do when they dream beyond their own comprehension. "Perhaps," she repeated as she walked back towards the marketplace where she was to meet Joseph and Mary on their return trip to Bethlehem.

****

Simeon had noticed the young couple enter the Court of the Gentiles and purchase the two turtle doves required for the sacrifice. He had planned on approaching the two, but was not fast enough. The tall man had ushered his wife and baby into the Court of the Women before he could get to them. But he kept an eye on the young girl after her husband had left her with the other women. He noticed that Anna had spoken to the young maiden as she had to so many women. He wondered what the old prophetess had said to her, and if she had recognized anything different about that baby. Apparently the Holy Spirit had not talked to her about that child. Perhaps he was not the One, either. Still, the old man watched and waited for the opportunity to speak to the mother with the father of the baby present. It would have been considered rude for him to approach the young girl without her husband by her side.

Finally, the tall, dark-haired man returned for his young wife. He held her arms, but did not show any public display of affection for that was considered rude to do so. But he did smile and stare deep into her eyes, and the young woman exchanged the greeting whole-heartedly. The man played with the baby for just a bit, and then the three of them headed back out of the Temple through the Court of the Gentiles.

"Forgive my intrusion," said Simeon politely as he blocked their exit, "but would you humor an old man for just a moment. Could I see your baby?"

Mary got that frightened look on her face again. She looked at Joseph to see if he recognized the man. Her beloved carpenter placed his large right hand on the old man's shoulder, grinned his have-I-got-a-surprise-for-you grin at him, and nodded his approval.

Simeon took the baby in his arms from his reluctant mother and unwrapped the blanket far enough to see the baby's face. The baby looked at him and smiled from ear to ear. The Holy Spirit fell upon the old man, and he stood straight for the first time in many years. He lifted the baby towards the heavens and said, "Blessed are You, O Lord our God, King of the Universe, Who keeps His promises to His people. O

God, You can now release Your servant; release me in peace
as You promised. For with my own eyes I've seen Your salvation; it's now out in the open for everyone to see. A God-
revealing light to the non-Jewish nations, and of glory for Your
people Israel."

Neither Joseph nor Mary knew what to say in response
to the words of the old man. They both just looked at him
incredulously. Both of them thought the same thing, but said
nothing. How did this old man know who Jesus was?

Simeon slowly brought the baby back to his chest to hold
him tightly. Mary and Joseph could see that the baby was
still smiling. "What is his name, Fair Lady?" he asked as he
handed the child back to his mother.

"His name is Jesus," she answered. By now her fear had
turned to wonder and amazement.

The old man placed his hand on Jesus' head and looked
straight at Mary as he said, "God's salvation! This child marks
both the failure and the recovery of many in Israel. A figure
misunderstood and contradicted. You will feel the pain of a
sword thrust through you. But the rejection will force honesty,
as God reveals who the detractors really are."

Anna had seen her old friend walk over to the couple
and had witnessed his testimony and blessing, as did many
others. She understood what Simeon was saying; the others
were not quite sure and were too intimidated by their lack of
spiritual awareness to ask. She walked up beside the young
maiden holding the babe in her arms. The old prophetess
placed one arm around Mary while placing her other hand
gently on her friend's shoulder. The old man looked up at
her with tears of joy streaming down his cheeks and nodded
his answer to the question that she couldn't seem to utter.
Anna looked at the woman standing beside her. Then she
focused her tear-filled eyes on the baby in Mary's arms. The
four adults stood momentarily gazing at the happy face of the
child. And suddenly Anna broke into an anthem of praise to
God. She began telling all those around her about the child.
Some of the people reacted with great joy for they, too, had

been waiting expectantly for the freeing of Jerusalem. Others simply shook their heads saying, "Messiah would not come as a baby. A baby could not kick the Romans out of Israel!" Still Anna told everyone who would listen.

A small crowd began to gather, with each person talking to the one beside them with authority about their interpretation of the events they had just witnessed. Joseph placed his arm around his young bride and ushered her out of the Temple area as fast as he could. Simeon stood his ground with his hands lifted to the heavens and praised God over and over again. The news of the Messiah had been made known to the people in Jerusalem. Some would believe, some would not, but no one would ever be the same again.

****

Chapter Sixteen

Homeward Bound

M ary was finally back in her own house, in her own hometown. While it was true that her dwelling was actually
just a room attached to her father-in-law's house, it was home,
and it was the place where she and her beloved carpenter
would spend their time together for at least another six months.

The former farm girl checked on her baby, Jesus, as he
slept so peacefully in the little crib that Joseph had made
with his own hands. "What a talented carpenter he is," she
thought as she ran her hands along the wood he had finished
shaping only two weeks before they had left for Bethlehem.
She glanced around their room and focused on the small
items he had brought from her father's house to make that
little room feel more like home for her. And she smiled as her
eyes settled on the bed Joseph had made for them fashioned
after a bed he had seen in Herod's Palace. She had never
slept off the floor before, and at first it had seemed so uncomfortable. But she got used to lying in the arms of her husband
each evening and awaking to see his smiling face greeting
her each morning. She giggled to herself just a bit as she
remembered how he had blushed when she told him about
the *mikveh*, the purification bath, she had taken just before
they left Bethlehem for home.

"Elizabeth told me of the *mikveh* ritual," she had said shyly the night after Joseph had offered the two turtledoves for her cleansing.

"*Mikveh*?... Oh, yes... the *mikveh*," he responded. Her big, strong carpenter turned his eyes away from her and pretended to be adjusting one of the bags that he had packed for their journey. And he tried to change the subject.

"Do you think I should try and make a stronger covering for the little cart?" he asked sheepishly. "So that you and Jesus will have more protection from the winds and the cool breezes as we head home in a few days? Mother will be riding with you again, and you know how cold natured she is. And I wouldn't want the baby to get sick... and..."

Mary could tell he was grasping for words... trying to find anything to talk about except the mikveh. "I went last night," she said softly.

"You... you went last night?" he repeated, with his back still to his young bride.

"Yes, Joseph," she answered. "Judith and Naomi took care of Jesus for me while you and your father and Eleazar worked out who would stay and put the finishing touches on the repairs you had been doing." Joseph looked up from his fidgeting with the strings on the travel bag, but still looked straight ahead.

"The whole ceremony didn't take long," she continued. "Did you know that there is a special bathing place for women just outside the synagogue here in Bethlehem? And Naomi's friend is in charge, so she arranged everything for me. After taking off my clothes and washing myself completely first, I immersed myself in the running water. Elizabeth taught me the prayer of purification. So, I covered my head and said, 'Blessed are you, O Lord our God, King of the Universe, who has sanctified us with His commandments and commanded us concerning ritual immersion.'"

Mary moved closer to Joseph's right side to see if he was responding positively to what she had done. "Then I immersed myself again and sang the words Elizabeth taught me, the

Y'hi Ratzon," she continued. "After the song, I immersed myself in the *mikveh* one last time as I was instructed. And Naomi's friend declared me to be purified. I understand every woman does the *mikveh* each month, after that special time is completed, so that she and her husband can know each other again. Funny... Rebekah never mentioned the *mikveh* to me."

Joseph slowly turned to face his beloved bride and found her grinning from ear to ear. At first he was puzzled, and then she spoke softly to him. "The boundaries we agreed to on our wedding day are no longer in effect, my Love," she whispered as he stepped closer to her. She had never spoken of her normal desires over the past seven months, nor had he. And now that Jesus was born and the law had been fulfilled, there was no need to ignore those feelings.

Mary remembered how gracefully and delicately her big carpenter had kissed her and caressed her that night. And she held the small pillow on the bed close to her, pretending that it was her beloved, and she dreamed of spending the night in his arms as husbands and wives are expected to do, taking pleasure by pleasing the other. And she closed her eyes and smiled broadly.

****

Sixty days had passed since Achim had told the prophetess, Anna, about his experience with the angels on the hillside outside of Bethlehem on the first evening of the Feast of Tabernacles. The importance of that encounter became ever so clear to her and to her dear friend, Simeon, less than a fortnight before this sad moment.

Anna had so enjoyed telling everyone who would listen to her about the story of the child Simeon had declared to be the Promised One of the Lord. With the exception of those who were nearby that day, most shrugged their shoulders and uttered something along the lines of "What can a mere baby do?" She had not minded that the people rejected her message, but it did hurt when they questioned the word of the old man who had so diligently awaited God's salvation, a baby who just happened to be named Jesus. Simeon had come to the Temple for several days after that day of proclamation, and she noticed the special glow on the face of the old man. But two weeks ago, her old friend had stopped coming to the courtyard to spend his day.

At first, the aged prophetess had suspected that Simeon was just walking about the city telling everyone he met about his dreams and about seeing the Messiah. After a couple of days, she inquired of others who frequented the Temple if they had seen or heard of the old gentleman who used to sit so quietly on Solomon's Porch. No one seemed to know what had happened to the old man, though they had noticed his absence.

Finally, Anna asked two of her friends to accompany her to Simeon's house to check on him. They found the old man sitting slumped over in a chair, a paper unrolled on the table. The writing on the paper simply stated that all of his possessions should be used to feed the poor of Jerusalem. Neither of the three women had touched the body, lest they become unclean. But Anna kneeled down to look at the face of the old man, and she saw no semblance of pain or agony... just peace... and a slight smile.

Anna had been given permission to wash and prepare his body for burial because he had no kinsmen to perform those duties. She had sung the Psalms as she did, placed the fragrances in the proper places on the body, and wrapped it in the burial cloths. One of the priests, along with two other men, carried the body to the family tomb just outside the city. And the four of them mourned his passing.

"Blessed art Thou, O Lord our God, King of the Universe," whispered Anna as the body of her old friend was positioned in its final resting place, "for He counts the tears shed for the death of a virtuous person, and He stores them up in His treasure house." Anna was saddened, but at the same time rejoicing in her heart because she knew Simeon rested with his ancestors and his beloved Martha in Paradise. Tears filled her eyes, but under her veil, she smiled as she thought about her old friend running around telling everyone in Abraham's presence that the Lord had kept His Word by sending the Anointed One. Surely they would listen to him there, after all, Simeon was an eye witness.

The small group of mourners slowly exited the cemetery, and as the elderly prophetess walked through the gates, she knelt down and plucked a handful of grass. As she stood, she tossed the clump of greenery behind her back and said, "God knows us inside and out, and He keeps in mind that we are made of mud. Men and women don't live very long; like wild-flowers they spring up and blossom. But a storm snuffs them out just as quickly, leaving nothing to show they were here."

Anna took a few steps outside the gates and stopped. Without looking back, she turned her head towards the heavens and said, "One day, Simeon, we will meet again."

****

Time seems to pass more slowly than usual when traveling to a place one has never seen, but has dreamed of for most of their life. So it was for Meshach, the Nabataean scholar who had convinced his uncle, the High Priest of AlQuam and Shamesh, to make a pilgrimage to Jerusalem in honor of the new born King of the Jews. And even though he was actually enjoying the journey and learning new things all along the way, the young court-teacher complained to his cousin, Abimael, at every stop.

"I don't think we're ever going to leave this place, Cousin," he had said with just a tinge of anger in his voice. "If I had wanted to live in Gerrha, I would have moved here myself a long time ago! Did you know these Chaldean exiles build their houses from salt? And when repairs are needed, they use some kind of salt water mixture?"

Abimael was getting far too much entertainment from his cousin's frustration at the slow pace of the caravan. "So, I assume you've heard that Aramazar plans on wintering here?" he mentioned while writing something in his book about last night's observance.

"Yes, I heard," retorted Meshach. "Do you have any idea how long this trip is going to take? We'll be too old to enjoy Jerusalem at this rate!"

"Don't exaggerate so, Cousin," replied Abimael with his new grin that he knew irritated his older kinsman. "We should easily be in Jerusalem... say in about a year... or so." The young astrologer played with some scientific instruments as if he were actually making precise calculations.

"A year... or so?" questioned the young scholar. "By that time..."

Abimael broke in, "By that time you and I will be a bit older... and a bit wiser. I know you've been speaking with the merchants as well as the townsfolk along the way. Take your time, Cousin, and study their ways... learn their habits. They are our kinsmen, too, you know... as much as are the people you so long to see who live in Jerusalem. These people are descendents of Abraham's son, Ishmael... and the Jews are descendents of Abraham's son, Issac. So whichever lineage you trace, you still come to the same conclusion... we are of Abraham's seed."

This was the first time Meshach had heard his younger cousin express his attitude towards family heritage. Perhaps, this journey meant more to the young star-gazer than what he had been letting on. Meshach stood tall, took a deep breath, and let it out slowly as he shook his head in agreement.

"Perhaps you are right, Abimael," he said matter-of-factly. "I suppose a wise man would take advantage of the situation to learn as much as possible about the cultures he came in contact with."

****

Rebekah could hardly wait to visit her little sister and her new baby. She and her husband had spent most of their time in Cana after the wedding of Joseph and Mary to avoid having much contact with "those carpenters". Ishmael had never particularly liked the tall carpenter of Nazareth and had decided that he and Rebekah would register at his hometown, even though he could just as easily traveled with the rest of the family to Bethlehem. And while a large number of the Jews journeyed to Jerusalem and the surrounding area for the Feast, some had to stay behind to perform the regular duties of husbandmen and shepherds. Ishmael owned a large flock of sheep and grazed them on the hills between Nazareth and Cana, home of his forefathers. His uncle, Jonas, still lived in the small village about three miles northeast of Nazareth.

Rebekah radiated a deep glow of excitement as she entered the room Joseph had built for Mary. The older of the two women found her sister sitting on a small stool next to a window which allowed the morning sun to brighten the dwelling place while allowing Mary to look out across the hills surrounding the village. Mary was nursing her baby and singing softly to him when Rebekah gave a familiar greeting.

"May the Lord's blessings be upon you, Sister," said Rebekah, her eyes sparkling. "I've missed you so. And I've longed to hold my nephew, too."

Rebekah was never any good at keeping secrets, and Mary could tell that there was something else that her older sister wanted to talk about other than her trip to Bethlehem or the circumstances of the birth of Jesus. But, the young carpenter's bride thought she would play Rebekah's game for awhile and let her think that she was unaware of the news that was about to explode from the older girl's mouth.

"Jesus is just about finished," stated Mary rather calmly. "Would you like to hold him now?"

"Most assuredly, I would like to hold him, Little Sister," gushed Rebekah as she extended her arms to receive the bundle from Mary. She gently bounced the baby in her arms while cradling him firmly. And then she looked directly into his eyes, and Jesus smiled. "He must have gas, Mary. He smiled so big… as if he's known me since birth," giggled the shepherd's wife.

"He's a friendly baby, Rebekah," commented Mary. "He smiles at everyone that way. Kinda takes after his father."

"I can't get over the look in his eyes," stated Rebekah. "They seem to be filled with such peace. And his smile… for such a little one… gives off a sense of acceptance and love." Rebekah very gently touched the face of the babe in her arms, and Jesus turned his head so that his lips touched her young finger. "If I didn't know better, Little Sister, I'd swear that he just kissed my finger… like he understood what I had just said. But he's much too young for that," she stated more to herself than to Mary.

Mary just grinned agreeably. Among the many words she had heard expressed in the past two months were the reactions of everyone who came in contact with Jesus about his eyes and his smile. All expressed their belief that he was not an ordinary baby, but only she and Joseph knew the truth. Joseph had convinced her that they should keep the truth of the baby being the Messiah, lest someone might try to harm him. "When the time is right," said Joseph one night back in Bethlehem, "the Lord will reveal to the world who Jesus really is. Some may suspect, others, like Simeon and Anna, may get a message from the Lord, but the general population will not accept the truth. So, we will raise him just like any other couple would raise their son, following all the Laws of Moses so that he can fulfill his destiny. Expect him to not act like the 'normal' child as he grows. Remember who he is… and what he will become."

"Do you think Jesus knows who he really is now, Joseph?" asked Mary humbly. "I mean… does he know that he is God's son? Is that why he looks at people the way he does?"

"I don't know the answer to either question, Mary," answered the tall carpenter, "but I do think there will come a time when we will know the answers."

Mary was pulled back into the present when Rebekah declared what she had come to say in the first place. "Mary, will you help me get prepared for my experience?" asked the elder of the two women.

"What? I'm sorry, Rebekah... I was daydreaming a bit. What did you say?" inquired Mary.

"I said that the Lord has opened my womb. I'm going to have a baby!" responded Rebekah with her joy bursting from within.

"That's so wonderful, Rebekah!" replied Mary with a huge smile crossing her lips. "When will this take place?"

"In about seven months, Little Sister," answered Rebekah. "I was hoping that you could help me get prepared since you were close to Elizabeth... and, of course, giving birth yourself. I'm feeling so many emotions right now; I'm not sure what to do next."

"You don't have to do much of anything, Big Sister," replied Mary with a grin. "Time will take care of everything for you. I wish you had stayed closer when my body was changing with Jesus, then you would understand. Tomorrow, you must attend the tree planting ceremony Joseph has planned. He will plant a cedar tree just outside this window which will grow into a great tree from which Jesus' *chupah,* his wedding canopy, will be made. Then we will talk about the days to come, but believe me, nothing will ever be the same again."

****

Chapter Seventeen

The Return to Normalcy

The city of Jerusalem appeared so elegant to Mary as she and Joseph entered the Golden Gate of the Holy City. The young couple had journeyed from their home in Nazareth along with several other families to celebrate Passover. The small caravan of pilgrims had traversed much the same course as they had some six months earlier down the Jordan Valley to Jericho where they crossed the river and began winding their way up to the city on the hill. Joseph and his family were accustomed to spending Passover in the great city, but for Mary, the entire journey was a new and exciting experience.

The young carpenter's wife, who was still considered a bride by most of the folks in Nazareth, had again shared the little cart her beloved had fashioned with her mother-in-law and, of course, her six-month old son, Jesus. Judith had again talked most of the journey as if she hadn't seen Mary for years, even though they shared the same roof back in their native village and took turns preparing meals for Joseph and his father. At least this time the stories were more historical in nature. The 50ish matron of the family spoke of family members long gone and their exploits during this life. She shared tales of adventures that her husband Jacob had experienced with his father while learning to be a carpenter. And she interspersed her stories with anecdotes about Joseph when he was a boy. Most of these narratives turned out to be quite humorous, and the young maiden couldn't help but look at her own son cradled in her arms and wonder if he, too, would get into such mischief.

"That boy," said Judith, speaking of Joseph when he was but three years old, "loved to explore. He had a hard time just sitting still long enough to listen to Jacob try and teach him the Scriptures. He could get distracted by the simplest of things like a butterfly fluttering amidst the flowers in the fields nearby. I don't know how he ever learned so much about the Torah, but I suppose those wandering times helped him bring the Words of Moses alive to anyone who would listen to him. He does have a knack for explaining the Scriptures, and he didn't get that from Jacob."

Mary smiled a bit as she thought of how nervous Joseph was that first evening a month before when he decided it was time to start teaching Jesus. "A father has a duty to train his sons and daughters in the ways of the Lord. I reckon this is as good a night to start as any," he had stated in a tone meant to convince himself more than Mary. The former farmer's daughter sat mesmerized as her beloved carpenter so patiently explained the beginning of the Jewish nation. She glanced ever so often at Jesus who was propped up on a small stool against the wall of their room. And she noticed that the baby didn't squirm or look inattentive as she had supposed he would, but he seemed to be hanging on every word that Joseph spoke. Perhaps it was her beloved's tone of voice, soothing, but authoritative. Or maybe Jesus was fascinated by the way Joseph used his hands to express himself, or the way he made characters come alive by changing his voice to match what he thought they might have sounded like. Regardless of the reason, her rough-handed woodworker held the attention of the baby and herself each and every night during those special times. As did most Jewish fathers, Joseph sang simple songs and recited special rhymes with scriptural themes as he taught the Torah to the small child. Jesus would be well prepared to participate in Sabbath and festival observances at their home, which would translate into future service in the synagogue at Nazareth.

"How wise the Lord must be," she thought to herself, "to have chosen Joseph to be the one to teach His Son about the book He wrote." And for just a moment she began to contemplate the idea that it was actually Joseph who had been specially chosen by God, and that she was just given her special place because of her attachment to him. She didn't labor on the thought for very long as she was rocked back into the present world by Judith's slightly annoying laugh and snorting that accompanied her mother-in-law's telling of a particularly funny story. Mary laughed, too, although she didn't know what she was laughing at, but she figured that she would probably hear the story again sometime in the future.

****

The caravan carrying some of the finest products ever gathered together under one master salesman continued on its journey from Susa towards Petra. Aramazar, the organizer of the caravan, had wintered his group at Gerra along the coast of the Arabian Sea. Several of the merchants who had originally joined the caravan had become discouraged with the long stop-over and had returned on their own to Susa. News of their demise had arrived just days before the Prophet of AlQuam had directed his two nephews to prepare the remaining traders for their departure. The group would follow the coast line of the peninsula fairly closely, while avoiding the Roman tax-gatherers as much as possible. The aging prophet had shared his plans with Abimael and Meshach during one of their evening meals.

"If we don't run into any resistance along the way," stated Aramazar, "we should be in Petra by late fall. I don't want to lose anymore merchants to thieves along the route, so I've hired more soldiers to protect the caravan. Word is leaking out concerning the value of the goods we carry. The value will, of course, fluctuate depending on how many businessmen we pick up along the way. Already I have received word from one of the tribal leaders about his willingness to join our caravan. He wishes to deliver some fine horses to Petra for running in the races at Jerusalem."

"We shouldn't have trouble keeping the merchants in line now, Uncle," commented Meshach, "since we've received word of Dagar and his group being slaughtered by robbers. None of the remaining men are as adventurous to set out on their own."

"The merchants are not blaming you, Aramazar," added Abimael. "They pretty much agree that Dagar and his followers were not under the blessing of AlQuam. They should have stayed with us instead of heading home with their camels overburdened with the gold they earned selling their goods here. Still the situation is a hazard that all are aware of and wish not to repeat."

"Then I'll be counting on you boys to help me keep the merchants satisfied," said Aramazar. "Perhaps talk to them about the overall goal of our expedition... or encourage them with prophecy interpretation... or heavenly signs."

The two younger men looked incredulously at each other. "You're not suggesting..." hinted Meshach with his eyebrows crinkled.

"I'm not suggesting anything," replied Aramazar, "other than that you two work together... use your wisdom and the experience you've gained on this trip to ensure the success of our journey. Failure will not be acceptable to King Aretas, and any combination of lesser gifts to present to Herod's son will be failure. We must keep this large caravan together... the success of our mission depends on it." Aramazar's tone bespoke the sincerity of his attitude.

Abimael was the first to break what seemed like an eternity of silence. "We'll do our best, Uncle," he said. "You can count on us."

The big prophet and caravan organizer shook his head at his two nephews indicating that he understood their comprehension of the situation. Then he leaned back in his chair and

stared into space as if in deep thought. His two young pro-
tégés excused themselves without a word of acknowledgement from their aging kinsman. Aramazar sighed heavily after
their exit.

The discouraged priest had spent a great deal of time
working out the details of this adventure that would eventually
free him from the burdens of his priestly duties. Aramazar
had heard of the crowds of people who gathered in Jerusalem
during the Feast times celebrated by the Jews. He was
counting on one of those crowds as well as the confusion
caused by a large caravan's entrance into the walled city
to supply cover for his escape. The larger the caravan, the
better things would be for him. Plus the good will fostered
by a large array of gifts for the new born King of the Jews
would help King Aretas quickly forget the loss of his trusted
religionist. And go a long way towards the former's forgiveness of Abimael and Meshach, neither of whom had any idea
as to the real mission of this trip. That would have to work in
their favor.

Aramazar walked purposefully to the entrance of his tent.
And looking out into the night lit by the campfires of almost
forty merchants and their entourage, he grinned while thinking
of what the future would hold for him. He closed the tent flap
and walked with confidence to his sleeping area.

****

Jacob and Joseph were unloading the family's belongings in the large upper room of a house they had rented for
Passover week each year for the past 35 years. The room had
been added to the house by Jacob and his father, Matthan, for
that very purpose just a few months before Jacob's father had
died.

"Israel is growing in population, Jacob," Matthan had mentioned one day so long ago, "We should seek out a friend
who will allow us to add a room onto his house... a room
large enough to accommodate our families... with our own

entrance, of course, so that we won't disturb the other family. And the room could be good advertisement for anyone looking to remodel or repair their own house." Jacob had agreed, and so the two carpenters met a man in Jerusalem who had two sons, one the same age as Eleazar. This man bought spices and frankincense from Nabataean traders and resold these items to the Hellenized Jews who brushed shoulders with King Herod. Later, their host became a trusted servant of King Herod. But the man had died five years earlier after a long illness, and now his son, Chenaniah lived in the house.

So, it was the custom of Joseph's family to stay in this upper room and to share the Passover meal there each year. Occasionally, they would use the room if they were called to make repairs on neighboring houses. The roof was also flat, like all the other houses in Jerusalem, and had two entrances, one for the owner of the house, and one for Joseph's family. Both families spent many evenings on the roof, relaxing or listening to the men talk politics.

Mary brought Jesus to the rooftop as the men unloaded the donkeys and the cart. She held her son upright so that he could see the magnificent white and gold Temple, which was the center of attention from most any spot in Jerusalem.

"Is this your first time to spend Passover in Jerusalem, Mary?" asked Joseph as he stepped onto the roof. She was only slightly startled, for she had not expected her beloved to join her so soon.

"No," she replied, with a sense of awe still in her voice. "Father brought us here several times when I was just a baby... before Mother died with the fever. I just don't remember much about those times. I am glad that he decided to journey with us this year. He usually stays behind to take care of all the sheep from the village. He said that the Holy City never seemed the same after Mother passed." Mary turned to speak directly to her adoring shaper-of-wood and to look into his dark eyes that always glistened so. "He's really lonely now, Joseph," she added with just a slight cracking in her voice. "I'm glad that he spends so much time playing with Jesus. And he is greatly anticipating Rebekah's baby."

"I know, my Love," whispered the tall builder from Nazareth. "Your father will always be welcome at our house. Did you see the Antonia fortress, Mary?" The big carpenter gently placed his large, calloused hands on his bride's shoulders and tenderly turned her around to face the Temple once more.

"No," she answered, "But then, I'm not sure if I'd know the Antonia fortress if I did see it."

Joseph held his young wife, who held Jesus, closely to him and raised his right arm to point in the direction of the fortress. "It's right over there... directly north of the Temple," he whispered in her ear. She grinned broadly as she felt his muscular arms encircle her. His breath tickled her ear, and for a moment her thoughts turned away from the spectacle before her.

"One of those towers there is where the Romans keep the beautiful robes of the High Priest hostage. He is allowed to wear them only on special feast days... like Passover, " added Joseph. "And over there," stated the woodworker as he carefully turned to his left, "is the great palace of King Herod."

Mary was indeed impressed by the extravagant architecture of the palace. Then her eye caught a glimpse of Jesus' arm protruding from under the blanket he was wrapped in. He seemed to be pointing to the hundreds of pilgrims filling the narrow streets of the city. With Passover only two days away, crowds gathered from all over Israel and even some foreign countries, milling around the streets searching for places to stay. The young mother glanced down at her son in her arms.

"Joseph," commented Mary with a questioning tone, "the wind must have blown some dust in the baby's eyes. They seem to be irritated... he must have something in them." She turned to face her beloved who looked into Jesus' eyes that seemed to be filling with tears.

The wise carpenter from the hills understood the look of compassion in his adopted son's eyes. "Yes, Mary," said

Joseph in a soft tone as he attempted to wipe the tears away, "He has something in his eyes, and he always will."

****

"May the Lord bless this house and all who enter here," recited Eleazar with a large smile on his face as he greeted his childhood friend, Chenaniah. The two men exchanged the normal greetings with little formality. "It's good to be back in Jerusalem again, my Friend," added the rugged carpenter from Nazareth. "And my family and I wish to thank you once again for allowing us to use the upper room of your house during Passover."

"You and your family are always welcome here," added Chenaniah with a big grin. "I understand that there has been an addition to the family since I saw you last. You have a new nephew, yes?"

"Yes," said Eleazar shaking his head, "a new nephew... and he came with a new bride for my brother, Joseph." The two men laughed aloud and shook each other's shoulders.

"So how goes your job at the Palace?" inquired Eleazar.

"It goes as well as can be expected," answered Chenaniah. "When you work for a crazy, sick old man, one never knows just what to expect."

"Be careful, my Friend," said the carpenter, "I understand that Herod has spies everywhere. Maybe in your own household." Eleazar raised his right eyebrow a little and flashed a sneering grin at his long-time friend so that Chenaniah could tell that he was only kidding.

The tall, skinny servant to the King sighed deeply as his countenance changed. "We are safe here, Eleazar," replied Chenaniah, "but I fear that there are many homes in Israel that are not safe." The two, old friends walked into the house as the city-dweller shared the latest news of Herod's activities.

"The old man is gravely ill," began Chenaniah, "and he sees enemies in every shadow of the Palace. Would you care for a glass of wine, Eleazar?"

"No, Chenaniah," answered the companion from the northern hill country. "Just how sick is Herod?"

"Sicker than the doctors let on, my Friend," answered the King's servant. "He flinches in pain at the least little outward touch to his skin, and he eats constantly... anything and everything... fruits, meats, exotic birds... everything. And because most everything he does brings on more pain, he does very little, except gain more weight and become more cruel each day. Sometimes he goes into convulsions that give him the strength of five men. I saw him break a man's arm the other day when he grabbed for him during one of those convulsions." Chenaniah poured himself a drink from the wine bottle sitting on a small table in the corner and continued his description of Herod's ailments after taking a drink from the wooden goblet that had become his favorite over the years.

"And the man stinks... literally... stinks to high heaven. His breath is such a vile odor by itself. He has difficulty breathing while sitting up, so his breath is heavy and foul of smell as to be noticed four feet away. But that's not the worst of it, my Friend. His body leaks a watery, clear liquid that makes his breath smell like the freshest roses. This liquid comes from his colon... and from sores under his fat belly... and, of course, all this runs down his legs and settles at his feet, which have their own sickening odor. We have to constantly change his clothes, and the old King is hardly useful in this endeavor at all. He cries out in pain at whatever place we touch his body. His clothes are too full of the stench from the liquid that pores from his body to ever be used again, so we burn them. We've tried hiding the smell with copious supplies of frankincense and myrrh, but to no avail. We try bathing him in highly perfumed water, but even that doesn't help mask the odor for long." Chenaniah swallowed hard the last of the wine in his cup. "But worst of all, Eleazar,... his privy-member is putrefied and produces worms."

"Have the doctors offered no cure for the man?" asked Eleazar more out of pity than real concern for the health of the hated King.

"Everything they try to suggest... every tonic or herb treatment... everything," replied Chenaniah, "the old King tries, but nothing works. He is being sorely punished by the Lord for past sins. Herod is dying... very slowly and painfully... but he is dying just the same. And the sicker he gets, the meaner he gets. Servants are punished for doing their jobs because he likes to see others in great pain. I was one of his favorites once... but with each day, I fear that the man will turn on me as he has done on his own family so many times over the years. I would rejoice at his death, but his new heir, Antipater, is not much better. Sometimes I wish I were a shepherd in the hills far to the north."

Eleazar tried his hand at changing the subject as Joseph would have done. He spoke of his family, his boys, and his new nephew. And he spoke of the repairs that he and his father and brother had made at the priests' quarters back in the fall. And he described Joseph and Mary's wedding, a wedding very similar to those even in the big city. He spoke of anything to try and cheer up his childhood friend. The small talk worked, and the two parted company that night with smiles and good wishes for the morrow, but both men kept Chenaniah's words in the back of their minds, realizing that as normal as things appeared, change was in the air. And nothing would ever be the same again.

****

Chapter Eighteen

Next Year in Jerusalem

Mary and her mother-in-law, Judith, arose early on Passover eve to visit the market in Jerusalem. Trouble was, many other women were also there. Some wore strange costumes from other countries, and many spoke languages that Mary did not recognize. All of this commotion was fascinating to the young farm-girl from Nazareth, but none of the activity seemed to phase Judith for even a moment.

"We are on a mission, Mary," said Judith earlier that morning. "We have to purchase all the herbs and wine so that we can prepare the Passover meal for our families. And as soon as we return to the upper room, we must bake the unleavened bread." Mary was well aware of the preparation involved in celebrating Passover. This was one of the most important feasts of the Jewish year, and everything had to be just perfect. Mary had spent the years before her marriage getting everything in order for Eli's household, including the annual spring cleaning that assured that no leaven could be found anywhere.

"I have a surprise for you, my Dear," said Judith. "Zachariah and Elizabeth and little John will be joining us this year for Passover. John will be a year old that day, so the celebration will contain a game or two directed towards him. Zachariah has been trying to get the lad to say, 'Next year, in Jerusalem', but so far the words just haven't come out right." The older of the two women smiled broadly. "Next year... it will be Jesus who offers that benediction to the meal as he runs to the door to see if Elijah has arrived," she added proudly.

Mary looked at her older companion and smiled. The young maiden was well aware how proud both Jacob and Judith were of their new grandson. They delighted in holding him and singing traditional, story-songs to the baby. Mary remembered how excited Joseph's parents were when the swaddling clothes Jesus had been wrapped in were finally discarded for good.

"Ahhhh, he has such large hands, Joseph," commented Jacob with the definite sound of pride in his voice. "And his arms are already strong, despite being held useless for these months past. He will make a fine carpenter... a true builder of great things, my Son. Yes, Little One," said the elder wood-smith, "you will make your mark in wood... as have your ancestors."

Mary recalled how she had caught Joseph's eye for just a moment and noticed that they appeared to fill with tears despite the huge grin on his face. She had wondered what her beloved was thinking in his heart of hearts about the words of his father. The young carpenter's bride shrugged her shoulders slightly and decided she would ask questions at some later time.

Again the young woman was jolted back into the present world of the marketplace in the Great City of God when Judith shoved a clove of garlic in her face. Mary flinched a bit, but Judith had not noticed at all for she was too busy feeling the other herbs there before her. The older woman wanted this Passover to be the best ever, and so she was quite selective when choosing just the right foods to prepare for the table. And time would become a problem for them both if she dallied too long in one spot. Mary simply sighed heavily and smiled. And the former shepherd's daughter followed her mother-in-law through the market as the latter woman went about her task of choosing the best herbs and spices.

****

The young scholar from Susa sat at the small table in his tent contemplating the words he would say to King Herod if the old King asked him how he had come to the conclusion that a new King had been born.

Meshach had not even thought about his response or even the question for that matter until his younger cousin Abimael had posed the scenario at the evening meal just a few hours before.

"Meshach," stated Abimael in his new irritating tone meant to keep his older cousin in deep thought trying to figure out some complicated philosophical question, "when we get to Jerusalem... and present ourselves to King Herod..." the young star-gazer purposefully took a mouthful of food in between partial comments to heighten Meshach's anticipation... "what will you say to him... if he asks how you came up with the idea that he had a newborn son?"

Meshach knew he was being baited, still he didn't hesitate to present his argument. "I'll simply tell him that I've made a life-long study of the Hebrew Scriptures, and that I consulted the ancient writings of our common ancestors."

A sly smile crept across Abimael's lips. "But Herod is not really a Jew, Cousin," said the young astrologer matter-of-factly. "Not ancestrally... and certainly not religiously. Do you suppose he will put much store in what some captured Jewish slave wrote over 500 years ago? What if he laughs at your theory? What if no baby has been born to Herod? What if...?"

Abimael's playful attempts at engaging his cousin in conversation was suddenly interrupted by a messenger at the tent door. "Pardon my intrusion, Master Abimael," stated Outriel, the personal assistant of Aramazar, "but your presence is requested in the tent of the High Priest immediately." Outriel's head was bowed, but he looked upwards at the two young men sitting before him. His extra-bushy eyebrows and wiry beard made the middle-aged messenger look ominous and just a bit un-nerving in the dim light within the tent.

"Thank you, Outriel," stated Abimael graciously. "Tell Aramzar that I will attend his invitation directly."

"The matter is most urgent, Wise One," commented Outriel, "a matter of plotting tomorrow's journey."

"I'll be right there," answered the young student of the stars without looking at the one who brought the message. Abimael did not like his uncle's assistant mostly because he did not trust the man. He had heard rumors in the palace in Susa about Outriel's plotting and scheming to take Aramazar's place as High Priest, and he had confronted Outriel with the accusations. Unfortunately, Abimael had no proof of the older man's conspiracy and had chosen not to mention the incident to Aramazar. Still he watched the pretender to the priesthood cautiously whenever he could.

"I will tell my master of your response," stated Outriel as he excused himself. Meshach started to say something, but his younger cousin motioned for him to remain silent. Abimael arose from his meal very quietly and walked noiselessly to the opening of the tent where he turned towards Meshach and announced loudly, "Well, I'll be leaving now, Cousin. I'll return shortly, and we'll continue our earlier discussion." Hurried footsteps could be heard just outside the tent as someone thought it most beneficial to not be discovered lurking in the shadows. Both Meshach and Abimael laughed out loud, and the younger of the two men brushed aside the opening and strolled into the semi-darkness outside.

That's when Meshach began pondering the answer to his cousin's questions about his explanation to King Herod. The young scholar was not sure if he had a good answer, but he knew that their journey would take awhile, so he would have plenty of time to practice his response should the question ever arise. "By next year... when we get to Jerusalem... I'll know just what to say," thought Meshach.

****

183

Chenaniah slowly looked around the main room of his humble abode in Jerusalem one last time just before blowing out the candles used to light the festivities surrounding the Feast of Passover. The celebration with his wife and children and other family members had lasted well into the night, but he enjoyed the games and the re-telling of the traditional stories and the laughter so very much. Passover was a time to remember, but for Chenaniah it was also a time to hope for a better future.

The forty-something servant of Herod was considered by many in the Holy City to be quite wealthy because of his position in the Palace and because he lived in a house that contained more than one room. The fact was, he had become Herod's chamberlain because that was the job held by his father just before he had died some five years or so before this night. And the house was also part of his inheritance, since Chenaniah was the only surviving son. Still, the household-organizer was proud of his position in the community, and he held his head high when he walked the streets of Zion.

Chenaniah held his hand close to the small flame on the candle he carried as he entered the chamber he and his wife used as their bedroom. While most people of his day slept on mats on the floor, Chenaniah and his wife slept in a simple bed, a gift from a grateful King Herod as a reward for doing some ordinary deed the second year the young Jewish man had worked in the Palace. There was a time when Chenaniah was the most trusted of Herod's servants, but the old King trusted no one since the execution by his own order of his beloved wife, Miriamne. Herod had accused his wife of plotting to overthrow him as an act of revenge for the death of her father. Chenaniah did not fear the shadows in his own house, but the shadows in the Palace might hide everything from assassins to conspirators to men willing to sell their own souls to retell a twisted version of an innocent comment from a trusted servant about Herod's activities. The Palace assistant had learned to be cautious in his words as well as his actions.

"We had a fine celebration tonight," said Betah while turning the top blanket back on the bed. Betah, Chenaniah's wife, was shorter than her husband by almost two feet. Her features were smooth and younger-looking than her actual age. She was often mistaken by strangers for a young girl, but the two had been married now for almost ten years. Still that was long enough for her to recognize when her husband was disturbed about something. "What's the matter, Chenaniah?" she asked.

Herod's servant of servants sat upright in the bed and leaned against the wall, sighed heavily and answered, "I'm just a bit concerned for our future, my Love. The old King leaves for his Palace in Jericho tomorrow afternoon. He hates Jerusalem, you know... and all the people who live here. He's frustrated because the people do not respect him despite all the building programs, including restoring the Temple to a greater grandeur than under King Solomon. Herod doesn't understand that the high taxes he enforces to build all of his toys is the problem... plus his trying to Hellenize the city... make it a little Rome."

"But aren't we safer when Herod is in Jericho?" asked Betah.

"To a certain extent... yes," answered Chenaniah. "But it is during these times that the workers in the Palace have to be even more vigilant. The old man sees enemies everywhere. And there are too many ambitious men like Dibon the Edomite who look for opportunities to increase their standing in the old man's eyes. I will have to be extra careful, for Dibon is after my position."

"What would happen to us... to Micah and Malcus... and to me... if Dibon were to lie to the old King about you?" asked Betah with a note of concern in her voice.

"Probably nothing... but then with Herod, one can never be sure," responded Chenaniah. He glanced over at his wife sitting beside him and realized that those words were not what she wanted to hear. So, he decided to change the subject as quickly as possible. "Did you notice Joseph and Mary's baby, my Love?" inquired the middle-aged Palace worker. "Did you notice how he looked around the upper room... taking in every piece of furniture and dish and decoration? It was as if he were inspecting it like Jacob must have done to the room Joseph built for Mary... like it was a place he would spend his final hours."

"Yes, Chenaniah," answered Betah with a smile on her lips. "I noticed, too, the way he looked at everyone... even our boys... like they were old personal friends that he had known for years. I guess some babies are just naturally inquisitive and friendly."

"And did he smile at you?" asked Chenaniah.

"Of course he did," remarked Betah. "He smiled at everyone... such an enchanting smile... peaceful, friendly... accepting."

"His parents couldn't have chosen a better name for him... 'Jesus'", added Chenaniah as he blew out the candle near the bed and assumed his sleeping position. "'God's salvation'... he is destined for greatness, my Love... you mark my words. When he grows up and assumes his role in society... I have a hunch he will change things wherever he is... and nothing will be the same again."

****

Chapter Nineteen

Time to Grow; Time to Learn

Rebekah lay peacefully on the small bed in Joseph and Mary's little room while recuperating from the ordeal of giving birth to her firstborn. The tiny baby girl nestled close to her mother, feeding at her breast.

"She eats so much, Little Sister," said the new mother with such a huge grin. "I pray that I can satisfy her."

"She's just hungry," commented Mary as she gently brushed her sister's long, black hair away from the face of the little one. "I'm glad Ishmael allowed you to stay with us so that we could be a part of the birth of your daughter. Too bad he had to miss seeing his little girl come into the world."

"I wish he could have been here, too, Mary," responded the young shepherd's wife, "but he had to go to his Uncle Jonas' house on a family emergency. Jonas is so very sick, and Ishmael is the closest kinsman. But Ishmael will certainly be here tomorrow."

Both women smiled broadly as each remembered the birth pangs of the previous hours in different ways. Mary had whispered into the ear of her older sister to calm her during delivery while one of the other women in Nazareth served as midwife. Judith was almost as useless for this birth as she had been for Jesus' birth, but she did help Eleazar's wife wrap the baby in swaddling cloths.

187

Jacob and Eleazar had paced outside the room loaned to Rebekah for her time, while Joseph sat in a chair by the table and held Jesus in his lap. The birth of a child was always a happy occasion in any village of Israel, but all were aware, too, of the many complications that could have led to the death of the baby or of the young maiden. Still the youngest of the three carpenters seemed to be taking all this activity as just a part of life. Jesus sat on Joseph's lap, swinging his legs back and forth, as he watched his agitated kinsmen busying themselves with useless activity. Occasionally, he would giggle, which in turn would cause the men to laugh at themselves. The two older woodworkers would relax for awhile until Judith scurried out of the room to fetch something needed for the delivery. What seemed like hours to the two nervous men was in actuality only a very short while. Jewish women had a tendency to give birth quickly once the process got started, and so it was with Rebekah. There was a baby's cry, and shortly afterwards, Mary came out to announce the arrival of the new family member.

"It's a girl!" she said, smiling from ear to ear. "Poppa would have been so proud," she added with tears in her eyes. Eli had suffered a stroke just after the family had returned to Nazareth after the Passover. He had died two weeks later.

"Gurworld," repeated Jesus as he looked into Joseph's smiling face. The slight mispronunciation caused all in the little room to laugh. Jesus had been growing rapidly since the village carpenters had returned home from Jerusalem. He was only eleven months old now, but had already started to take his first steps and utter a few words. He had grown heftier, too, husky and tall like Joseph with a head full of black, curly hair. And he continued to look at people he encountered as if he had known them all their lives. Some of the people in Nazareth were astounded by the young boy's ability to recognize them, while others were just a bit irritated by his gaze. But then he would smile at them, and their hearts would melt as that smile of his disarmed them.

In addition, the young wood-shaper's son was a fast learner. Mary marveled at how quickly the child learned the scriptures Joseph had been teaching him. Just as soon as Jesus started putting sounds together to form a word, Joseph had begun to teach him to say "Moses gave us a regulation from the Lord, the special possession of the people of Israel. 'Listen, O Israel! The Lord is our God, the Lord alone!'"

"Joseph must have repeated those verses a hundred times over the next two days," Mary had commented to Rebekah while the two women were making final preparations for the birth of the latter's baby. "And sure enough, Jesus started saying the words on the third day! That boy is just constantly learning. I can't wait 'til he starts asking some really tough questions... like 'How can birds fly?'... or 'Why doesn't the ocean flood the shorelines?'... that's when I will refer him to his father!" The two women looked up from their preparations and giggled like teenagers on a sleep-over.

*****

Almost an entire year had elapsed since Abimael and Meschach had left Susa with their Uncle Aramazar on a huge caravan carrying spices and other goods to Jerusalem in an effort to win the approval of King Herod. Now they were finally entering the gates of Petra, capitol of the Nabataean empire and home of King Aretas. Aramazar had arranged for a large reception at the Palace of Aretas for the leading merchants of the caravan and his two nephews in an effort to sway Aretas into allowing the caravan to continue immediately on the planned-journey to Jerusalem, where the tired priest and his kinsmen would salute the birth of Herod's new-born son while bringing conciliatory gifts from the Nabataean Kingdom.

All the travelers were tired from their arduous expedition following the coastline of the Arabian Peninsula. There had been so many stops and so many merchants leaving or attaching themselves to the caravan, that it did not resemble the original group of businessmen at all. Still, the trade-goods were virtually the same. The caravan arrived in Petra with 150 camels loaded down with frankincense, myrrh, persimmons, dates, bitumen, pottery, and copper. And, of course, there was a large herd of sheep and horses.

By the time the caravan reached the Walled City, the supply of frankincense had been cut in half because everyone along the way wanted to be paid off in that precious commodity. Fixed portions had been given to Aramazar and to his two nephews who helped organize the trip and kept things moving as much as possible. And the guards received their payments with this expensive spice as did various servants and gate-keepers in the towns visited along the way. And, of course, frankincense served as the medium of exchange for water, fodder, and occasional lodging along the trade route.

But now the pilgrims from the northeastern edge of the Nabataean kingdom were at the beautiful city of Petra. Petra was a city carved out of rock, smooth and level. The external wall was steep and sheer, but within, there were abundant springs of water both for domestic purposes and for watering gardens, making the inhabitants safe from invasion. Beyond the city itself, the country was, for the most part, a desert. The shortest road to Jericho led through the Judean desert, but it was a journey of only three or four days, days that would seem like only a few hours compared to the months already spent on the road by Aramazar and his crew. From Jericho, the journey to Jerusalem would take about a day and a half. The spirits of all three men were quite lively with the thought of finally reaching their destination.

Aramazar sat next to Aretas during the feast. Other rich merchants sat nearby while Abimael and Meshach sat towards the end of the long, Roman-like table covered with an enormous variety of foods... most of which the travelers had not seen in quite some time.

"I trust your journey was pleasant, Aramazar," commented Aretas as the two men shared a clump of sweeten dates.

"I have greatly enjoyed the trip, Sire," answered the old priest, "despite some difficulties along the way. It's been a long time since I traveled with my father to visit Petra. I was only a boy... about 10 years old as I recall. Our journey did not follow exactly the same route as this caravan and did not take as long. But I have always cherished the memories of seeing this city for the first time."

"There's nothing like it anywhere, My Friend," said Aretas with a nod. "Not even in Rome itself. Is this the first time that your nephews have been here?"

"Yes," was the old priest's reply. "They have visions of grandeur... of serving you, O Great King... and of walking the streets of Jerusalem."

"So you still envision presenting yourselves to Herod, then?" asked Aretas. "As a representative of my Court... to pay homage to the new born King of the Jews?"

"Of course," answered Aramazar. "That has been our plan all along. We plan on presenting our portion of the caravan as a gift to Herod's new son... on your behalf... to placate all the ill feelings between the two of you."

Aretas leaned more closely to his High Priest and longtime friend so that the two could share their conversation more privately. "Do you not think the marriage of my daughter, Phasaelis, to Herod's son, Antipas, was enough to placate that old fool?" inquired the Nabataean king.

"It probably should have been," responded the priest, "but you know Herod. He sees enemies everywhere and twists events into diabolical intrigue at every chance. He might assume that you are out to capture his kingdom if you don't send expensive gifts to honor the birth of his son."

Aretas relaxed and stared at his dinner companion directly, looking for some sign of self-ambition in the eyes of the man he had trusted to bless his caravans for so many years. "We have received no word of any of Herod's wives giving birth," said the king after a deep sigh. "What makes you think that the birth of a new king has taken place?"

Aramazar's face lost a bit of its color at the news delivered to him by the man who literally held life and death in his hands. Aretas was not vindictive, but he hated to be embarrassed or "used" by those who served him to further their own ambitions. The old priest swallowed hard. He could remind the superstitious ruler of the appearance of the star that Abimael saw almost a year earlier, but he feared the rage of the old monarch at the suggestion that ancient writings from a Jewish prophet had anything to do with the organization of the caravan or the plan to go on to Jerusalem.

"We have heard in Susa that the old King has been sick... even to the point of death," answered the wise man from Aretas' summer palace. "I believe that Herod's ego is such that he would do anything to secure his throne for all of eternity if possible. And as we discussed so many months ago, Abimael spotted the creation of a star in the constellation of Coma close to the constellation Virgo and Pisces, the latter of which is closely associated with the Jews. It is the appearance of that star along with certain mystical forecasts long ignored by most scholars that we came to the conclusion of the birth of someone extraordinarily special in the vicinity of Jerusalem, O King. Perhaps that old fox, Herod, is hiding the birth from the public to maintain the safety of the child until the most appropriate time. What a jewel in your crown it would be for us to offer gifts in your name, and to be among the first to do so, in honor of the baby's birth... a birth proclaimed by the heavens and the gods." Aramazar carefully chose each word of his discourse so that Aretas might feel the importance of the opportunity to honor Herod and completely mend the rift between the two. Getting into Jerusalem was the key to unlocking the old priest's chains of service to gods he no longer believed in. Aramazar was too close to freedom to let anything as insignificant as Aretas not hearing of the birth of the new born King of the Jews to stand in his way. "Perhaps," continued the old prophet of Shamesh, "the birth the stars have proclaimed is your own grandson, O Great King... the offspring of your daughter and Herod Antipas. Perhaps Herod is waiting for just the right moment to announce the birth to the world. Perhaps he has ordered Phasaelis to not tell you anything about this birth in order to put you to shame. Consider how brilliant you will appear to Herod and his Court when we arrive and announce that we have seen the star of the newborn."

Aramazar looked squarely into the eyes of the old King sitting at his side and perceived that this latter statement appealed to Aretas' ego tremendously. How foolish Herod would appear to try and keep quiet the news the heavens had declared. Aretas leaned back in his chair once more and stroked his beard with his right hand. And then he smiled, ever so slightly at first, but from ear to ear before agreeing with his ally. Afterall, the High Priest of the eastern portion of the Nabataean Kingdom should know all about the heavens declaring the glory of the gods.

"We will speak of this more in the morning," stated Aretas with that look men often get when they think they are about to outsmart their opponents in some game of skill. The old King turned to his left to answer a question from one of his guests, while Aramazar sighed slightly, raised his wine goblet to his mouth and peered over the rim towards his nephews who were wrapped up in the glamour of the occasion. The three of them would soon walk the streets of Zion... and nothing would be the same again.

****

Chapter Twenty

A Time for Every Purpose Under Heaven

"Will we ever get to Jerusalem, Uncle?" asked Meshach in his ever so prevalent complaining tone while sharing an evening meal with his cousin and the High Priest from Susa. The three were again eating in a tent somewhere southwest of Petra. They had been leading a caravan carrying rich trade goods from Susa and other Eastern territories to Jerusalem under the disguise of paying homage to the new born King of the Jews. At one point, just a few months earlier, they had been within a week's journey of their intended destination. But now they were on the Nabataean trade-route once again heading not to Jerusalem, but to Gaza along the Judean coast.

"Yes, Meshach," answered the old religionist, "we will get to Jerusalem." It had become obvious to both Abimael and Meshach that their Uncle Aramazar had become a bit aggravated since King Aretas of the Nabataeans had requested that the trio continue the caravan to Gaza before going to Jerusalem with a much smaller caravan of trade goods. Aretas was not completely convinced of the existence of another son born to Herod. The old Arabian king had received word of Herod's arrest of his favorite son, Antipater, for treason just a few months before the three pilgrims from Susa had arrived with a large caravan in the capitol city of Petra.

Aretas had decided that Aramazar's caravan should take the secondary trade-route that went down from Petra and the mountains of Adomia to the Arava. From there, the group would travel the scorpion trail eventually heading to Beer Sheba and on to Gaza. It was at that great port city that most of the trade goods would be sent further west to Rome. Only a small caravan of ten camels was to travel along the road from Gaza to Jerusalem. Aretas trusted his old friend, Aramazar, enough to know that the old priest could easily explain a small caravan entering the gates of Jerusalem, especially if they had traveled the normal Incense Trade-route.

"Do you think we'll arrive in Jerusalem in time for the festivals?" asked Abimael. The young star-gazer's attitude had changed, too, during the course of the pilgrimage from Susa. He no longer concerned himself with dreams of working in the capitol city of Petra. And he no longer kept copious notes of the stars each night as they stopped for rest or for food and water. He had begun engaging his scholarly cousin, Meshach, in historical or philosophical conversation. Meshach had glanced at Abimael's diary several weeks earlier and discovered that it contained notes about the people they met and answers to questions he had asked them about their understanding of the gods or their dreams and fears. The young teacher was impressed with the comments his older cousin made regarding the dialogue with the natives along the trade-route. Abimael was thinking almost like one who was trying to solve an unanswerable puzzle.

"If we don't have any unusual delays... we should arrive in Jerusalem sometime before or perhaps just after their Passover celebration," responded the old priest. "Depending on the actual day we arrive, there may be great crowds of people in the streets... or the streets may be deserted completely despite the thousands of pilgrims who come to celebrate the feast."

The three anxious men discussed the weather for awhile, noting that the area was cloudy most of the time and subject to sudden showers. And the summer months could contain scorching heat. Still, agriculturally, the farmers in the area produced bountiful crops and excellent herds of mules, horses, sheep, and even swine. Abimael noted the various species of birds he had documented since leaving Gerrha. All this production with a population estimated at less than ten thousand in the entire Nabataean Kingdom.

Abimael and Aramazar tried to mask their discontent and their disappointment at the length of the journey. Meshach was a bit more obvious in his desire to walk the streets the great prophets of Israel once walked. He had shared with both men on various occasions his belief that he would walk closer to Jehovah just by being in the city. The young teacher was just a bit puzzled that neither of the other men questioned his loyalty to Shamesh when he made his statements about the God of the Israelites. Aramazar simply nodded in an understanding manner. Abimael tried changing the subject each time his younger cousin ventured into the topic of religion. Each man had his own interpretation of how being so close, yet so faraway meant.

****

The young shepherd-boy, Simon, sat on a large rock situated half way up a small hill on the common field just a short journey from Bethlehem wondering whether he had a nephew or a niece by now. The skinny sheep-herder grew impatient to hear the news of his brother, Nathaniel, and his firstborn. Nathaniel and his wife, Johanna, had been trying to have children for some five years or so, but the young Bethlehemite had been barren until just after that night over a year and half ago. She had lost her first child in an accident just after the Feast of Passover the previous year. And her pregnancy had not gone well this time, despite her extra care, which made young Simon the more nervous. He glanced over at his father, Achim, who stood several feet away and gave words to his eagerness for some news.

"Father," said the young boy. "Father," he repeated just a bit louder. "Father!" he shouted loud enough to frighten the lambs close to him.

The older shepherd had been leaning against his staff and was about to doze off because of the routine of watching the sheep graze. Achim was startled at his youngest son's declaration and momentarily suspected that some creature was after his flock.

"What is it, my Son?" asked the old shepherd, still a bit dazed at his sudden return to reality.

"Shouldn't we have heard something by now?" inquired Simon as he rose from his rock and took a few steps towards his father.

"Heard something about what?" responded Achim with a slightly puzzled look.

"Heard something about Joanna's baby!" answered Simon. The young shepherd just could not understand why his father was not more concerned about the birth of his grandson.

The old shepherd placed his large left hand on the boy's shoulder and said with a slight grin, "Women have been giving birth for a long time now, Simon. You should know from watching our sheep that it will happen when it will happen. Worrying over something so normal as childbirth won't hurry things along. Joanna is strong and healthy... and Nathaniel is there in case there is any trouble. I am sure he will send word just as soon as he can once the child comes into this world. In the meantime, we have a flock of sheep to watch... and a bunch of young lambs to protect and check regularly to make sure they have no blemish. They will be used for the Passover next week, so we have to be careful that no harm comes to them in any way."

Simon knew his father was right. He had witnessed the birth of lambs several times... enough for that miracle to become common. But this birth was different. This was the birth of his nephew. And the young boy wanted everything to be perfect including the baby. The young shepherd remembered the night he and his father and brother had visited the little baby who had been born in the manger near Bethlehem and wondered if angels would announce this birth. Simon had already made plans for the education of this little gift from God. He daydreamed about teaching his nephew how to run... and climb the rocks in the fields... and fish in the brook close to their house. There were just so many things the two of them could do together. Actually, the pint-sized herdsman was more concerned about Johanna giving birth to a little girl than he was about her safety. He couldn't play with a little girl. "They don't know how to do anything!" he thought out loud.

"Who doesn't know how to do anything?" asked Achim trying to coax the small one's fears into the open.

Simon looked into the wise, clear eyes of his father and answered, "No one in particular, Father. I was just thinking about something that I guess doesn't matter." He sighed heavily, shrugged his shoulders, and turned around to walk back to his rock where he kept a watchful eye on the chosen lambs that would soon be offered as a sacrifice in the Temple. "Nobody really cares what I think anyhow," he mumbled under his breath as he walked away.

As the two resumed their watch over the flock, a man came running up the hillside, waving his arms and shouting, "It's a boy, Father! It's a boy!" At first neither Simon nor Achim could make out the voice, but within seconds, they both beamed with pride and delight as they recognized Nathaniel bringing the good news.

****

There is an unmistakable sense of pride that radiates from the face of a parent who watches his or her youngster performing even the most mundane activity, especially when that parent has been coaching said offspring in the activity. Joseph and Mary were no exceptions to the rule as the two Nazarenes witnessed their son, Jesus, asking the four questions the youngest child of the family asks each year during the Passover seder. Although Jesus was only 18 months old and merely toddling around the room, Joseph felt sure that his little man had nailed the questions perfectly, just as they had practiced for the previous month. Mary had grinned from ear to ear while looking into the faces of the other family members reclining around the table in the upper room of Chenaniah's house in Jerusalem.

"He says the words with such feeling," whispered Miriam into Mary's ear. "Neither of our boys did that well when it was their time. You must be very proud, Mary." The young, former-farmer's daughter looked at her sister-in-law and smiled while patting the hand of the older woman.

"Yes, Miriam," replied Mary, "we are very proud of Jesus. He is a very fast learner and remembers his lessons so well. He seems to hang on every word his father says." Mary's thoughts turned to Joseph's patient teachings as he skillfully explained the Passover to Jesus. She recalled how artfully he drew a picture with his words describing every detail of the Seder, the order of the Passover meal, and the questions that their young son would be expected to ask that night. She had thought at the time that her carpenter was teaching the young boy too much as an adult, after all he only had to recite the questions... he didn't need to understand why he was asking them. But the eyes of her little man sparkled with interest as Joseph gave his simple but thorough explanation of the significance of the Passover meal. She remembered looking into the eyes of her son and convincing herself that he actually understood what her husband was saying. Jesus' interest in the stories seemed uncanny to her...for he was just a small boy.

Zachariah and his small family had once again joined with Jacob's family to celebrate the Passover. But this year, he insisted that Jacob read from the Haggadah and perform the function of head of the family. Jacob had glanced at his older cousin several times during the first portion of the meal to make sure that everything met with the old priest's approval.

The elderly wood-shaper had presided over the setting of the Seder table by his wife and his two daughters-in-law. He had double checked the arrangement of the parsley, bitter herbs, charoset, roasted egg, and the shank bone of the lamb on the family's heirloom Seder plate. And he supervised the placement of the four wine goblets and the three matzahs on the table.

Jacob had followed the Haggadah several times before, but this night was special. It was the night his young grandson, Jesus, would ask the questions. The old carpenter felt just a bit uneasy in Zacariah's presence as he began the Seder with the traditional blessing. He wondered if the old priest would have said anything differently. And then Jacob secretly thanked God that the ancient Jews had written every detail and prayer into the Haggadah so that all families would be unified in the celebration.

Joseph knew of his father's desire to put just the right feeling into each part of the Seder while not losing the joy of the celebration of their ancestors' freedom from slavery in Egypt so many years before. And the young carpenter knew that someday he would be the leader of the feast for his family, so he watched and listened even more closely than ever before. Joseph memorized every move Jacob made as the latter washed his hands to prepare for the eating of the *karpas*. He noticed how his father held the parsley and dipped it into the water, and he took a mental picture of exactly how the older man unceremoniously took the middle of the three matzahs, broke it in two, and wrapped the "best part" in a clean linen cloth and placed it away from the Passover table. Then Jacob gently placed a pillow over the severed half proclaiming it buried and a stone placed over it.

Eleazar, too, had been watching his father's movements and his constant referral to the Haggadah. And like the others, Joseph's older brother was impressed with the feeling expressed in Jesus' asking of the questions that led to the story of the Exodus from Egypt.

"Why is this night different from all others?" Jesus had asked in his childish, but distinct voice. "Why tonight do we eat only unleavened bread?" he continued. "Why tonight do we eat bitter herbs? Why tonight do we dip them twice?" Eleazar noticed that his young nephew had only slight trouble with the enunciation of the words. They were in fact clear enough to be understood by all no matter how many times they had heard them. And he noticed, too, that the boy looked directly at the adults reclining around the table as if he were asking them the questions. When he finished, Jesus looked at Joseph and smiled.

"He is his father's son," thought Eleazar. "No one can resist that smile and those sparkling eyes framed by those boyish curls."

In answer to his grandson's questions, Jacob retold the age-old story of Moses and the children of Israel being freed from bondage to Pharoah so many years previous. While doing so, the older carpenter drank from the second cup of wine, the cup of instruction, and recited the *dayenu*, the story-poem which lists the miracles that Jehovah performed for the Jewish people as well as the gifts given them. After each item was enumerated, the other members of the family responded with "*dayenu*"... or "we would have been satisfied". The celebration continued on into the night with more rituals and stories and the serving of the Passover meal.

Finally, Jacob called for the *Afikoman*, the buried piece of matzah, to "come forth", or be brought forward. This was to be like a dessert. But the children in the family had played their part and hidden the *Afikoman* during the meal while the adults were "distracted" by story-telling.

"The stone, the pillow, has been removed, and all we found was this linen cloth," said the oldest of Eleazar's sons, as innocently as he could without laughing. The adults and children then searched the room for a few minutes until the *Afikoman,* in Hebrew "it is finished", was found and restored to the leader of the feast.

Jacob took the matzah and said, "Blessed art Thou, O Lord our God, King of the Universe, who brings forth bread from the earth." He then broke the bread and passed it around the table so that each family member could share the dessert. Then he lifted the third cup, the cup of redemption, and said, "Blessed art Thou, O Lord our God, King of the Universe, who brings forth fruit from the vine." After taking a sip himself, he passed that cup around.

Finally, long into the night, Jacob asked Zachariah to pro-nounce the *hallel,* the blessing of praise, on the family's cel-ebration. And right on cue, just before drinking from the fourth cup of wine, the cup of praise, Jesus ran to the open door to look for Elijah, as did all the Jews that night. He turned slowly, looked first directly at his slightly older cousin, John, and then to the family gathered, he said, "Next year... in Jerusalem."

The family members repeated the phrase which more or less ended the Seder dinner. Still there were more stories shared, and psalms were song, and praises made to Jehovah for His countless blessings. This had been a special night for all, and the next day was a special day of rest which started the week-long Feast of Unleavened Bread. That day would not be just a day of rest, but also a day of reflection followed by more family meals shared together. Joseph, Mary, and Jesus had been invited to spend a day or two in Bethlehem with Malachi and Naomi in their caravansary. The pilgrims in Jerusalem would be thinning within the next eight days as families returned to their homes.

Zachariah, and his wife, Elizabeth, watched John and Jesus playing in the corner of the room. The old priest glanced at Joseph and Mary, each of whom were cataloging memories of that evening in different ways. He caught the eye of the young carpenter from Nazareth, and the two men stared momentarily at each other as if they shared a secret about that Passover that the others would not understand. Then they both looked at the two young boys playing together, unnoticed by most of the family... and the two men grinned.

****

As had become their custom over the years, Chenaniah and Eleazar met on the roof of the humble house where the two families had shared the Passover meal. Only twice before had the two families reclined at the same table, for Chenaniah's family usually met downstairs with their extended family. But this year Herod's servant had decided to spend the evening with his friends from Nazareth. The two men shared their usual greeting as if they had not seen each other in years despite the fact that it had only been a few hours since they ate together.

"What a year this has been," commented Chenaniah after the two men positioned themselves along the edge of the roof on the former's abode. "Herod has become more ill with each day. Fortunately for his servants here in Jerusalem, he has spent most of the year in his summer house in Jericho."

"We heard of his order to arrest his son, Antipater," added Eleazar. "A traveler passing through Nazareth told us that Herod had accused Antipater of trying to poison him, and now the old king awaits word from Rome for permission to execute his own son. He sounds like a man possessed by the demon of fear... or jealousy."

"Or both, my Friend," answered Chenaniah. "He suspects everyone of trying to kill him... especially his own family. I would not want to be one of his sons right now." Both men chuckled a bit at the double-sided meaning of that statement. Rumors spread throughout Israel that Caesar himself had said something very similar on one occasion. "I think that he is crazy enough to perform even the cruelest act to secure his place in history," added Chenaniah. "He just cannot understand why the people don't adore him for all the buildings he has built to make Jerusalem more beautiful. That was his main purpose in rebuilding the Temple... to buy the people's love. It hasn't worked because the people know that he is a fake King of the Jews. He's not even a Jew by birth, but he tries his best to keep that secret under wraps. But everybody knows." Chenaniah just shook his head in disbelief.

"The Lord has blessed us greatly this year, Chenaniah," mentioned the carpenter from Nazareth. "We have been busy. Our carpenter shop has many orders for furniture and repairs to houses. My two sons are old enough to lend a hand, but we are still swamped with work. Still, Father insisted that we spend Passover here in Jerusalem. We're leaving the day after tomorrow, but Joseph and his family are going to stay a day or two with our cousin in Bethlehem. That brother of mine... says he felt it necessary to spend some time with Malachi and Naomi. He's a dreamer, that one," added Eleazar.

Both men laughed, and then Chenaniah pointed out the flickering lights all over the city indicating that most of the people in the overcrowded town were still awake. The two old friends continued sharing family happenings as well as local news that bordered on gossip. Then Eleazar got a strange look on his face as he began to share a story with his childhood acquaintance.

"You know, Chenaniah," began Eleazar, "a funny thing happened about a month ago in our shop in Nazareth. Jesus was playing in the corner while Joseph and I were making a table for one of the young families in a nearby town. I accidentally knocked over the box containing three rather large nails that we use to help hold roof beams in place. Those nails made an awful noise when they hit the floor. Neither of us paid much attention to the nails on the ground until Jesus walked over to where they were laying. He looked at them for a moment... and then he bent down and picked up one of the nails. The little tyke had to use both his hands to pick up that one nail because of the size and weight. Joseph stopped what he was doing rather abruptly, and that little boy toddled over to where we stood. With all his strength he held that nail up to his father. I could have sworn that Joseph's eyes filled with tears. But that little boy simply shook his head ever so slightly... and smiled. Joseph reached down and took the nail from Jesus as gently as possible... like he was taking a thorn from a lamb's ear... you know, trying not to hurt him, but relieving him of the burden. And that little fella repeated that routine with the two other nails. My boys would have been scared by the noise of the nails falling onto the dirt floor at that age... but not Jesus. After handing the third nail to Joseph, that little boy just went back to his corner and resumed playing with some little tools my brother had made for him. Joseph stood there, dumfounded, for several moments before muttering some scripture that I could barely hear. I asked him what he said, and he looked me in the eye and said, 'Nothing, Eleazar. Nothing that would make sense to you now.'"

"Did he ever explain?" asked Chenaniah.

"No," answered the Nazarene. "Every once in awhile, Joseph gets this strange look on his face... especially when he observes Jesus... almost like he's looking into the future or something. And he'll mumble some scripture, but he never explains."

The two men stood silently looking at the stars twinkling above them as each tried to bring some meaning to the previous year. After several minutes, they gave the usual nightly blessing to each other and returned to their families. There would be more evenings to share with one another in the future. Plenty of time to exchange stories of family and work and even their personal feelings about the political situations of the day. For now, each man was content in knowing that the future was secure in the hands of an all-knowing, all-caring God. And each man felt secure that they were protected by unseen angels.

****

Entering the holy city of Jerusalem was quite an experience for the weary travelers from Susa. Aramazar, the leader of the caravan and the personal envoy of King Aretas, had visited the City of Jehovah for the first time when he was a young boy. He had journeyed with his father on a mission to set up new markets for the spice traders that his father had represented. The old priest recalled how impressed he was with the activity of the people even back then. He remembered how the people gazed at the strangers as they entered the gates of Jerusalem, and he noted in his mind that this day seemed to be no different. Like the others in the caravan, Aramazar noticed how majestic the buildings appeared to be. He was an educated man, and he knew well the history of the Jews. He had traveled to many cities on behalf of King Aretas, including Rome itself, but there was just something about Jerusalem that made him just a little awe struck. But on this day, after all the planning and managing of the trade caravan that had taken almost two years to complete, the burned-out religionist focused more on the dress of the people and how he would attempt to blend into the crowds of people leaving the city. His escape from the routines of paying homage to a god he no longer believed in would soon be over.

Abimael, the King's astrologer, thought of the people, too. They did not seem to be in a rush to leave, but still there were many exiting the city. He recalled the words of his uncle at the dinner he and his cousin, Meshach, had shared with their mentor on the previous evening. He was just overcome with the sheer number of people inside the walls of Zion who had made a pilgrimage just for the Feast of Passover. Two days had passed since that celebration, and now many families led wagons and heavy laden beasts of burden through the gates towards their own villages scattered across Israel. The young star-gazer, too, was an educated man, and at least nominally familiar with the history of the Jews. He knew that his profession was forbidden by the Hebrew Scriptures, but he wondered just how many of the pilgrims used the stars and the moon as reference points for planting and mating their animals or for travel guides. Thus, Abimael justified his occupation as being nothing more than what a farmer does on a regular basis to ensure a good crop. The only difference in the astrologer's mind was that his "crop" was trying to please the King and other court officials with agreeable forecasts of deeds yet undone.

Meshach, the teacher, was the most awed of the three adventurers by the spectacle of the people and the buildings in God's City. For him, this journey marked, what he believed to be, a great discovery of and reconnection to his Jewish heritage. Ever since he had stumbled on an old piece of parchment hidden in an old trunk belonging to his mother, the young philosopher had longed to walk the streets of Jerusalem. The parchment contained names of his ancestors, names of young children and pre-adults who had been forced to leave their homeland by Nebuchadnezzar almost 600 years earlier. As Meshach gazed at the faces of the people, he recalled how that piece of parchment had inspired him as a young boy of six to learn as much as he could about the Jews and the role his ancestors played in shaping the history of the place he called home as well as the history of the world. He read everything he could find about the captivity of the Jews in Babylon, and the eventual return of some of his family members to rebuild Jerusalem. The young scholar had marveled at the writings of the prophet Daniel each and every time he studied them. Today, he was walking the same streets that his forefather, Mishael, had walked. Meshach studied the faces of each person he passed and wondered if any of them might be his kinsmen.

The three ambassadors from King Aretas bore gifts for the newborn King of the Jews and would approach the palace of King Herod the next morning to pay homage to Herod's new son. They had spent the better part of two years traveling Arabia and had experienced cold, wind, sandstorms, and heat, while making new friends at each and every stop along their way. Each of the men had had a different motive for making the journey from Susa. Now they were entering their planned destination of Jerusalem, the capitol of Israel, the Holy City, Mount Zion, and each knew in their hearts that nothing would be the same again.

******

Chapter Twenty-one

Where Is He?

"**S**o tell me, Mary," said Naomi while the two women prepared the evening meal for their men-folk, "how is life in your new home… without Judith looking over your shoulder all the time?"

Mary looked at the older woman kneading the bread in the extra large bowl on the table between them with just a hint of curiosity. The younger woman was still considered a bride by many in Israel despite the fact that she and Joseph and been married for almost two years, for the two of them had only recently taken up dwelling in their own house. Mary was not quite sure just how honest she could be with her husband's cousin-by-marriage. Then Naomi grinned slightly. The wife of the caravansary keeper, and sometimes midwife, had grown up with Judith, Mary's mother-in-law, and knew that the woman could, at times, become annoying with her unintentional comments that could make even the strongest person feel inadequate about something.

The young, former shepherd's daughter understood Naomi's grin and returned the facial expression. "Pretty much normal I suppose," she answered. "We moved into our own house just two weeks before leaving for Jerusalem and this year's Passover. I am anxious to return home, but I am also thankful for the opportunity to spend some time with you and

Malachi. You've been so gracious to us these past two years. I'm not sure I ever really thanked you for your kind consideration of my need for privacy the night Jesus was born," said Mary with a grin. "At the time, I was more concerned with just getting the birthing done!"

Naomi smiled and nodded in an accepting way. "I understand that Joseph built a small room attached to the main structure so that the two of you could have some privacy in your own home," added the older woman.

"Yes, he did," commented Mary, "he said we'll need a place where we can escape once we start having other children." Mary looked down at the chicken she was preparing for the shared meal that evening and blushed a little. "And that won't be much longer," added the young carpenter's wife.

"Mary!" exclaimed Naomi, "you're going to have another baby? Judith didn't tell me that!"

"She doesn't know yet," answered the shy bride from Nazareth. "Joseph doesn't know yet, either. I'd planned on telling him tonight... when we are alone."

"Don't worry, Young Lady," said Judith with a smile spreading from ear to ear, "your secret is safe with me! But be sure and tell your woodworker husband tonight... for I'm not sure how long I can keep your secret." Both women giggled.

"Does the baby spend most of his time with you or with his father?" asked the innkeeper's wife while placing the loaves she had shaped over to the side to rise for a couple of hours before placing them in the oven.

"Jesus splits his time between us," answered Mary. "He'll go with me to the market each day... he does so enjoy seeing the people milling around the tables. He seems to be listening to every word said... the deals being struck by the merchants and farmers... the responses of the women buying the vegetables and such," added the young Nazarene woman. She pointed the knife she was using at her host more for emphasis than anything else and said, "You know, he gets this funny little grin on his face and wrinkles his brow when he hears one of the farmers arguing with one of the women over the price of their merchandise." She shook her head and went back to plucking another chicken. The meal the two of them were preparing would have to serve the caravansary guests as well as their own families.

After less than a minute of concentration on what the two were doing, Mary continued her story. "Jesus dearly loves being in the carpenter shop with Joseph. He doesn't get in the way even though he is a very curious little boy. He wants to know how everything is put together. Joseph tells him stories about Jewish history... and about the folks he's done work for... all the time waving his hands, even if he has tools in them... changing his voice to be another character... and Jesus loves it. He hangs on every word. He's going to be just like his father... kind, loving, a friend to everyone... and a great story-teller!" Mary grinned proudly as she thought of her husband and her son playing and talking together. She cocked her head to the side a bit as she pondered that new little grin that both her boys had developed... a grin like they were sharing some kind of extra secret that she wouldn't understand. And the young bride from Nazareth determined in her mind that she would coax that secret from one of them before much more time had passed. After all, she felt she had a right to know what they were hiding since she had hidden that other secret of theirs so well.

****

The blare of trumpets announced the arrival of the three ambassadors from King Aretas in Herod's Court. The sickly, old King of the Jews had not been accustomed to holding Court or receiving emissaries from foreign governments in quite some time for fear that the visitors might be spies sent to discover his weaknesses. But Herod had decided that he would allow these visitors from his enemy to approach him, especially when he learned that they came bearing gifts. Herod had hoped that the three men would offer a chest of frankincense to him... he needed that special fragrance for personal reasons, not for reasons of worship.

Aramazar noticed that the Court was practically empty as he and his nephews entered the highly ornate chambers. The old prophet of Shamesh also noticed that Herod was almost reclining on an overstuffed, cushioned-couch behind a thick veil that only allowed for shadows of the arrogant old King to be seen. The priest, the astrologer, and the teacher from the far corner of the Nabataean Kingdom were stopped by Chenaniah, the King's servant, some thirty feet in front of Herod. All three of the wise men from the East noticed an unusual odor coming from the direction of the King's position... an odor that was only half-masked by the pungent smells of expensive ointments and spices. It was the unmistakable odor of death. The three men looked inquisitively at each other. But before any of them could say anything, they noticed the wrinkled brow of the man before them and the ever so slight movement of his head that indicated it would not be in their best interest to mention the smells.

"Why do you wish to have an audience with the King?" asked Chenaniah in his most diplomatic sounding voice.

"We wish to pay homage to King Herod. We bare gifts from King Aretas to pay tribute to you, O Great King," answered Aramazar. "and to your son. Where is he who is the new-born King of the Jews?" The three Eastern scholars had not anticipated the reaction they received. The look of horror that stifled a look of amusement on the face of the young man standing before them told them all they needed to know. Each man very carefully glanced at the handful of soldiers and Courtiers for some type of acknowledgement that might include joyful expressions, but none were at all evident. Then there was a period of hushed silence that was deafening.

"Did Aretas send you here to harass me?" asked Herod in his old, authorative manner used just before pronouncing judgment on one who was about to be executed. "What makes you think there is a new-born King of the Jews?"

"We observed an unusual star while back in our home of Susa," interjected Abimael rather quickly. "The star was in a constellation closely associated with the Jews and usually indicates the birth of someone great. And who could be greater than yourself, O King? We have come on a pilgrimage to worship your new son." Again, there was a long period of silence. Chenaniah had ever so gracefully backed away from the Nabataean ambassadors, an indication that he did not want to be in the line of fire that was expected by everyone in the room.

"When did you see this... star appear?" asked Herod in a gravelly, but stern voice.

"Almost two years ago," answered Meshach. He spoke before his younger cousin could say anything. The young teacher was not afraid of Herod or his soldiers and so he stood tall and straight. "I am a scholar, O Great King," added Meshach. "And I have studied the writings of your prophets, especially the one called Daniel. His writings indicated that a great leader would be born about the same time we saw the star hovering over the direction of Jerusalem. And so we came as quickly as we could... not to mock you or him... but to pay respect to the one who would bring even more honor to the name of Herod the Great."

Aramazar looked at his nephew with a slight bit of admiration for the tone of voice used by the young philosopher. There was more to this impetuous dreamer than met the eye. The young man had a way of diplomacy about him. Again, there was a long period of silence interrupted by a deep sigh.

"I have no new-born son," stated Herod in a rather matter-of-fact manner but with just a twinge of disappointment. "I will do some research... ask some questions of those who should have told me of this incident of which you speak. And we will talk more later. In the meantime, you will be entertained as you should be... as my guests." The old king waved his hand, and Chenaniah bowed before motioning nearby guards to escort the three travelers out of the room and to the quarters reserved for foreign dignitaries.

****

Rebekah watched the rain gently hit the ground outside her new home in Cana, wishing that she could share her dreams with her younger sister. But Mary had journeyed to Jerusalem for the Passover with her husband, Joseph, and their baby and Joseph's family to celebrate the Great Feast. Rebekah and her husband, Ishmael, had gone to Cana to look after Ishmael's uncle's flock. The old man had died just two days before the Feast, and Ishmael claimed the flock and his property as the closest kinsman. And since Uncle Jonas' house was much larger than the small house the two shared with their baby daughter in Nazareth, Ishmael had moved his young family to Cana.

Cana was not all that far from Nazareth, but somehow Rebekah felt like she might never see her sister again. Ishmael had still not gotten over his dislike for Joseph, and so the two women had to create excuses to see one another. The shepherd's wife wanted to tell Mary about a dream she had had concerning the wedding of her granddaughter to one of the most influential men in Cana.

"Funny," Rebekah had said to Ishmael that morning after the dream, "our daughter is just a year old... and I'm having dreams about our granddaughter! Mary would know what this all means, I'm sure of it!"

Ishmael had not responded in a way that was satisfactory to Rebekah. He simply shook his head, grunted, and left their house to tend his sheep. He didn't even kiss her good-bye the way Joseph always did Mary, even though his carpenter's shop was just a few yards behind his and Mary's house.

Rebekah also had real news to share with the youngest of her siblings, too. She and Ishmael were going to have another child, probably sometime in Heshvan, or mid-fall. The shepherd's bride hoped that the news of God's blessings would bring her and Ishmael closer together. Ishmael had grown so business-like in the past few months... interested only in making money. He planned on selling off some his uncle's sheep to buy two fields on the southeast side of Cana where he could plant and grow crops to sell in the market. Ishmael was noted by all as being a hard-worker, but recently he seemed to be obsessed with building more barns, like he was anticipating a drought which would make all his stored possessions even more valuable. He had shared his vision with Rebekah, not to get her approval, but to impress her with his business sense. And all the while she just wanted him to hold her close, especially on cold nights. But he was mostly too tired. Even the rain did not stop him from completing his day's work.

Rebekah listened to the gentle sound of the rain through the window... and prayed for a torrential downpour.

****

Chenaniah walked slowly down the hallway from the room where the three travelers from Susa were being "entertained" to Herod's private meeting room. Even though only an hour had passed since the announcement of the purpose of the visit by King Aretas' envoy, the favorite servant of the King of the Jews knew that their revelation had caused quite a stir in the Holy City. News spread fast amongst the Israelites who had not yet left town after the Passover Feast. And this news was bad.

Each and every adult inhabitant of the city knew of Herod's irrational fear of being assassinated by his enemies. They knew, too, that his illness caused him to react sometimes even more irrationally than usual, and the news of a leader of the Jews being born would make the old Kings' mind even more unstable. All Jerusalem was troubled and perplexed over how Herod might react.

"Chenaniah," said Herod as the trusted servant entered the King's chambers, "you have served me well over these years. I have never had any real cause to doubt your loyalty, although I would not be surprised to find out that you do not trust me." The wise servant stood silently, not really knowing just what to say. "Will you answer me truthfully now?"

"I have always answered you truthfully, Sire," answered Chenaniah, "if I knew the answer."

"Have you heard... talk... of this new leader these three Nabataeans spoke of?" asked Herod in his seldom heard "soft" voice... a gentle, questioning voice.

The attendant to the King recognized a hint of remorse and fear in the question. He too was troubled over Herod's potential violent reaction to the visit by the Eastern scholars. But something from deep within him led Chenaniah to speak the truth. "I heard of an old man's ramblings in the Temple many months ago," he said calmly. "I understand the old man visited the Temple everyday in search of the Messiah. One day he proclaimed to a handful of people waiting for the priests to offer their sacrifices that he had seen the face of the Messiah. Apparently no one paid him much attention except for a very old woman who used to run errands and cook for the priests."

"And why didn't you inform me of what these people said?" asked Herod.

"Because I considered them just idle talk from two very old, very worn-out people who wished folks might remember them after their deaths," answered the King's helper.

"And are they... dead?"

"Yes, Your Majesty," replied Chenaniah. "Both have long since departed this life."

After a long period of silence broken only by the heavy breathing of the old king, Herod propped himself up on one elbow and said, "Get word to the High Priest... and to his religious experts... that the King demands their presence in his private chambers immediately. I must see them within the hour... understood? They are to drop whatever they are doing and come at once... or suffer the consequences of a disgruntled King!"

"Your wish is my command, O Great King," said Chenaniah as he excused himself.

"And Chenaniah," exclaimed the King in his usual rough voice. "Have Dibon the Edomite wait outside my chambers. I have a job for him, too."

Chenaniah bowed once more and quickly exited the room, fearful that Herod might change his mind or want some other action to take place. It was obvious to the long-time assistant that the King was angry... which meant that someone, someplace would suffer the brunt of that anger.

****

Simon, the young shepherd-boy from Bethlehem, sat on a stool in his brother's house, gently rocking his two-week-old nephew. The young boy made gentle cooing sounds as he rocked... mimicking the sound a dove makes as he courts his true love.

"It's not right to keep a boy wrapped up so tightly in these old swaddling clothes," he said softly to the babe in his arms. "Don't grown-ups know that boys have lots of things to do? You need to wave your arms and kick your legs... get strong... like young lambs after their born. Nobody wraps them up so they can't move around."

Johanna, Simon's sister-in-law, smiled in an understanding way as she answered Simon's objections. "He'll grow up strong soon enough, Simon," she said. "And he'll probably want to follow you everywhere you go. You'll get tired of him tagging along and wished he hadn't grown so strong," she said with a laugh.

"No, I won't, Johanna," remarked Simon. "Me and little Benjamin are gonna be the best of friends! We'll go fishin' and swimmin' together... and I'll teach him how to hunt and how to protect the sheep with a slingshot just like King David did when he was a boy!"

"I'm sure you'll have lots of great adventures together," said the dark-eyed village beauty, "but in the meantime he needs to do what all babies do... eat and sleep and..."

"Yeah, I know that last part," said Simon with just a hint of despair in his voice. "I don't think I'm ready for that part yet."

Johanna laughed. "Well you can't do anything about the eatin' part now, either, Young Man," she said with a grin. "So hand him over, please. I expect he's probably getting hungry right about now. And so are your pa and brother. You might want to take them their food."

Simon reluctantly handed over the little bundle of joy and picked up the towel-covered bowl off the table. He raised the cover a little to make sure his sister-in-law had included enough sweet dates and bread for him to eat with them in the fields. With his curiosity satisfied, he skipped to the door of the little farmhouse on the edge of Bethlehem and waved good-bye to Johanna and little Benjamin who was obviously enjoying his meal.

****

"Gentlemen," said Herod from behind the thick veil that always surrounded his presence, "you've been holding back on me. Why didn't you tell me of the birth of this new-born King of the Jews?... the Messiah, I think you call him."

The mesh of the material from which the veil was made allowed the old King to view those standing in his presence without them seeing him too well. The High Priest, Matthais, and all his religious experts were indeed agitated by his inquiring statement. Their obvious fear of finding disfavor with this mad-man who claimed to be their King did nothing to give them any redeemable qualities whatsoever. Herod grinned viciously as the team of spiritualists conferred with one another. Finally the High Priest spoke.

"We know nothing about what you speak, O Great King," said Jehovah's spokesman in a nervous manner. "We have heard nothing from the Lord about the birth of His Messiah!"

"Perhaps you are not as in close communication with the Lord as you suppose," commented Herod in his most sinister voice. "Have you not heard anyone in the Temple proclaiming that Messiah was born... say some two years ago?"

Again the scribes and priests put their heads together to find a satisfactory answer. "We heard of the ramblings of a senile old man named Simeon and his equally senile friend, Anna, speak of the Messiah. But we rejected their claims because we ourselves had not received any such proclamation from the Lord," stated the High Priest in a don't-you-know-who-I-am manner. Another long pause followed so that the silence might penetrate the minds of those being interrogated.

"Then tell me this... since you are so in touch with... God," replied Herod, "If Messiah was born... where was that blessed event to have taken place?"

Once again the men who had been entrusted with the spiritual development of Israel conferred with one another. "In Bethlehem... in the territory of Judah," answered one rather sheepish-looking scribe. "The prophet Micah," continued the sawed-off legalist, "wrote it plainly." The young religionist looked at his peers for courage, but they were all looking at the floor. "It's you, Bethlehem," he continued, "in Judah's land, no longer bringing up the rear. From you will come the leader who will shepherd-rule my people Israel." Again there was silence, and the little man stepped back into the small group in a cowardly fashion as if to hide himself.

"Chenaniah," said the King in a rather loud voice, "escort these... hypocrites away from my sight... and turn them loose again on the gullible subjects in Israel. Bring me the three wise men who came from the East... and tell Dibon I wish to see him now."

****

"I wish we weren't leaving the day after tomorrow, Naomi," said Mary as the two of them set dishes on the long table of the caravansary. "I enjoy visiting with you. You remind me so much of my mother... kind, generous, always helping others."

Naomi blushed a little at the complement paid to her by her cousin-in-law's bride. Naomi had lived all her life in Bethlehem and never traveled farther than to Jerusalem. She had lost her parents shortly after marrying Malachi, who himself had inherited the family caravansary business from his parents just three years before the two of them had married. Their own boys had both died young from the fever many years past, so the two innkeepers had thought of the pilgrims who graced their establishment as their family. The older woman had tried at first to not form attachments to any of the guests, but her heart was too large, and more often than not, she cried when the travelers moved on. Naomi had found a special place in her heart for the young girl from Nazareth who had come for the census with her husband some 18 months earlier. The innkeeper's wife had served as a mid-wife or the assistant on several occasions, but she could never get out of her mind what she witnessed on that night of the Feast of Booths.

Joseph had tried to explain to her the miracle that took place that night... the miracle of a virgin giving birth to a son. She only partially understood because medically, she knew that what happened wasn't practical. But she believed strongly in the Lord God Jehovah, and like many others, had been expecting the arrival of the Lord's Chosen One. She just didn't think she would be involved in his entrance into Israel. Still, she couldn't tell anyone what she experienced... because she knew that they simply would not believe her. So she kept the secret to herself, not even telling Malachi. Perhaps, some day, a medical doctor might visit the little caravansary in Bethlehem, and she would try telling him her story about the birth of Jesus that night. Until then, she would remain silent and just pretend that it didn't happen.

"I wish you could stay, too, My Dear," replied Naomi, "but there are several folks heading out on the northern trails tomorrow or the day after. You need to be with them for protection. There are just too many crazy people hiding in the hills between here and Nazareth who would not think twice about attacking a young man and his family on the roads."

Mary nodded her head in agreement. She recalled quickly in her mind the stories Joseph had told her about different merchants he had heard about who had thought that they could disguise themselves and slip past the thieves. None of those ideas worked, so most folks joined together and traveled in groups. Some would pay a nominal fee to travel with a caravan.

"What did Joseph say about your special news?" asked Naomi.

"He was excited and began reciting scriptures about 'having his quiver full'," replied Mary with her contented grin. The young carpenter's wife continued arranging the caravansary table with food for the guests that included vegetables from Naomi's garden, fresh baked bread, and some figs and melons purchased from the market earlier in the day. She paused to inspect the arrangement of the food and the bowls which would be piled high by the individual guests. The caravansary had two vacant rooms that night, but Naomi always spread an abundant table. The innkeeper's wife wanted to make sure that no one left her table hungry.

"I think Jesus will make an excellent big brother," stated Mary as if she were halfway dreaming. "He's attentive and helpful and so very calm in everything he does. He's a lot like his father in that respect. And by the time the baby arrives, he'll be old enough to do more of the little things around the shop. He already tries to help by bringing Joseph small boards and pieces of wood needed to make some repairs. And he's such a quick learner. I think he'll be a patient teacher towards his little brothers and sisters." Mary looked up at Naomi who was bringing over the wine for the evening meal and blushed a little. "Yes, Naomi," she said with a grin, "we plan on having our quiver full."

Naomi grinned from ear to ear and said, "Perhaps we should call our men-folk and the guests to supper... and maybe change the subject to politics or something that will allow the men to take charge of the conversation. Knowing Joseph, he'll find a way to direct the table-talk to tell a story about one of our Jewish ancestors." And both women giggled.

****

Aramazar and his companions had stopped for a few moments at one of the last of the merchant stands still open for business in the market place of Jerusalem. They pretended to be discussing a bunch of grapes, but were in fact, planning on how they could get rid of Herod's spy who dogged them. Dibon the Edomite thought he was being clever in his trailing the visitors from the East when he would duck into a doorway to avoid being seen by them. But they knew he was there. They were on their way to the little village of Bethlehem less than five miles south of the Holy City in search of the one whose star lit up the western sky almost two years previously. They spoke in their native Chaldean tongue pretending to not understand the Aramaic spoken by the merchant.

"I don't trust the old King anymore than he trusts us," said Meshach to his companions. "Did he really think he was fooling us when he told us to go search for the child, let him know when we found the boy, so that he could join us in our worship of the child?"

"Did you see the look on the Chamberlain's face when Herod pretended to be so devout?" added Abimael. "I'm glad for his sake that Herod couldn't see the disgust in Chenaniah's eyes."

"Herod is an old fool," commented Aramazar, "and he's afraid of being overthrown. He knows the Jews resent him and his attempts to turn them into Romans. I think he is not long for this world. His sores are putrefying by the minute. But at least we know to look in Bethlehem."

"Then you do believe that the Lord's Chosen One has been born, Uncle?" asked Meshach.

"I believe that Herod believes he has," replied the old priest.

221

"So how do we shake Herod's spy?" questioned Abimael. "And where we do start looking in Bethlehem?"

"I've got an idea about the former question, Cousin," said Meshach with a mysterious and devilish wink. "That is, if we are in agreement that we want to lose the man following us." The other two men shook their heads in agreement, and Meshach tossed a small silver coin towards the merchant while the three pilgrims walked away eating the grapes the young scholar had been pretending to examine.

Within five minutes, the trio spied a woman standing in the shadows who appeared to be more than willing to spend a little time with a man... for a price. Meshach looked at his companions and motioned for them to linger in the street for a moment or two while he made a deal with the woman. The young scholar walked nervously up to the woman.

"Pardon me," he said rather sheepishly, "how much would you charge to keep someone entertained for half an hour?"

"For you, Sonny," she said with a broad smile, "I'd do it for free!"

"No... no," stammered the Eastern teacher, "not me... someone else... that man over there." He motioned to his right with his head towards the Edomite.

"The old man?" replied the woman.

"No... not that man," answered Meshach, "that other man... the one leaning against the building on the corner pretending to be drunk."

"Him?" repeated the woman. "For him, probably more than you've got or want to spend."

"How about a gold coin?" asked Meshach. "My friends and I think he is following us. We're trying to lose him. Would you keep him occupied for half an hour in return for this gold coin?" Meshach handed the coin to the woman, who inspected it carefully.

"All right," she replied, "for half an hour... but not a minute more." The woman placed the coin in her pocket, and Meshach returned to his cousin and his uncle.

"Meshach," interrupted Aramazar, "tell me you didn't just do what I think you did!" The young teacher cocked his head to one side and grinned broadly. "I don't care to know the details, Young Man, but I'm sure you should be ashamed of yourself," added the old priest. Then he matched the young man's grin, and the three travelers continued walking down the narrow street.

Abimael pretended to get a rock in his sandal so that he could stop and lean against a building long enough to glance back at their "shadow" being distracted by the woman in the doorway. Dibon was trying to pull away from her, but she was stronger. Before he knew what had happened the Edomite spy was inside her small dwelling.

"You're plan worked, Meshach," said the young star-gazer. "We won't have to worry about that fella for awhile." Abimael grinned broadly himself as he looked at the faces of his two smiling companions. Suddenly the young astrologer's eyes grew wide as if he had seen a ghost. "Look!" he said pointing towards the sky behind his two kinsmen. "Do you see that... that light? It looks like a star!"

Aramazar and Meshach turned slowly to view a shin-ning light in the general direction of Bethlehem. Their jaws dropped, and they turned their heads back towards Abimael for some explanation. "I didn't do it," insisted the young sky-mapper. All three stood in their tracks not knowing whether they were capable of moving. Then the light started moving as if it beckoned them to follow. And so they followed. ·

The three men were unaware of time or distance for they soon found themselves in the streets of the little village of Bethlehem. The light continued to lead them until it hovered over the small caravansary. All three of the light-followers took deep breaths at the same time and slowly advanced toward the little inn in the City of David. Just as they got to the door, the light they had been following slowly disappeared.

Meshach, looking first to his left and then to his right, was the first to break the silence. "Have you noticed that no one else seems to have seen that light?" he asked in a half-question, half-statement kind of tone. The three pilgrims from Susa stood in front of the door to the caravansary and began canvassing the handful of people milling about the streets of the small village. The sun had just set, so there was not a lot of activity, but still there were merchants hurrying home as well as others who should have noticed the light, but apparently didn't.

"I'm an educated man, Uncle," said Abimael softly, "and I've seen some strange sights in the heavens... all of them could be explained by science. But this... light... I can't explain."

"It seems, Gentlemen," replied Aramazar, "that we may have stumbled onto something much more mystifying than we could have imagined. I believe we need to see this through to the end." The old priest turned to look at Abimael and then at Meshach before resuming his speech. "Either of you two boys want to knock on the door?" he asked. All any of them could do was just stand there with their mouths open.

Suddenly the door of the caravansary opened. "Ah... I thought I heard someone approaching the inn," announced Malachi, the innkeeper. "You look like you've come a long way. Please enter my humble dwelling, eat with us, and rest. We do have a room available if you are seeking shelter."

The warm smile of the innkeeper pulled the three men back into the reality of the situation. None of them knew where this adventure was taking them, but each felt compelled to complete the journey. They had indeed come far in search of new beginnings, and for the moment, each one's plans and ambitions seemed to be taking new directions. Without knowing the final results of their search as yet, each one believed that once they entered that door, nothing would be the same again.

****

Chapter Twenty-two

The Escape

Meshach was the first to arise to welcome the dawning light through the window of the room he shared with his cousin and his uncle in the small caravansary in Bethlehem. The young scholar from Susa had been awake for several hours, not because of his inability to sleep, but because of the discovery of Jehovah's Chosen One the evening before. Meshach had actually spent a very restful night in deep slumber until awakened by a dream. He wondered if his traveling companions had had a similar dream as he watched the early sunlight cast shadows in the room. Then his Uncle Aramazar, the High Priest of Shamesh, began to stir, and the noise and movement caused Abimael to arise also. The three men looked at each other... and smiled like heavy burdens had been lifted off their shoulders or they had found a field with a hidden treasure.

"Good morning, My Kinsmen," said Meshach with just a hint of an I-told-you-so attitude in his voice.

The two other men exchanged the usual morning pleasantries with Meshach and each other. Aramazar walked over to the bowl of fresh water that Naomi had brought the pilgrims just before she had turned in for the night. He stood there looking at his reflection in the basin for just a moment before splashing handfuls of the liquid onto his face to aid the process of awakening from a sound slumber.

With water dripping from his beard, the old priest wiped his hands on his tunic and started the morning conversation. "I trust you both slept well," he said with a grin. "I most certainly did. We've each had time to think about the events of the last 24 hours... especially meeting the young child for whom we started this journey two years ago. I know what I must do, but I will not require that either of you follow in my footsteps on my next journey."

Abimael busied himself with rolling up the large, leather-covered, feather-filled mat he and Meshach had shared on the previous evening. He had not shared much of his personal feelings with the other two men as yet because he was trying to analyze all the consequences of his future actions. The young star-gazer looked at his older cousin and grinned slightly.

"I slept with a peacefulness that I've never experienced before," commented Meshach. "You both know that I've spent a great deal of time studying the writings of the Hebrew prophets and researching everything I could find about the Jewish thoughts concerning Jehovah. I will admit to you now, that I never really believed that Herod had fathered a child. I used the prophecy as an excuse to get to Jerusalem... to walk the streets my... our... ancestors walked." Meshach paused to let his pronouncement sink in a bit. "I had dreamed of finding a job here... perhaps in a school... that is, up until last night when we found that little boy sitting in his mother's lap. The moment I looked into his eyes and felt him looking through me... into my inner most being... not in a judgmental way... but in an accepting way, I knew we were in the presence of the One mankind has been searching for since the time of Abraham. I believe that child, Jesus, is the Chosen One of the Lord God Almighty... the Lord's Messiah. And I can't go back to my old way of life... but I also know that I can't stay here, either... because of Herod."

"I felt the same way, Nephew," stated Aramazar. "I can tell you now that I've not believed in Shamesh or AlQuam or any other god for a long time. I had planned on running away once we got to Jerusalem... perhaps to Asia Minor... ply my skills as a tentmaker once again. I never wanted to even hear the name of Shamesh or AlQuam or... even Jehovah. But last night... as we were introduced to that little boy, Jesus, and he smiled at me as he brushed back those ebony curls, I felt like a new man inside... like I had been reborn with a fresh purpose. I cannot return to Susa or to Petra right now... maybe sometime later. I believe that I should travel for awhile... and tell everyone I meet about the One who brings real life to anyone willing to accept Him. And I will not tell Herod of our discovery, lest that old fool try and harm the child. That will make me an outlaw of sorts... at least as long as Herod lives."

Aramazar and Meshach looked at Abimael who had been silently packing his belongings and dressing in plain traveling clothes. For just a few seconds, the young scientist spoke not a word. Then he grinned.

"I, too, have discovered the answers for which I have searched... not in the manner I had assumed that I would... but in the eyes of a curly-headed little boy. Those eyes... so full of... fire... yet so very peaceful. And that magical smile." Abimael's grin widened and tears filled his eyes. "Yes, Cousin," he continued, "I believe he is who you claim him to be. Like my learned uncle, I, too have become disillusioned with pretending to know the future by studying the stars. For years now, I've wondered who put those stars in place... for whoever He is must be greater than the stars themselves. I've done a bit of research myself, Cousin... into the beliefs of the Jews. And now I believe I understand more than I ever did... because we looked into the face of God's Holy Child." The former-astrologer sat on his belongings and wiped his hand across his beard in a thoughtful manner. "The question now is... what are we going to do with the information we have?" asked Abimael as he looked first at Aramazar and then to Meshach.

"Let me tell you about a dream I had early this morning," stated Meshach. "It was about Herod... and the child, Jesus... and us."

****

Chenaniah entered he private chambers of King Herod as he had done on countless occasions, but this time there was trouble in the air. The longtime attaché to the hated Hellenistic King of the Jews could feel the tension growing with every bellowing order made by the sickly, old regent. That same feeling of tension had been the focal point of a discussion Chenaniah had had with his wife in the hours reserved for rest.

"Betah," said the King's servant quietly as the two lay in their bed. "You've been rather silent about... about Herod's visitors tonight. Did you not hear about the men who came from King Aretas?"

"Yes, my Husband," replied Betah in her softest voice, "I heard in the market this afternoon about the men seeking the new born King of the Jews. I think most everyone in the City has heard the story, and most everyone is frightened at what that old madman might do next." She whispered the last words.

"I understand your feelings, my Love," replied Chenaniah. "Everyone in the palace shares those same concerns. Those three men are supposed to report back to Herod in the morning... about the result of their search." Chenaniah turned to face his wife. "Herod sent them to Bethlehem... to look for a child under the age of two... who might fit the criteria for the Messiah. He told them that he wanted to worship the boy himself. But I know him to not be religious... not even now that he is so close to death. I've heard him curse the Lord many times. He will not worship the child... he will try to kill him."

"Oh, Chenaniah," responded Betah with even a deeper fear in the tone of her voice. "Didn't Eleazar say that Joseph and Mary were spending a few days in Bethlehem? Are they still there? Is Jesus... with them?"

"I don't know, Betah," answered Chenaniah. "I don't know. I've been praying that Eleazar's brother and his family have already left the little village. Or at least, that the men from the East won't find them. Jesus fits the description of the child Herod seeks. And as small as Bethlehem is... I don't think there could be too many young boys under the age of two there." Betah scooted closer to her husband to find some comfort in his arms, and she wept. The picture in his mind of his wife weeping for their young friend brought Chenaniah back into the present.

"Dibon the Edomite awaits your summons, O Great King," announced Chenaniah who chose not to look at the shadow behind the silk screen.

"Send him in at once," bellowed Herod, "and for his sake, he'd better be bringing me the news I want to hear!"

Chenaniah opened the door and stood just inside the doorway, leaving enough room for the king's spy to enter. But Chenaniah noticed the look of fear and consternation on the face of the little man who had been so unrelenting in his quest to please the King that he would manufacture lies about anyone in order to impress Herod. Something was not right, so Chenaniah decided that he would evesdrop for a moment to assess the situation. Dibon entered the room slowly and deliberately.

"What news do you bring me, Edomite?" asked Herod with a slight change of tone from belligerent to conniving. "Did the three scholars from the East find the child they sought?"

"I... I don't know, Your Majesty," stammered Dibon. "What I mean is... I'm not sure. They might have... they must have... by now." Dibon tried to say something without saying anything.

"You are not a diplomat, Dibon," sneered the old King. "You are a spy... a cutthroat... of little more use to me than a rat. Tell me what you know... and tell me now... before I have your lying tongue cut out and your head paraded on a pole throughout Jerusalem!"

"Well, O King," started Dibon, trying to choose his words carefully, "I followed the men as you instructed. And I am positive that they never knew that I was watching their every move. Suddenly... without warning... a woman grabbed me... and... and she started having her way with me." Dibon was almost in tears as he tried to explain without explaining.

"A woman grabbed you?" repeated Herod. "And you were too weak to fight her off? Or were you too puffed up with pride that a woman... any woman... even a prostitute would seek to have her way with you?"

"It wasn't my fault, Sire," answered Dibon, trying as best he could to give himself an alibi. "She was bigger than I am... and as strong as any man... and... she forced me to please her!"

For a full minute, there was silence in the room. Outside the door, Chenaniah had to work hard to suppress a belly-laugh at the picture he imagined of the little spy and the strong street-walker.

Finally, Herod spoke in a disgusting tone, "And the three spies sent by Aretas... what became of them?"

"I don't know, Your Excellency," answered Dibon in a mousy, terrified voice. "The last time I saw them, they were headed towards the village of Bethlehem. I am sure they found the lad you sent them to find... and they're probably on their way here now... to tell you all about their search."

"If they're not here by noon, Little Man," stated Herod hatefully, "you will be sent to find them. Don't even think about returning to me until you do find them. Understood?"

"Understood, O Great King," answered the Edomite with a sense of gratitude that his life had been spared for at least a few more hours.

Chenaniah walked away from the door hurriedly so that Herod's ambitious little spy would not discover that he had been listening. The faithful servant to the King had heard enough to convince him that the men who had spent the better part of two years searching for a child were indeed wise enough to know that Herod had lied to them about worshipping with them. He also knew that if they did not report to the old monarch soon, that they would be declared outlaws and brought into the chambers in chains. And since they were ambassadors from King Aretas, this incident could be enough to start another war between the Roman-backed kingdom of Herod and the Nabataeans who controlled the spice trade. And Chenaniah also knew that the Romans would only nominally support Herod... again. For their demand for frankincense and myrrh far surpassed their need to keep a dying man on a puppet throne.

****

Joseph watched with great interest as the half dozen soldiers watered their horses at the village well just a short distance from the caravansary run by his cousins, Malachi and Naomi. The strong carpenter from Nazareth had been repairing the gate on the inn's corral that housed the animals of the two guests still remaining at the inn. Joseph's donkey and the cart he had built for Mary stood over in the corner near the back door of Malachi's place of business. Joseph noticed that a little man with the face of a rat questioned several people near the well. Wiping his hands on his carpenter's apron, the young woodworker walked to the front door of Bethlehem's best and only inn. All the while he kept an eye on the little man and the soldiers.

As he pushed open the entrance, Joseph couldn't help but remember the conversation he had had with the three travelers from the East just a few hours earlier.

"Joseph," stated the older of the three visitors, "we've come to bid you and your family farewell. We will be leaving within the hour, all taking different routes that will eventually lead us back to the land from which we came." The young shaper-of-wood noticed that the men were dressed in very ordinary clothes much different from the fancy duds they had worn the night before. It was obvious to the tall Nazarene that they did not want to be discovered.

"It will be better for you and your family to not know which direction we are traveling," continued Aramazar. "We leave this place as wanted men because we will not do Herod's bidding. But we leave this place as changed men. We each came seeking something different which actually was the same... a new meaning to life itself. We found that meaning after meeting Jesus and hearing your story about his birth. We believe him to be the Son of God, just as you say."

"We brought gifts with us to present to Herod's new born son," added Abimael, "or so we thought. Meshach was off just a bit in his interpretation of the writings of the Hebrew prophet Daniel. He failed to link that prophecy with that of Micah." Abimael grinned as he placed a friendly hand on the shoulder of his older cousin. "Still," continued the former star-gazer, "we found the One we had been searching for... with the help of a very bright, star-like light."

"Unfortunately," interrupted Meshach, "we don't have all the gifts we brought to honor the new born King of the Jews with us at this time. Most of the treasures are back in Jerusalem at the inn near the Temple. But we can't go back there. Herod will be looking for us. He wants us to tell him about Jesus. He means to harm the boy, Joseph."

"Please accept what we do have," said the former priest. "Take this bag of frankincense, this bag of gold, and this bag of myrrh... gifts from us to Jesus to celebrate his entrance into the world." Joseph was humbled by the gifts presented to Jesus... gifts from the heart... gifts of gratitude... gifts of sacrifice... gifts of great value.

"But won't you need these on your journey?" asked the carpenter from Nazareth. "If you can't return to Jerusalem for your possessions, how will you pay for your journey home?"

"We'll get by," replied Abimael. "We will find work along the way... and the Lord will take care us." All three men grinned broadly. Each made his way to express their sincere thanks for the hospitality shown by their hosts, Malachi and Naomi. Then the three approached Mary and Jesus, who clung to her skirt. And the three scholars bowed themselves before the boy child. Jesus walked to where they were kneeling and gave each one a strong hug around their necks, then he backed away. The men arose and with tears in their eyes, bid the household adieu.

Aramazar handed a large sack to Naomi and whispered, "Please take care of these clothes for us. You might be able to sell them in a month or two... after the storm settles. Or burn them if need be... we won't need them any longer."

Joseph walked the men to the corral where they had kept three horses purchased earlier that morning from one of the traveling merchants who had left for Petra an hour or so before this departure. Aramazar placed his arm around Joseph and handed him a purple bag filled with frankincense and whispered, "Herod will try to kill the child if he gets a chance. There's a caravan leaving for Egypt late tonight... led by a friend of mine. Give him this bag... he'll recognize it... and he will help you blend into the caravan so that you can get far away. Use it only if it is necessary." Aramazar mounted his Arabian mare and with a wave of his hand said, "I'll pass through Nazareth on my way to Damascus. I'll explain everything to your folks. Good-bye, my Friend." Then the three men reined their horses and trotted off in different directions.

****

Chenaniah was accustomed to visiting Herod's chambers several times each day, partly to see if the old King needed anything and partly to see if Herod had died. This day of turmoil caused by the disappearance of the three men from Susa had forced the longtime servant to open the door more times than he wished to count. But Dibon the Edomite had returned empty-handed, and the old regent insisted that the little spy be brought before him at once. Herod was in a terrible mood. He did not like the idea that he had been outsmarted by Nabataeans.

"Dibon the Edomite, Your Majesty," announced Chenaniah. And with that announcement, he left the hallway. He did not want to hear this interview.

Once again Dibon entered the room sheepishly. "Live forever, O Great King," he said in his mousy voice.

"I assume you have failed once more, Dibon," stated Herod matter-of-factly. "You don't have the three men with you."

Dibon always stuttered when he got nervous, and the more he stuttered, the more nervous he became. "I... I.. came close to finding them, Sire," stammered Dibon. "I think maybe someone kidnapped them."

"Dibon, you are so close to losing your head," grunted the old king.

"They were in Bethlehem... I think," interjected the little spy. "I found some people who thought they saw them at the caravansary. And... and... and I asked the owner of the place... a man named Malachi about them... and he just laughed and said 'Why would men of such importance dressed in fancy clothes stay in his humble dwelling?'"

"You are trying my patience, Edomite!" bellowed Herod.

"I tracked them to the inn just to the east of the Temple," stated Dibon hurriedly, "but they weren't there, either. And all of their belongings are still there... no sign of them... no one's seen them. They just vanished, Sire."

"Vanished?" repeated Herod. "You mean they skipped the country! Those three tricked me!" screamed the old King. Herod began spitting blood in between words and coughing. Dibon was glad he could not actually see the King through the veil.

"I'll show those three who is the smartest in the land!" shouted Herod in between coughs. "Take as many soldiers as you need... go back to Bethlehem... and kill every male child in the city... every male two years old and younger! They messed up... they told me when they saw that blasted star... two years ago! Kill them all!

"Uh... Sire...," said Dibon falteringly, "The sun has gone down."

"I don't care what the sun has done, you fool!" shrieked Herod.

"It's the last day of the Feast of Unleavened Bread, O Great King," began Dibon. "And all the palace guards have gone home... you graciously gave them the evening off, remember... so that they could celebrate with their families. They've all gone. It would take hours to gather them all."

"Fine," sneered Herod. "Do it tomorrow... but do it!... or I swear, it will be the very last thing you don't do!"

****

"Mary," whispered Joseph as he tried to awaken his sleeping wife. "Mary," he said a little louder with just a bit of a jostling of his bride. "Mary," he repeated still a little louder.

"What is it, Joseph?" asked the carpenter's young wife. "Is it morning already?"

"No, Mary," stated Joseph calmly, "it is still the middle of the night. But we need to leave Bethlehem... and we need to leave right now."

"But why?" inquired Mary. "What's going on?"

"An angel spoke to me in a dream," replied Joseph. "He said, 'Take the child and his mother and flee to Egypt at once. Stay there until you are told that it is safe to return home. Herod is on the hunt for this child and wants to kill him.'"

"Oh no!" sighed Mary, "it's just like Aramazar said. I'll hurry and pack our belongings."

"I've already done that," responded the tall Nazarene. "And I've loaded everything onto the cart and hitched up our donkey. Take Jesus and hurry to the little wagon. I'll tell Malachi that we're leaving, but I won't tell him where we are going, lest he and Naomi get into trouble. Now hurry... we've no time to waste." The urgency in her carpenter's voice caused Mary to respond quickly. She trusted her husband because she knew that he loved her and Jesus completely. And if Joseph said an angel told him to take the family to Egypt, then to Egypt they would go. Mary wasn't sure how they would get there, but she believed that Joseph had been given instructions by the Lord God Almighty.

Joseph and Mary left Bethlehem under cover of darkness and journeyed the five miles to Jerusalem where they found a small caravan about to leave for Egypt. The young carpenter sought out the leader of the caravan, a man with a patch over his left eye, and handed him the purple bag filled with frankincense.

"Where did get this bag?" asked the leader in broken Aramaic.

"A friend by the name of Aramazar gave it to me," replied Joseph. "He said we could trust you to get my wife and child safely to Egypt."

"Aramazar, huh?" repeated the one-eyed man. "I haven't seen that old scudder in probably 20 years... but he saved my life once... way back when we was both just pups. He must have thought pretty highly of you, my Friend," added the caravan leader while hefting the bag as if he were weighing its contents. "His father gave him this bag a long time ago... before he went to war and was killed. Aramazar cherished this bag like it was a part of his own body." The one-eyed man looked squarely at Joseph and then at Mary and Jesus in the little wagon. "I'll get you safely into Egypt," he stated. "All of you. We'll be leaving in about an hour. Fall in line behind that second wagon over there. If you need any supplies, like extra water, then you best be gettin' it now."

The caravan boss handed the bag back to Joseph and said, "We'll settle up later. In the meantime, you might want to keep this. Every stop along the way will want some of what's in that bag, but they'll treat you right because they know who owns the bag." That was the first time the one-eyed leader of the caravan smiled at Joseph and his family. It would not be the last.

By the time daylight had conquered the shadows of the night, Joseph and his family were out of Jerusalem and well on their way to Egypt. The tall woodworker knew that he and his family would have to stay in Egypt at least until Herod died. As he walked beside the little wagon, he reached out and touched Mary's hand as he often did on their journeys from Nazareth to Jerusalem. He smiled at her as he remembered the words of the prophet Hosea, "I called my son out of Egypt." So many lives would be touched during this Egyptian exile, just as many lives had already been touched by Jesus… and nothing would be the same again.

****

Chapter Twenty-three

The Consequences

By the time young Simon got to his brother's house, the residents of Bethlehem were mourning the vicious murders by Herod's palace guards of the innocents. Blood was everywhere… flowing in the streets… smeared on the walls of buildings… oozing from the bodies of men and women who had tried to protect their babies from senseless slaughter. Simon hesitated entering the small, one-room house. He stooped down and picked up a silk scarf laying in the doorway… the blood-soaked scarf had been a gift to Johanna on the day that she had given birth to little Benjamin. Tears filled the eyes of the young shepherd boy as he realized that the bloody scarf was not a good sign.

Simon had spent the night in the fields along with his father and brother, Nathaniel. They had just awakened and stirred the fire when Nathaniel noticed the soldiers again entering Bethlehem. But this time, the soldiers were fully armed. Nathaniel looked at his father as if asking permission for something.

"Perhaps you should go back to town, Nathaniel," said Achim calmly. "Just to see why the soldiers have returned to our village. And on your return you can bring us some of Johanna's fresh baked bread."

The old shepherd grinned. Simon just shook his head. Nathaniel was always finding excuses to go back to town to check on Johanna or on little Benjamin. But Simon was supposed to be too young to understand these things.

Less than half an hour later, Achim turned his head towards the little village at the sound of what seemed like shrieking and wailing and crying. At first, Simon thought that it was just the wind. But the screaming continued and became more ominous. Then the young shepherd saw the soldiers leaving. He couldn't quite see Nathaniel's house from his vantage point on the hill, and he could not make out Nathaniel among the people pouring into the narrow streets. The pre-teen glanced at his father for only a moment, and then began running down the hill towards Bethlehem. Achim made no move to stop him. The old shepherd turned his face to the skies, closed his eyes, and prayed.

Simon moved slowly into Nathaniel's house, trying to force back the tears that blurred his vision. Then he saw Johanna lying on the floor just inside the doorway, her back ripped open from her left shoulder to her right hip. The young shepherd boy put his hand to his mouth because he felt sick to his stomach. Then he turned his gaze to the body lying sprawled on the floor near where little Benjamin had slept. It was Nathaniel. The insides of the normally peaceful shepherd lay in his blood-soaked lap. There was a puncture wound on his left hand, which was stretched across the lifeless body of the baby. Simon could tell that the little bed was saturated in blood. Nathaniel apparently had tried to save his son from the sword of the soldiers, but his only weapon was his shepherd's staff. Simon found the staff lying close to his brother's body. There was blood on the larger end, an indication that he at least got in one good jab at the assailant. The staff was cut in half.

Simon turned from the horrible scene and threw up everything he had eaten in the last two days... or so it seemed to him. He could not control his sobbing. The young shepherd boy walked to the doorway, took one step outside, and simply collapsed. The lament of the villagers became deafening to the lad. He looked for someone to give him answers. What had Nathaniel and Johanna done that Herod's men would attack them so? And what about the other bodies that were being brought into the streets... men, women, and three small children... all boys. Simon knew each of the boys... none of them were older than two years.

****

Betah walked quietly towards her husband. Chenaniah stood in the darkness atop their humble home in the middle of Jerusalem, leaning on the parapet, deep in thought. Betah approached him and placed her arm around him and gave him a little squeeze. He did not respond as she had hoped.

"What has you so troubled, my Love?" asked Betah.

"A multitude of things, Betah," replied the King's chamberlain. "The land of Judah is on the edge of revolt, I fear. And that could bring the Romans here in greater numbers."

"Are you thinking about what happened at the Temple today?" she asked.

"Yes," responded Chenaniah. "Judas and Matthias were right in talking those men into tearing down the image of the golden eagle which Herod had erected over the great gate of the Temple. Too bad that the captain of the guard caught them and 40 others as they were destroying the image. Herod was so angry when he received word of this 'great desecration' he called it... mostly the old King thought of all the money he had spent on the image. Herod never has understood the Jewish teachings concerning how and how not to worship Jehovah. The men stand trial tomorrow. Herod will claim that the men acted against God by destroying something dedicated to Him. But everyone in town knows the men acted as they did because they had heard that Herod had died, and they were simply showing their disrespect for the 'pretender' as they call him."

"Herod grows more evil each day or so it seems," added Betah. "I can't imagine how truly satanic the man must be to order the death of those babies in Bethlehem last week... and their only crime was their age."

"The old King returns to Jericho next week," added Chenaniah. "His departure won't be too soon for me and most of the palace. Herod received word the other day from Rome... that the fate of his son, Antipater, rested in his own hands. And the old man sent word to Antipater in the palace dungeon... to let the boy sweat a little longer. Antipater has tried to bribe several guards with promises of riches if they let him live after Herod dies. He does not know that Herod has changed his will once again... and left Antipater out entirely. Herod intends to execute Antipater, but in his own time."

Betah placed her hand on Chenaniah's arm and gently squeezed it. "You've never been so concerned about the actions of Herod and his family. Why now?" she asked in a coaxing manner.

"Because of the potential repercussions," answered Chenaniah. "Herod is trying to keep everything secret... especially about the slaughter of the innocents in Bethlehem. He had Dibon thrown into the dungeon today... to be executed on the day Herod dies. And he had Jonadab, his faithful captain, transfer the six soldiers who participated in the murders to the summer palace in Jericho. They will never return. And there are no written accounts of Herod's orders. He made sure of that. But all this and all the other atrocities that this madman has committed will one day come out... and the Romans won't be happy."

"What will the Romans do, my Love?" asked Betah.

For the first time since his wife had walked up to him, Chenaniah turned and looked deeply into her eyes. "They'll probably send someone to take over the governing of Israel who will be worse than Herod ever dreamed of being," he said. "They don't like for folks to show signs of rebellion... especially in the outlying areas of their territory. Herod has changed his will so many times... the Romans probably won't even recognize whoever the old King names as his successor. He will be dead soon, Betah... more than likely before the month is out. His sickness grows worse each day. He told his sister, Salome, to round up all the important men in Israel, put them in the Hippodrome, and have them speared to death when he dies... so that all Israel will mourn his death."

"And what about his servants who have been faithful all these years?" asked Betah. "What will he have done to them? Will he give them money... or will he order their deaths also, fearing that you know too much?"

"I don't know, Betah," was the Chenaniah's slow answer. "I have no way of knowing what might go through Herod's mind when he finally dies."

The two wrapped each other in their arms and held each other's embrace for quite awhile before retiring to their sleeping quarters downstairs. The opening to the roof was located in the corner of the upper room Eleazar and his father had added to the house so many years ago. Chenaniah stopped for a moment and glanced around the room, recalling fond memories of the Passover meal they had shared just a month before. He remembered the games and the laughter of the children and the adults. And he remembered the little boy, Jesus... and he smiled.

****

"Jacob," said Judith softly as she placed a bowl of sweetened figs and a loaf of cinnamon bread on the table in front of her husband, "I'm worried about Joseph and Mary and Jesus. They should have returned to Nazareth over two weeks ago. Shouldn't we send someone to find out what's happened?"

Jacob sighed deeply as he cut a slice of the bread for his wife. He tried to not appear to be as anxious about his youngest son's absence as she, but the truth was, he had been wondering himself. Joseph was usually a dependable man... a man who understood his responsibilities to his own young family and a man who took his work seriously, too. It just wasn't like Joseph to be this late without some word.

Jacob tried to answer Judith's concerns without adding to her fears. "Who would we send to find them, Woman?" he asked politely. "Neither myself nor Eleazar can go... we are much too busy. And besides, whoever we sent might not take the same route that Joseph and Mary are traveling. The messenger could simply miss them on the road. No, my Love, we just need to be patient. They will arrive when they will arrive." Jacob bit a piece of the figs that Judith had prepared and smiled in a don't-worry-about-it manner. "Eat," he added, "the food is good, it's been a long day, so relax... and eat."

Judith played with her food the way a child does when the young one doesn't really want to eat what's been placed on his plate. Mostly she simply rearranged the bread and the figs nervously. In her mind, she imagined all sorts of evils had befallen their youngest son and his family... thieves along the way, soldiers in one of the small towns who wanted to display their authority, or some strange illness that made them leave the protection of the caravans that headed north almost everyday. Perhaps they were lying in a ditch somewhere, hungry, wet from a sudden cloud burst, and being stalked by evil men.

The old carpenter's wife had lived with her husband too many years to be fooled by his passive manner. She knew in her heart that he was also worried. But Jacob kept his feelings bottled up inside. Jacob was a strong man, physically, and a good husband and father, but he never shared his emotions unless she prodded him. Judith had learned over the years when to prod and when to back off. This was a time to back off. Still she could see his fears and feel all of his own "what-ifs" when she looked deeply into his eyes. And she could tell by the way he kept avoiding looking into her eyes that her man carried a burden of supposed guilt. Her big, strong carpenter would blame himself if any evil happened to his son or to Mary or to his youngest grandson.

Jacob was about to share his usual scripture-time from the Torah... his favorite story about the destruction of Jericho... when a light knocking sound came from outside their front door. For a moment, a small sign of delight flashed in the eyes of the old couple, as both wanted to believe that the knocking was made by the small hand of Jesus. Judith hurried to the door, fidgeting and fussing with her apron while Joseph stood grinning and holding a piece of bread in his hand. But the grin left the old nail-bender's face as he heard his wife's reaction to the person standing outside their home in the night.

"Oh," said Judith with just a hint of disappoint in her voice, "I was expecting someone else, Sir. May I help you?"

The tall, elderly man wearing traveling clothes held his hands out from his side to indicate that he wished the woman in the doorway no harm. He grinned slightly and said, "I'm looking for the home of Jacob the carpenter. I have news from Joseph and his precious family."

"Judith!" exclaimed Jacob, "don't just stand there! Invite the man inside." Jacob had already taken a step or two towards the door... a door that Joseph had recently repaired.

"Come in, Friend," continued Jacob as Judith opened the door widely and turned her eyes for a moment to the man's feet. It was obvious that he had been walking for some time from the dust that had accumulated on his sandals.

"May God's blessings be on each one who dwells in this house," said the stranger.

"And to you, too," answered Judith.

"Please make yourself at home," added Jacob. "We were just sitting down to supper. Won't you join us, Sir? And tell us the news you bring of our son." Judith brought an extra dish and a goblet of wine to the table as the weary traveler sat on the floor next to her husband.

"I do thank you for your hospitality, my Friend," said the pilgrim. "My name is Aramazar. I've been traveling from Susa for the better part of two years in search of someone. I found that someone sitting on his mother's lap several weeks ago...

in Bethlehem... in the inn of a man named Malachi, your kinsman, I believe."

"Are you speaking of Jesus?" asked the big carpenter. "He is our grandson. But what about Joseph and Mary?"

"They are safe," replied the former priest of AlQuam. "They were forced to flee Bethlehem on just a moment's notice... because of the rage of that madman who sits upon the throne of Israel."

"Herod?" gasped Judith.

"Yes, Ma'am," responded Aramazar, "Herod. He ordered all the male children under the age of two years old in Bethlehem to be murdered. Joseph and Mary and Jesus escaped just a matter of hours before the soldiers came and carried out Herod's orders."

"But why?" asked Jacob, realizing the scope of the slaughter. "What had the little children done?"

"Nothing!" answered the stranger. "Except being born. I must tell you my story as part of the explanation. Almost two years ago, my nephews and I left Susa on a journey to Jerusalem to find the newborn King of the Jews as had been foretold by the Jewish prophet Daniel during his exile in Babylon. One of my nephews, an astrologer, witnessed a new, bright star shining just above the horizon, in the direction of Jerusalem. That star had something to do with the birth of your grandson, Jesus." The old man paused for a moment to let that revelation sink into the hearts of his two hosts. He took a bite of the bread and continued his story. "Of course, we went to the palace in Jerusalem... the obvious place of birth for a future king. Herod had not heard about the star... and there certainly was no newborn in his family. He asked questions of the High Priest and the scribes there in Jerusalem, and sent us to Bethlehem in search of the Messiah promised by Jehovah. We found him... the boy child Jesus." Again, the former, big city preacher paused and looked into the eyes of the old carpenter and his wife. He could tell by the look on their faces that they were not aware of Jesus being the Messiah.

"That can't be," said Judith, the disbelief apparent in her voice. "He is only a child... and he was born in a cave used as a stable by our kinsmen."

"Yes," replied Aramazar shaking his head, "Joseph told us the story about Jesus' birth, and I have met your kinsmen. Fine folks. But let me continue my story." Aramazar lifted the cup of wine that Judith had set before him and downed it all in one big gulp.

"My companions and I were under orders to report back to Herod after we found the child," continued Aramazar. "He said that he wanted to 'worship him with us'. But we knew he lied. So we left town, parted company, and chose different routes back to our homeland. I told Joseph to buy passage with a friend's caravan heading to Egypt as soon as he could, and I gave him the means to buy that passage. I stayed at the house of one of Herod's personal servants... another friend of yours, I believe... Chenaniah."

Jacob and Judith both nodded in agreement that they knew the household of Chenaniah. Both of the Nazarenes listened attentively to every word spoken by the traveler from the East.

"It was Chenaniah who told me about Herod's proclamation to kill all the male children of Bethlehem under the age of two," continued Aramazar, choking on his own words. "The old King picked the time based on our sighting of the star. There were only four babies slain that day... but their parents resisted the soldiers, and they were murdered, too. All because Herod feared one of the babies would grow up to take his throne. We did not expect Herod to take his wrath out on innocent children. We thought that he would send soldiers to try and track us down and bring us back to Jerusalem in chains. But my nephews and I are just as much to blame for the mourning in Bethlehem. Had we not come to Jerusalem, those babies and their parents would all still be alive."

Aramazar hung his head in shame and wept. Jacob placed his large hand on their new friend's shoulder while Judith grasped his hand. Both tried to console the man who had eased their worries about Joseph, but neither could find any words of comfort that could be suitable. Aramazar and his companions would share a heavy burden of guilt for the rest of their lives. Still, they had found the Messiah.

****

Simon sat in a slumping position on a large rock located on the hillsides overlooking the village of Bethlehem. His father's sheep grazed peacefully nearby, undisturbed by the sorrow of the young shepherd. The twelve-year-old boy could not erase the sight of his murdered brother, sister-in-law, and young nephew from his mind. He pondered over and over again the cause of the slaughter, the decree made by Herod to kill all the male children in Bethlehem under the age of two.

The young shepherd boy had grown up with the ruthlessness of a madman sitting as the King of the Jews and had echoed his father's opinions about the foreigner who stole the title while claiming to love the Jewish people. Simon, like most of the Jews in the area, admired the building projects Herod had completed during the years of his reign in an effort to purchase the respect of his subjects, but he hated the man himself and the heavy taxes imposed to fund those massive endeavors.

Like most of his fellow countrymen, Simon also hated Herod's attempts at Hellenizing the Jews, thus taking away their heritage, their culture, and their religion. Herod stayed in power only because of the backing the old King received from the Romans. Roman soldiers walked the streets of the Holy City and were stationed in several locations across his beloved homeland, in a demonstration of the control Caesar had over the everyday activities of the Jews. The young herdsman concluded that the deaths of the innocents were a direct result of the Romans. If they had not supported their puppet-King, Herod would have been overthrown years ago... or assassinated as he deserved.

"As the Lord is my witness," stated Simon out loud as if the sheep milling around him were listening to his vow, "I will avenge the massacre of my kinsmen. I will train myself in the art of fighting, and someday… I will join with others. Together, we will kill the Romans and those who wish to be like them… one by one if we have to… in a dark alley… on a lonely back road… even in a crowded market… anywhere I find those pagans. But I'll be careful… I will not get caught until I've taken vengeance against the Romans a hundredfold for each life they took in my town. They will be sorry for butchering my people."

Simon had heard rumors of a secret organization of Jewish patriots, zealous in their hatred for all Romans and Roman sympathizers. He would seek out these men and join their group. The Roman Jew-haters had forever changed his life and his ambitions, and nothing would ever be the same again.

****

Chapter Twenty-four

The Finish of the Beginning

Herod's illness grew worse with each passing day. Even the cool winds that flowed through his palace in Jericho could not relieve the pains he felt with every movement of his body. He had tried everything the doctors prescribed including bathing in the warm baths at Callirrhoe. The old King even tried drinking from these waters which eventually flowed into the Dead Sea. Nothing helped relieve the pain or stop the smell of the putrefying sores that covered his body.

Not long after returning to Jericho, Herod soaked in a tub of oil and became so relaxed that his attendants assumed that he had died. Their mournful lamentations, or were they sighs of joyful relief, aroused the ailing king. Herod, himself, feared that his end was at hand. So he ordered each of his soldiers paid fifty drachmae. The captains of the guard were given extra money. All this in an effort to bribe the guards into keeping death away, as if a mere sword could do such a thing.

Just a few days later, Herod called for his sister Salome to visit him. "I will be dead hopefully in just a few days," he told her. "And death will be such a release from the pains I have suffered these last few years. But I fear that I will not be mourned like a great king should be mourned by his subjects." The old regent gasped for each breath he took.

"Do not worry about such things, my Brother," whispered an ever faithful Salome. "Do not speak of dying, O Great King. If that time comes, you will be mourned by all those who loved you."

"But that does not include the Jews," replied Herod. "Unless they have a reason. You have sent out the orders to the principle men of Israel... to come to Jerusalem under penalty of death for refusal?"

"Yes, Your Majesty," replied Salome, "the request has gone out and even now the men enter Zion. They will be herded into the Hippodrome as you instructed."

"Kill them all, my Sister," said Herod. "The same day that I die... kill them all. Otherwise any mourning from the Jews will be in mockery and jest, for they see my death as a desirable thing. I wish them to mourn from their very souls."

"It will be done as you have instructed," said a teary-eyed Salome.

****

Joseph washed his face and hands in the basin outside the small house where he and Mary and Jesus had taken up residence in Alexandria, Egypt. Then he strolled inside the simple structure to share the evening meal with his family. He gave thanks to the Lord silently as he entered their dwelling, grateful for Jehovah's protection and guidance.

Many years before, Ptolemy, who had inherited the rule over Egypt when Alexander the Great had died, had set aside two of the five districts of the city for the Jews so that they could keep their cultural laws. And unlike most other cities controlled by the Romans, the citizens of Alexandria treated the Jews with respect. Joseph had found work in one of the carpentry shops in the city of the Great Lighthouse and spent most of his time with several other carpenters repairing municipal buildings that had fallen into ruin.

Mary spent her time much as she had in Nazareth... choosing the daily foods from the market place, baking bread, and making thread to make or repair the family garments, and preparing for the birth of her second child as she had done for Jesus.

Within a few days of the family's arrival, some eight months earlier, the women in the Jewish community began to notice that the fair maiden from Nazareth was with child. Two of the older women, widowed sisters who lived nearby the pilgrims from Galilee, decided to become surrogate mothers to Mary. The two sisters gave the couple a *mezuzah* for their front doorway, and they loaned Mary all the furnishings and pots that she would need to set up housekeeping while in exile in Egypt. Of course, they did not know that the couple from the north were in exile, just that the three of them had left Israel in a big enough hurry that they had few of the essentials to set up housekeeping. Neither Mary nor Joseph spoke of why they had journeyed to the southeastern shores of the Mediterranean Sea, despite the prying questions of their neighbors.

Deborah, the older of the two sisters by some four years, reminded Mary of her special duties during the latter's pregnancy. Deborah's gray hair and kindly face caused most everyone to trust her. She seemed to know all the gossip about every family in the Jewish section, but she refrained from sharing most of the "stories" or tales of woe with Mary, for the carpenters' wife was not supposed to listen to such idle tales, as was the custom for women who were expecting in Jewish households. Still, the elderly mother of six, all daughters who had long since married respectable Jewish men and moved back to Israel, always had a name for her young protégé who needed some kindness shown them, allowing the young carpenter's wife to increase her "good deeds" each day. Deborah even presented the former-shepherd's daughter with a charity box that she herself had made during her early child-bearing days. The charity box stored small coins, usually deliberate change given to Mary by merchants from transactions in the market place. These coins were then given to the poor. The

Jews believed that charitable acts during pregnancy helped to insure a safe and easy time during the actual birthing period.

Sarah, Deborah's younger sister, reminded Mary of Naomi. Sarah always had a smile on her face and a word of praise for the Lord over some minor miracle she had witnessed, like a flower growing through a crack in the brick streets. Sarah helped Mary design new *mezuzah* cases, which Joseph fashioned after working during the day. Sarah had been spending time with Gideon, an old friend from Israel. Gideon was a scribe by trade and a widower himself. He wrote the *mezuzahs* that were placed in the cases on each doorway in the small house rented by Joseph. The *mezuzah* symbolized that God and the Torah were entering the room.

The two older women also helped the young carpenter's wife sew the *gartel*, the sash for the Torah scroll. If the child were a son, the sash would be used on the Torah at his *bar mitzvah* and again when he got married. The sash Mary had sewed for Jesus was safe in a small box that would hold memories. Joseph had created the little box back in his shop in Nazareth.

Mary truly enjoyed her daily visits with the two older women because they brought the young bride a sense of family, something she dearly missed.

"When can we go home, Joseph?" asked Mary one evening while Joseph was preparing to recite his nightly rendition of Psalm 20.

Joseph looked into the eyes of his beloved bride and felt deeply her yearning to return to their little home in the village of Nazareth. He, too, longed for the familiarity of his boyhood surroundings, and the tall carpenter missed working beside his father and his brother. He even missed the way his mother would nag him sometimes... over small details that didn't really matter. The displaced woodworker reached out his hand and gently touched Mary's cheek, the way he had done so many times before Jesus was born. Mary liked that touch of his... strong, yet so gentle and reassuring. He didn't have to speak... that touch made everything all right... that touch plus the love she could see in his eyes... and that special grin he had just for her.

"I don't know, my Love," answered Joseph in a calm voice. "I remember Eleazar commenting about how Chenaniah had described Herod's sickness. I believe the old King will die soon. But we can't risk returning until Herod is dead. Until then, the Lord will look out for us." Joseph placed his hand over the candle and snuffed out the light, leaving only shadows in the room from the moonlight shining through the window.

"May the Lord answer you when you are worried," he whispered gently to Mary. She sighed and snuggled as close to her husband as she could, being over eight months pregnant. He gently kissed her cheek, and the young bride from the hills of Galilee smiled her special smile that only Joseph was aloud to see. Her carpenter placed his muscular arms about her and continued his recitation. "May the name of the God of Jacob protect you. May He send you help from the sanctuary and grant you support from Zion. May He remember all of your sacrifices and accept your burnt offerings." Joseph paused for a moment so that Mary could meditate on the Word of God. His thoughts turned to the synagogue where quiet music would be played for a few seconds to allow for deeper concentration. Then he continued, "May He give you the desire of your heart and make all of your plans succeed. We will shout for joy when you are victorious and will lift up our banners in the name of our God. May the Lord grant all of your requests. Now, I know that the Lord saves His anointed; He answers Him from His holy heaven with the saving power of His right hand. "

Joseph paused to glance in the direction of the small mat under the window where Jesus lay sleeping peacefully. And the big shaper-of-wood grinned once more as he continued. "Some trust in chariots, and some trust in horses, but we trust in the name of the Lord our God. They are brought to their knees and fall, but we rise up and stand firm. Save us, O Lord! Answer us when we call!" Joseph had been looking at the angelic expression on the face of his beloved. She was asleep. He tenderly brushed her coal-black hair from her face. And once more kissed her softly.

"May He send you help from the sanctuary," he whispered in a barely audible voice, "and may He grant you support from Zion." Joseph moved his forehead so that it touched hers, and he closed his eyes and slept.

****

Gabbal, the head of the household servants in Herod's palace at Jericho, brought the sickly monarch an apple and a small knife during the latter's afternoon repose. The disease-infested King of the Jews enjoyed eating an apple each day, and he insisted on paring the luscious fruit himself. Herod had become quite adept at skillfully removing the peel in one long, curly piece. This simple routine was one of the few things that gave the ailing ruler of Israel any joy.

Herod took the small, silver platter in his hands and placed it on his bloated belly. The old king was only partially listening to his cousin, Achiabus, spinning some yarn about a young woman he had met the day before somewhere or other. Herod held the apple in his left hand and picked up the knife with his right. Suddenly, a strange look came across his face, and Herod lifted the knife in an ominous fashion as high as the pain in his arm and shoulder would allow.

"No!" screamed Achiabus, "No, your Majesty! You must not do this!" Achiabus grabbed Herod's arm just as the old king was about to plunge the knife into his own chest. Achiabus was much stronger than Herod at that point and easily stayed his attempt at suicide, wrenching the knife from the King's grasp.

"Leave me alone, Achiabus!" commanded Herod. "I don't want to live in this agony any longer. Let me die with honor!" Gabbal rushed to aid Achiabus and the two men tried as best they could to restrain Herod's actions. At that moment, Herod screamed maniacally and pushed the two men away.

Hearing the commotion and screams from the King's chamber, several of the servants nearby assumed the worst. "The King is dead! The King is dead!" squealed Michalah. The young maiden had been on her way into the chamber to cleanse the sores on Herod's feet. She threw the pan of water mixed with spices and a special nerve-deadening herb into the air and began running down the palace corridor proclaiming tearfully what she had presumed to be true. Within minutes the entire palace was mourning the death of Herod. It would be several more minutes before the news spread that their mourning was a bit premature.

The news of Herod's supposed death reached even the prison where Antipater had been kept awaiting his execution. "Release me, Jailer!" implored the formally loyal son of the King, "Release me," he repeated with his head stuck as far between the bars as was allowed by his imprisonment. "I am now the King of the Jews! Obey this very second, and I will make you rich beyond your wildest dreams!" coaxed Antipater.

Demus, the younger of the two guards took the keys from their place on the wall and stepped towards the cell to release the King's son. "What are you doing, Demus?" asked Jonah, the grey-haired Sargeant of the Guards, as he stepped between the man with the keys and Antipater's cell.

"Releasing the new King," stated the young prison-keeper in a bewildered tone.

"Are you absolutely positive that the old King is dead, Boy?" grunted Jonah. "We have heard only rumors. Nothing official. We had best wait." Jonah gave his young protégé a determined look that meant business as he grabbed Demus' arm.

"Listen to me, Jailer," urged Antipater. "Release me now... and I will pay you handsomely. Delay more than one minute, and the both of you will pay with your lives."

The big, burly jailer turned slowly to face the young man who might hold the keys to his future. He stared at his prisoner and then at the young man by his side who had turned pale as a ghost. "Do with me as you wish," he growled. "If you become King."

About five minutes later, one of the other guards appeared in the doorway to the damp prison beneath the palace of Jericho and announced to the two men guarding the condemned son of Herod that the old King stilled lived. The news of his demise was a false alarm. Antipater melted into a defeated heap with his hands still clinging to the bars above him.

"What would have happened to us, Jonah," asked the young jailer, "had we let Antipater go?"

"We would have taken his place," answered the older prison officer, "in there… and at the chopping block."

Upon hearing of Antipater's bribe, Herod ordered his son executed immediately, just as Jonah had suspected. The old ruler of the Jews smiled at the news of Antipater's beheading and seemed to revive in spirits somewhat. Deathbed or no deathbed, pain or no pain, Herod was not about to let a little thing like family or the idea of forgiveness cloud his judgment or his brutality. His end had not come just yet.

****

Chenaniah walked through the door of his humble house in Jerusalem some three hours earlier than usual. Betah had just started preparing the evening meal of fruits and chicken when she heard her husband enter their dwelling.

"Chenaniah," said Betah with a puzzled tone. "You're home quite early today. Is everything all right?"

Herod's Chamberlain stood for a moment surveying his home, built by his father, and inherited by Chenaniah upon his father's death. Then he looked at his wife, cocked his head to the right a bit, held out his arms wide, and smiled like Betah had not seen him smile in a long, long time.

"Everything is fine, my Love," he answered with a great sense of relief mixed with just a touch of joy. "A runner came from Jericho this morning… straight from the palace. Herod is dead!"

Betah dropped the bowl of fruit she had been taking to their table and ran to her husband. The two clung to each other in an embrace that resembled that of a groom with his young bride. Betah sobbed softly.

"Is it true, Chenaniah?" she asked. "Is the madman truly dead?"

"Yes, Betah," answered Chenaniah, "he is truly dead. The message was confirmed by another runner sent by Salome, Herod's sister, just a couple of hours later. We had been told to not tell anyone about the news from the first messenger until after the second messenger arrived."

"How?" asked the faithful servant's wife, "how did he die?"

"In extreme pain," commented Chenaniah as he released his wife to pick up one of the dates that had hit the floor. He bit into it after wiping off a little dirt. Chenaniah continued his report. "The old King had just finished changing his will for the umpteenth time, leaving vast sums of money to his remaining family members and to Caesar and his wife, Julia. And he died… just five days after he had ordered the death of Antipater."

"Herod has been king a long time," added Betah, "he's the only King of the Jews that I've ever known."

"Thirty-seven years," remarked Chenaniah. "He will be remembered for his great cruelty towards everyone, especially those he feared in his own family. But he did amass a great deal of wealth. Some will say that Herod lived an unfortunate life, always scared of losing his throne, forced to accept the disrespect of his subjects, overcoming treachery in his own family… and dying in a most excruciating manner. People will not forget his heartless and merciless treatment of his real and supposed enemies."

"Oh, Chenaniah," gasped Betah, "what about all those men that have been herded into the Hippodrome here and in Jericho? What has become of them?"

Chenaniah grinned once more and shook his head. "They've been sent home," he said. "That was the message of the second runner. Salome, Herod's sister, had them all released... told them that the King wished them to return to their own lands and take care of their affairs. Shortly afterwards, she announced that Herod had died. Then she told all Herod's soldiers about their inheritance and spoke of how he had appreciated their service. She read a letter to them from Herod asking the soldiers to be loyal to Archelaus. I read the same letter to the servants and soldiers here a few hours ago."

"At least the uncertainty of what tomorrow might bring is gone," noted Betah. "Surely Archeaus will be a more predictable leader."

"Perhaps," added Chenaniah. " or perhaps he will be predictably worse. We'll just have to wait and see."

****

Mary cradled her three-month-old son to her breast while watching Jesus playing with some wooden carpentry tools that Joseph had fashioned for him. Her and Joseph's young family would be leaving for Nazareth soon. She had fulfilled all the scriptural obligations a woman giving birth was required to do, as she had done when Jesus was born. The only difference was the ceremonies were offered in the local synagogue instead of the Temple in Jerusalem. But that was the best she and Joseph could do, for there was no Temple for the Jews in Alexandria, Egypt.

Pilgrims arriving from Jerusalem confirmed what the angel had told Joseph in a dream just the night before. Herod had died. Her beloved carpenter had been told that it was now safe for them to return home. They would miss all the new friendships that they had forged over the previous months, but they would be headed home to Nazareth. Joseph figured that they would be able to celebrate Passover in Jerusalem with their family as they had always done. She looked forward to that with great anticipation.

Joseph had found a caravan headed for Gaza and had purchased passage with them using the frankincense Aramazar had given them. She and her much-adored nail-bender had packed most of their belongings and had said their good-byes to those who had befriended them in the little Jewish community.

As Mary placed her baby, James, in the little box used as a bed, the young carpenter's bride fondly remembered the little one's *brit milah* in the home of Deborah and Sarah. The two elderly sisters had insisted that the ceremony take place in their house so that they could prepare the feast of celebration in honor of the baby's circumcision and naming. The two older women also knew that their young friends would be leaving on a northward journey back to their hometown as soon as they could. They wanted the feast to be a going away celebration, too. Mary grinned as she recalled the way Jesus had hugged both of the older women that night, as if he was saying good-bye to a family member.

Jesus was losing his baby fat, and his face was taking on its own personality and distinction. His eyes grew brighter with each day and sparkled almost all the time, especially when he looked into the face of someone speaking to him. And his smile was so catching... no one could be in his presence for very long and not respond to that smile. The little boy was already developing his own style and imitated his father with his hand gestures whenever he talked to folks about the things that interested them the most. And he had become so inquisitive, even asking strangers what they were doing. He appeared to have a deep desire to understand why the people around him were doing what they were doing. And his smile would alleviate their objections to his inquiries. Mary wondered if Joseph's folks would notice the slight changes in her little man's personality that indicated that he was growing up.

Mary was often asked by folks who lived close to the Nazarene family if Jesus were showing signs of jealousy because his little brother was monopolizing so much of her time. And the answer was always the same.

"No," the former farm-girl would say in her proudest voice, "Jesus is not the least bit jealous. He willingly shares his toys and gently kisses James' forehead. You should see the way the baby smiles when Jesus talks to him. And James just makes the funniest noises back. I'd swear the two of them were carrying on a conversation that only they understood."

Joseph expected the trip to Jerusalem to take two to three weeks, depending on how many times the caravan stopped along the way for rest and supplies. Their Egyptian exile would soon end, after a very long year, and Mary could hardly wait to talk to Rebekah about her adventures in the land that had been the scene of Jewish slavery so many years ago. Plus, she wanted to show off her new son.

****

Archelaus had not only taken control of the kingdom, but he also took control of his father's funeral procession from Jericho to Herodium, just over a mile. The young monarch decided that Herod's funeral would be remembered if for nothing else, its elegance.

Herod's body was carried on a golden bier, embroidered with a great variety of precious stones. Upon the old king's head, Archelaus placed a diadem and a gold crown above that. The body held a scepter in his right hand. The entire bier was covered in a purple cloth, indicating royalty. Around the bier walked his sons and other kinsmen.

The body was followed by his personal body guards and soldiers, all decked out in their full armor as if prepared for a victory march through a conquered territory. The soldiers were followed by 500 of the old sovereign's servants, all carrying spices.

Archelaus mourned the death of Herod for seven days, according to the law of Moses. Afterwards, the new King returned to Jerusalem and went to the Temple among shouts of praise from the people gathered there. Archelaus thanked the crowds for their shouts of encouragement and for not blaming him for the prior grievous actions of his father. He told those gathered that he would not claim the title of King until Caesar actually bestowed the same on him, but in the meantime, he would do his best to run the government in a civil manner.

The crowds went wild with acclamations of praise for the young ruler, and asked for lower income taxes, for the release of political prisoners, and for a release of the sales tax imposed by Herod. But Archelaus promised them nothing. The crowd simply assumed that life in Israel would be better under the rule of Herod's son. After receiving the praise of the multitude, Archelaus entered the Temple, offered a King's sacrifice to God, and then left to feast with his friends.

****

Joseph had spent the last hour repairing one of the wheels on the little wagon he had made for Mary almost three years before in his carpenter's shop in Nazareth. The repair was considered routine, and since the leader of the caravan in which the Galilean pilgrims traveled had decided to spend a couple of days in Gaza before turning towards Jerusalem, the tall hammer-slinger took advantage of the stop-over to re-work and mend his craftsmanship.

Mary felt a bit uncomfortable in the main room of the caravansary where she and her family were staying for the next two days. Most of the other travelers were men, and some looked at her in a sympathetic, dreaming-of-home kind of manner. Some didn't. The young carpenter's wife felt like she was being sized-up by two of the men who sat across the room in the opposite corner, despite the fact that she held two children in her lap. Then Joseph walked in, and the two men immediately turned their gaze to one of the young girls who brought food to the weary pilgrims.

"Are you alright, Mary?" asked Joseph as he stood between his beloved and the rest of the travelers. His tone of voice indicated that his young wife should ask the same question of him.

"I'm fine," she replied, "but you look troubled, my Love. Is something wrong with the wagon?"

"The wagon's fine," answered Joseph. "But I overheard some men in the corral say that Herod's son, Archelaus, has taken control of the government. He might be just as crazy as Herod. I think we need to by-pass Judea... not go to Jerusalem, but follow the trade route along the coast to Azotos and up to the mountains... then across to Nazareth. It might take a little longer, but I think it will be a wiser journey. And it means we will miss our family as they travel southward. And we won't be celebrating Passover in Jerusalem this year."

Mary saw the disappointment backed by true concern in the eyes of her carpenter. She trusted his ideas and admired his wisdom. She knew that he would do nothing to endanger the lives of their two boys. She smiled and reached out her hand to her beloved woodworker. Joseph took her hand in his and grinned, knowing that she had approved of his plan.

Two hours later, Joseph had found another caravan traveling up the coast of Israel. He and his family would be safe, and the leader of the caravan promised that they would be in Nazareth within ten days. That was news that the muscular wood-shaper gladly shared with his young wife. They would be leaving the first thing in the morning.

****

Jacob handed the note to his wife; a note that Malachi had given him as they arrived in Jerusalem, as was the family's custom, in time for Judith and Miriam to prepare the upper room of Chenaniah's house for the Passover celebration. The old carpenter grinned broadly as he said, "Read this, my Dear. This will make the celebration joyful for you again."

Judith slowly unfolded the small parchment and read aloud, "We are safe... we are on our way home... but we will miss you at Passover. J." Tears filled the old woman's eyes as she realized the implications of the message that told them enough without telling them much. She hugged her husband with all her strength and just wept for a few moments.

Eleazar stood with his arm around Miriam and held her close also, nearly dropping the bundle of provisions he carried under his left arm. The family would be reunited soon. Jacob suggested that they stop what they were doing and give thanks to the Lord for His protection and guidance. No one in the small room cared how Malachi had received the note, or from whom... at least not at the moment. There would be time to discuss that little detail later.

The family trek from Nazareth to Jerusalem had been a sad one that year, because Jacob had not heard from Joseph since that visit from Aramazar so many months previously. But now the journey homeward would be one of enormous expectation. This day was a time of immense celebration and joy.

****

It was springtime in Israel, and Joseph noted with pride how observant Jesus was as they passed other pilgrims along the way. The talented carpenter from Nazareth delighted to watch the young boy sit in the fields of lilies at one particular rest-stop. He touched the flowers so gently and breathed in their fragrance deeply and then would smile his broadest as if he were showing them off to Mary and his baby brother sitting nearby.

On another occasion, the young lad leaned way over the side of the little wagon he shared with his mother and little James when they passed a man sowing seeds in a rocky field. "He's watching where each seed falls," whispered Joseph to himself. Most children... most adults might pay attention to the man doing the work, but not to where the seeds ended up as did Jesus.

Just down the road from the farmer, Joseph noticed how Jesus gazed so intently at two men building the foundation for a house upon a large rock. "House will stand strong," said the young boy to Joseph as the two walked hand in hand beside the wagon. Joseph grinned at the boy and nodded his agreement. Sometimes even Joseph was awed at the child's perception, but then the skillful hammer-slinger would remember just who Jesus really was.

The caravan leader kept to his schedule, stopping for planned rests several times a day and allowing the merchants to sell their goods at towns along the trade route as well as the oasis stops. By the evening of the ninth day since Joseph and his family had joined the travelers in Gaza, the troupe camped in the Galilean hills just 20 miles southwest of the little village of Nazareth. The journey northward had gone as expected, and the next evening would find the weary pilgrims resting in their own home once again.

Joseph checked on Jesus and James, both of whom were sound asleep. The big carpenter dreamed of his family's arrival back in their hometown and the welcome that he knew they would receive from his folks as well as the other villagers. He knelt down and brushed the dark curls from around Jesus' closed eyes. He loved that little boy just as much as if he was his physical offspring. But Jesus was the Son of God, the Messiah, the Chosen One of Israel. Many would accept His message and follow Him, but many more would reject that same message of love. Joseph knew in his heart that everyone would have to make a decision about who Jesus really was. That decision would determine their own destiny. Jesus' smile and his words would touch the hearts of many before his ministry was completed. God's plan for the ages was coming to fruition and no one would escape the message of life and hope that Jesus would spread. People all over the world would have to decide just how they would respond to Jesus.

"One thing is certain," whispered Joseph, "nothing will ever be the same again!"

CPSIA information can be obtained at www.ICGtesting.com
Printed in the USA
LVOW13s0347090813

347025LV00004B/9/P